THE PROPHET

Also by Martine Bailey

AN APPETITE FOR VIOLETS
THE PENNY HEART
THE ALMANACK *

* available from Severn House

THE PROPHET

Martine Bailey

SEVERN
HOUSE

First world edition published in Great Britain and the USA in 2021
by Severn House, an imprint of Canongate Books Ltd,
14 High Street, Edinburgh EH1 1TE.

Trade paperback edition first published in Great Britain and the USA in 2021
by Severn House, an imprint of Canongate Books Ltd.

severnhouse.com

British Library Cataloguing-in-Publication Data
A CIP catalogue record for this title is available from the British Library.

ISBN-13: 978-0-7278-9103-7 (cased)
ISBN-13: 978-1-78029-765-1 (trade paper)
ISBN-13: 978-1-4483-0503-2 (e-book)

All Severn House titles are printed on acid-free paper.

MIX
Paper from
responsible sources
FSC
www.fsc.org   FSC® C013056

Typeset by Palimpsest Book Production Ltd.,
Falkirk, Stirlingshire, Scotland.
Printed and bound in Great Britain by
TJ Books Limited, Padstow, Cornwall.

The virtuous man contents himself with dreaming of that which the wicked man does in actual life.

Plato, *The Republic*, Book IX

Dearest, bury me
Under that Holy-oak, or gospel tree;
Where, though thou seest not, thou mayest think upon
Me, when you yearly go'st procession.

Robert Herrick, 'To Anthea'

ONE

I say that in 1753,
A second saviour will descend to thee

The New Prophet of the Forest

12 May 1753
Old May Day

They had been riding for more than an hour when they entered the forest. Tabitha enjoyed the cool green shade dappling her skin as they passed along avenues of trees illuminated by shafts of sunshine. Nature had woken for May-tide; they passed an abandoned arbour that had doubtless been used at the climax of moonlit revels. A hoop of rowan twigs hung on a tree and a single stocking lay abandoned by a pond's edge. It was said that the curtain between this world and the uncanny realm was torn aside at May-time and hung open till Midsummer. She could certainly believe that, as she moved through a kingdom of leaves as lustrous as green stained glass.

Married for only three months, Tabitha had spent May night alone in her great curtained bed at Bold Hall, subject to Doctor Caldwell's enforced separation from Nat. Growing big with child, she had luxuriated in lavender-scented sheets and a goose-feather mattress, safe from the nips and arrows of the single life. In her wild London days she would have scorned ever becoming such a dull creature; even now she felt a small pang of envy at the signs of a night's frolics.

In the distance the wolfhound, Hector, was leading their way, dashing and panting, his nose to the ground. It had not been easy for Nat to persuade Sir John that his hound was in need of a hard run. At ten years old the dog was content to spend long hours by his master's bedside, but from his first scent of the forest he had yapped and leapt like a puppy.

Behind Hector was Tabitha's young friend, Jennet, laughing at some remark passed by their young footman, Tom. Jennet had begged to come along that morning, expressing great enthusiasm to visit the forest. So far on the journey she had only made eyes at Tom, who was that day on duty as their groom. Oh, fiddlesticks, Jennet's father the constable would no doubt disapprove.

Tabitha glanced over to Nat, heir to the western tract of this forest since Sir John had acknowledged him as his only, though love-gotten, son. He turned around in his saddle and smiled at her, his tortoiseshell eyes warm with love. 'You are not too tired, sweetheart? We can turn back.'

After an hour astride her gentle mare her backbone ached yet she would not spoil the others' pleasure. Tabitha shook her head. When Nat had first studied the maps of the Bold Hall estate and remarked on a tree being honoured with a title, Tabitha had insisted on accompanying him. 'It's the oldest tree in the forest,' she insisted. 'It's venerated, especially by womenfolk. I should like to call upon the tree spirit with you and ask for a safe childbirth.'

She had risen to join him at the map table and he had wrapped her in his arms. She often wondered how such good fortune had fallen upon her, of all women. In her hidden heart, she struggled to believe she deserved such contentment.

Nat was sensitive to her needs; now he seemed to sense her discomfort. 'Wait here. I'll see how far ahead the oak tree is.' He clicked his tongue and moved forward on his black stallion, Jupiter. She watched him disappear into a green glade and then stretched her neck as a gentle wind showered gold and green flashes of light upon her.

A short while later Nat returned, trailed by two small girls of eight or nine years old. They were as bright-eyed as hares, garbed in hand-me-down rags, their feet bare and filthy.

'These children say we are not far from the oak,' Nat called. 'They'll lead us to it.'

Nat reined in Jupiter to wait for Tabitha and then spoke quietly. 'Odd children. They are full of a tale of a sleeping May Queen lying beneath the oak.' They both observed the two girls skipping ahead, thrashing the nettles with wands of wood.

'A May doll, perhaps?' Tabitha asked. 'Old customs are not forgotten by the foresters. Children parade a wooden effigy around the lanes and show it for pennies. Perhaps they then leave it at the oak?'

The Mondrem Oak at last came into view. 'Great God, it's a giant,' Nat said, halting at the edge of a circular clearing beside Jennet and Tom. The tree stood entirely alone, the king of the forest, raising its branched arms as high as a house in all its springtime glory.

'I hear that trunk is near fifty foot in girth,' Tom said. 'Why, you could fit a dozen men inside it.' He looked inside the narrow entrance in its hollow trunk that showed a dusky interior as large as a carriage.

Nat was impressed. 'They say it could be twelve hundred years old. It was growing here when the Roman legions invaded Britain. Tacitus tells us the oak was the Druid's tree and these groves were a place of worship. And sacrifice.'

Tabitha coaxed her horse forward. She was admiring the decorations hanging from scores of branches, what the foresters called the 'bawming' of the tree for May-time. A rainbow of ribbons and bows made up most of it, but as she grew closer she saw strange objects: a playing card, a child's bonnet, and offerings whittled from wood of a solitary leg, a dangling eye, and a carved baby.

Only after Nat had helped her carefully dismount did Tabitha remember the two little girls. The turf beneath her feet was as springy as an ancient grave as she walked to where they stood. A heap of forest debris lay on the far side of the gigantic trunk. She studied it, then recoiled to clutch the corrugated bark. It was not a May doll lying on the ground but a life-sized figure reposing beneath a blanket of foliage. Her first thought was of the mannequins she had seen at an exhibition in Chester. But no, this woman had recently been mortal. Her nut-brown hair fanned out luxuriantly around her head like the sun's rays. Her lean face was composed, though her lashes were not quite closed and showed an eerie rim of white. And the flesh of her cheeks had sunk a little, suggesting the ridges of the skull beneath.

'What's happened to her?' moaned Jennet, who had just

appeared at her shoulder and now hung back. Tabitha was inspecting the covering that must have been placed over her, sometime after the girl's body had been so carefully arranged. Yellow primroses, pink anemones, frothy cow parsley and wilting bluebells had been laid upon a blanket of leaves with such neat attention that they might have been the dressing of a holy well or rush cart.

Nat pulled hard on Tabitha's arm. 'Stand away. Don't look. It will do you no good.'

Tabitha stood firm though she knew precisely what he meant. She had just experienced a violent shock and felt it behind her ribs, as if the child within her had reached up and clutched at her heart. Many said that such a shocking sight might leave a powerful impression on her child's mind or body. There were tales of mothers-to-be frightened by the sight of blood who then delivered a bloodily birthmarked child, or an encounter with a hare that doomed a babe to a hare-shotten lip. She for one did not believe them.

'Wait. I have laid out many a dead body before,' she insisted, trying to sound braver than she felt. For an instant she recalled that worst of all occasions when she had laid out her own dead mother. Since then until her marriage she had worked as the village Searcher, tending to the dead and entering the reasons for their deaths in the parish register. She had grown used to the fixed stillness of the dead, and learned to read the tales that death wrote on a corpse in his curious alphabet. She leaned closer over the motionless face. That scattering of bran-like freckles across the cheeks. Hadn't she met this girl somewhere before?

'For pity's sake,' Nat muttered, trying to pull her away by the elbow.

'A moment,' she insisted. She crouched unsteadily beside the dead girl. The bodice of flowers wilted across the girl's chest. Tabitha moved them aside, surprised by the death-chill on the girl's skin. Some blooms were stained rusty brown and the girl's gown was slashed in several places. Underneath, the white skin had been butchered, so that her stomach had swelled from the savage attack. Blood had dried treacle-dark on her chemise. 'God save us,' Tabitha gasped, glimpsing sticky entrails in the centre of the bloody mess.

Grasping Nat's hand, she let him raise her up, feeling suddenly dizzy. 'She has been murdered,' she whispered. 'Help me over to that fallen log. I can go no further at present.'

It was then that Tabitha noticed her husband's agitation. 'Hector!' he cried. His summons alarmed a flock of birds and sent an echo through the forest. 'I need to report this to the authorities. Where is that dog?'

'Tom! When did you last see him?' she called. The lad broke away from where he was comforting Jennet.

'A while back he were pawing at a rabbit hole, my lady.'

Far above the forest canopy a cloud slid across the sun shedding gloom upon the scene.

'He ran ahead. I reckon we'll catch him up,' Jennet added.

Nat stared into the surrounding trees. 'Tom. You go back fifty paces to check he's not following some creature behind us. Then come straight back. I'll go on ahead and do the same.'

Tabitha rested on the fallen log, conscious that the carefree adventure of the day had been ruined. And worse, she had a premonition that the glorious honeymoon months of her marriage would forever be blackened by today's discovery. Surely her child would be safe? She laid a protective hand over her stomach and recited a silent prayer of her mother's, for protection against all the dangers and pains of her travail. Her eyes kept returning to the corpse; its presence made the forest appear uncomfortably watchful.

'Is the baby well?' Jennet approached her older friend and anxiously patted the swelling beneath Tabitha's riding habit.

'The baby is sleeping, I think. Lucky little darling.' Jennet's clear grey eyes met hers with a crinkle of concern. 'I know,' Tabitha spoke before the girl could interrupt. 'Doctor Caldwell instructed me not to ride far. I had forgotten the distance. How I detest taking orders from such a pompous toad.'

'But if it's—'

'Yes, yes,' she interrupted. 'I do think of the child. I shall not ride again.' Oh Lord, her back was burning with pain. She had persuaded herself the jaunt would be healthful – wrongly it would seem.

Soon after, Tom returned with a sorry shake of his head. Then Nat returned looking very stiff and grave. 'Pox the dog,' he cursed. 'What a time to run away.' He pointed at a plume of smoke rising above the trees. 'There is a settlement ahead. We need to make inquiries about this poor dead woman.'

'Aye,' called the larger of the two girls. 'We're almost home.' The children began walking forwards while the others followed more slowly.

'There was no village near here on the map,' Nat confided, drawing close beside her. 'I'm curious to see where exactly these children came from.'

'Perhaps they are tramping folk crossing your land, sir,' suggested Tom.

Nat frowned. 'We must find out. And despatch someone to fetch Constable Saxton to move that tragic creature to a more dignified location.'

Tom cast a worried look towards Jennet. 'Should we not wait here for Jennet's father? Is it wise to go after strangers when we're so few, sir?'

Nat opened his coat to reveal a pistol. 'It is all the more reason to discover them before they run away. You have your hunting knife, lad?' Tom nodded though he looked scared, and adjusted the blade at his belt. Nat turned to call for Hector and then remembered. 'Dammit. Where the devil is that dog when you truly need him?'

TWO

The two scrawny children ran ahead, one moment whispering with lowered heads and the next looking backwards with sly glances. The four on horseback followed them into a tunnel through a thicket of thorns and the sky vanished in a thatch of branches. The air was thick with midges and Tabitha blinked in the gloom, rubbing her forearms and face. She was nagged by a growing insistence that they should turn back for home but knew that was impossible. Nat was for all purposes the local magistrate now that Sir John's apoplexy left him an invalid. As news had spread that Nat Starling, a man largely known as a scurrilous writer, was the heir to a baronetcy, disbelief and derision had rippled through the neighbouring gentry. Here was his first test. If he failed to behave according to his rank and uphold the law he might never be accepted by his peers.

At last they emerged into the sudden dazzle of a woodland clearing. Tabitha and her companions hesitated, scrutinizing the bizarre sight before them. Two ancient yew trees formed the foundations, part-walls and ramparts of a curious structure. The space between the two branching trunks had been entirely filled with dried turf walls in which a timber-framed doorway was the only visible entrance. It was hard to tell the growing trees from manmade walls and hazel thatch. Tabitha thought it looked like a dwelling from a fable, where a witch or woodland spirit might wait for unwary humans.

'Squatters,' muttered Tom. 'So long as they put up a hovel between sunset and sunrise and get the chimney smoking they tell themselves it's their land.'

Smoke was indeed rising from a hole in the roof, signalling to all-comers that the inhabitants had taken possession of a part of Nat's birthright. The culprits numbered a dozen or so young folk and a scattering of children, preoccupied with washing clothes at a pool or hanging them to dry on branches.

Nat was clearly rattled. 'Damned scavengers. That may be the

Welsh way, to throw up a house in a night, but by English law
they cannot stay here on my father's land.'

'Look at the door.' Tom pointed to a fine head of antlers hung
above the entrance.

Nat shook his head. 'We keep no deer. They've helped themselves to our neighbour's venison.'

When their two young guides walked into the sunlight the
dogs stirred, barking uneasily. Tabitha and her companions walked
their horses to an open spot and all those in the clearing fell still
and watchful. She was aware of how they must appear: Nat in
his gold-buttoned velvet coat, and herself in a smart sapphire
riding habit. Little would these folk know that she had spent
much of her life in the roughest homespun. Breaking the tension,
a young man of pleasing appearance showed himself at the treehouse's entrance and strode towards them, extending his open
palms in a gesture of welcome.

'Welcome, good people. What a pleasure, sir, and madam, to
have visitors. I am Baptist Gunn, man of God and saver of souls.
At your service.'

Gunn bowed low. His voice was cultured and he alone of the
squatters was stylishly dressed in a blue frock coat and he wore
his chestnut hair long to his shoulders. Tabitha felt his gaze upon
her, his eyes large and curiously wideset. He could not have been
more than thirty years old and she guessed that he strove to
appear of a rank higher than those who surrounded him. As if
recognizing an old friend, Gunn said, 'Mister De Vallory of Bold
Hall, is it not?'

Nat did not reply. Undeterred, Gunn turned to Tabitha. 'And
you are . . .' He hesitated, then appeared to consult a memo-
randum book inside his brain. 'Mistress Tabitha De Vallory. What
a pleasure—'

'Enough,' Nat snapped. 'What the devil do you think you're
doing here? This is not common land. You cannot live here.'

Gunn backed away, smiling. 'You mistake us, sir. We don't
settle here. We are merely journeying through the forest. We stay
here no more than six weeks or so and then sail for America at
Midsummer. We are journeying to Pennsylvania to build a farm
on a piece of God's earth that is free of any landlord or lawyer's
title. Do not begrudge these poor folk and their children the loan

of a tree as shelter for their heads. We live in peace, gathering roots and berries and drinking the clear water of your streams.'

'Aye, and the rich meat of another man's venison.' Nat indicated the head of antlers.

'Ah, that. We found a wounded creature by the wayside.'

'And we have just found a young woman murdered. What d'you say to that?'

'No.' Gunn's face stiffened as he stepped backwards. Tabitha thought him a good actor if he were lying. 'Where?'

'Not two hundred yards away. Beneath the Mondrem Oak.' Nat sat high in his saddle and cast his eyes coldly across the assembled company. 'So, you people. Who was she? Who carried out this barbarous act?'

His question was met only by fidgeting and head shaking. He turned back to the young man. 'What do you say, Gunn? I cannot believe you know nothing of such devilry. It was two of your children that led us to her.' Nat beckoned to the two ragged girls who solemnly stepped forward.

'Girls,' Gunn asked gently. 'The woman you found. Did you know her?'

The two shook their heads in silence, their eyes round and dutiful.

Suddenly Gunn cried loudly, 'We must pray for this poor unfortunate stranger.'

At this signal, all those assembled save for the Bold Hall company sank to their knees. Mister Gunn began importuning the Lord in a melodious voice.

Nat looked to Tabitha and cast his eyes heavenwards. 'Mister Gunn,' he interrupted. 'Rather than vex the Almighty I look for human remedies. I need a good runner to go at once to fetch the constable from The Grange at Netherlea. And then I need to question you.'

Gunn lifted his palms and quickly made an 'Amen'. Then signalling that his followers should also stand, he addressed Nat. 'Please, sir. Take refreshments with us and I'll tell you all you wish to know. Mistress De Vallory has, I observe, a deal of discomfort in her back. She should dismount and I'll call my herbal woman to ease her pain.'

Though surprised by the preacher's acute perception, Tabitha could not deny her need to rest. It was decided they would halt awhile. Crude wooden benches were gathered and the contents of a vast barrel of ale were passed around. An older woman with an apple-wrinkled face gave Tabitha a cracked china cup of hot water and leaves which, she mumbled, were gathered from the forest. Draining it down to the last astringent drop, Tabitha at last stretched back into a large, cushioned chair and closed her eyes.

Tabitha woke to see black tree branches forming a lattice against the late afternoon sky. Those seated at the benches had been joined by a dozen more young folk, carousing and drinking. The air was sweetly sour with ale and pipe smoke. Nat was deep in animated conversation with Gunn. No longer discussing the dead woman, the two men were speaking of liberty and she understood at once from Nat's flushed cheeks and overloud speech that he was in the full flow of an enthusiasm. Gunn was matching Nat quote for exuberant quote, calling on the works of Messrs Hume, Voltaire, and all the rest. Tabitha stretched and wished she could remove her boots, which were squeezing her swollen ankles. Her back at least had eased. And, surprised though she was, it was good to hear her husband enjoying lively conversation instead of bending over his quill in silence. And even better, she remembered that this Gunn fellow would soon be sailing off to America.

'My dear. You are awake.' Nat was at once at her side. 'You slept for most of the afternoon.'

'Is there any news of Hector?'

Nat frowned as he tidied a strand of her hair. 'No one here has seen him. But he's a clever dog. No doubt he'll find his own way home.'

The sky had lost its former radiance. She pictured old Hector, more used to warm fires than mazy paths, still roaming the forest alone.

'And the girl beneath the tree? Did you send for Joshua?'

An echo of distress crossed Nat's countenance. 'Yes, the constable has just left. Gunn sent a lad to fetch him and he brought some men and a cart from the nearest lock-up. At least the unfortunate creature will have the dignity of lying at Bold

Hall tonight. Next there must be an inquest. I've sent for Dr Caldwell to inspect the body tomorrow.'

She yawned and stretched. 'You didn't think to wake me? We could have travelled back with Joshua.'

'I could not bear to disturb you. And Jennet and Tom begged to stay.'

Tabitha looked over to the young couple, sitting far closer together than Joshua would have allowed. And as for you, my husband, she thought, you have been too busy exercising your radical opinions. She caught Gunn watching them and turned to address him. 'Tell me. Who was that dead young woman, Mister Gunn?'

Gunn's expression was muted as he cast down his large, inquisitive eyes. 'None of us knows,' he said firmly. 'She'll be a village girl, no doubt. Even so, I've set up guards around our camp and I've forbidden any woman from walking alone in the woods. Now, supper is almost ready. You will honour us by dining here?'

Deep sleep in the open air had left Tabitha hollow with hunger. It would take an age to reach Bold Hall and there were no respectable taverns nearby. It would be good to stay and eat.

Excusing herself, she rose to take a look around the camp before the light faded. Most of the women were gathered at an outdoor kitchen to the rear of the tree dwelling. A meaty scent rose from cooking pots. She dawdled, watching women chop roots and herbs, as they sang a psalm in a pleasant chorus. They were all dressed in drab gowns like Quakers or Methodists, for such ranters infamously forbade lace, colours or any mark of fashion. Yet their costume was curiously attractive; they wore their hems high above their ankles and neat white kerchiefs over their hair.

When the singing ended they gathered to question her. A pox-faced woman with pinched features looked Tabitha up and down. 'Got a little 'un on the way, 'ave you? Baptist has sired seven of our own babes. And I've another coming along.' She touched her apron proudly to show how it was tied extra high below her breasts.

'That's only at the last count,' giggled a plump young woman with the scorched complexion of a labourer. Eyeing Tabitha's diamond ring, she added, 'We don't favour marriage vows round here, you know.'

'Ah, so how does that work in practice?' Tabitha asked, surprised. A couple of small children had crept up to inspect the guinea-like buttons of her riding habit. Without a word she lifted a small grubby hand from out of her pocket.

'There ain't no rules. We just does as we pleases.' A third giggling girl grinned, showing a couple of broken teeth. 'We want lots of babies to fill our New Jerusalem.'

'So who chooses who at bedtime?' Tabitha asked mischievously. She had spent long enough in a bawdy house to know it was the men who always did the picking.

The giggler dreamily wiped a steel knife. 'Oh, Mister Gunn is a lusty man. And there's plenty of other fine lads.'

The pox-faced woman jabbed at the speaker in jest. 'Tall ones, dark ones, even a pair of twins. This girl here don't even know which of them twins be her child's father. Go forth and multiply is what the scriptures command.'

'That is true,' Tabitha said. 'Have any of you yet remembered seeing that young woman with freckles and brown hair? She had been savaged in a violent fury, I'd say.'

The women turned to their tasks, shaking their heads. 'Never seen such a one,' was the general response.

Tabitha excused herself and went in search of a private spot in the bushes. After emptying her aching bladder she looked about for a place to sit in solitude. At the side of the path stood a felled log where she eased herself down and unbuttoned her boots, then wriggled her stockinged toes in the cool grass. She sat very still, hearkening to Mister Gunn's followers as they passed behind a stand of shrubs. It was all inconsequential conversation, save for one tiny fragment. A woman's voice she had not heard before said, 'Remember, we mustn't breathe a word about t'Trinity.'

'I know. Now shush . . .' replied her companion.

The Trinity? What was that supposed to be – some form of religious heresy?

THREE

The food was surprisingly good, sharpened by outdoor hunger, the best of sauces. The rabbits in the stew no doubt belonged to Sir John but the nuggets of hasty pudding, wild garlic, green-tops and barley were plain fare of a sort Tabitha had missed since dining in the grand style at Bold Hall. A blazing campfire had been lit and the Bold Hall party were given places at a long plank table beside Gunn. After the bowls had been cleared the singing began and strong nettle beer flowed. The hymns and psalms were interspersed with ballads, all sung as well as any balladeer at Covent Garden could. A fiddler was called upon, and then a lad with a penny whistle whose fingers flew faster than the wind. Someone else found a drum that boomed like a giant heartbeat.

Tabitha leaned on Nat's shoulder and let herself enjoy the entertainment. Above them the full moon was rising in the blue-bell dark of twilight. She considered the curious connection between the moon's waxing and waning and her own monthly courses. Last October, after the calendar had lost eleven days and the calculations she had always used to prevent conception had faltered, she had conceived this baby. Now she wondered how many full moons were left before her confinement. Only one, or two? If she asked Doctor Caldwell he would doubtless lecture her on her womanly ignorance. She wished her mother were still alive to see her first grandchild's birth. Widow Hart had attended many a birthing, guiding terrified mothers through their great travail.

She reached for Nat's lean hand and stroked it. It was foolish to worry. The music was fast, her head and heart vibrated with the drumbeat, till it seemed that all the listeners' bones shook in unison. Here was a rare moment to surrender themselves: they were part of the circle of amber-lit faces, watching orange sparks ascending like fireflies, as the swell of song and fiddle sounded out across the listening darkness.

'Speak! Speak!' Tabitha must have dozed again, for she woke to find the camp still rowdy. Through heavy lids she watched Gunn stride towards the bonfire and turn to face his congregation. She blinked and leaned forward. His form was dramatically backlit by the firelight, his hair wild, his face a mask of bronze. He began to speak of love and the common bonds of mankind. Of how kings and coin had corrupted the goodness of the human race. Of how the slavery of work for profit set man against man. Of how the slavery of marriage turned lovers into enemies. And of how the tyranny of schoolmasters beat the God-given innocence from humanity's greatest blessing, their children. Liberty was the answer. Freedom in a new land without lords and judges, lawyers or tax collectors.

'Without property,' he cried, 'there is no sin! No theft, no adultery, no murder. You are the fortunate ones to be reborn as God's innocent children. In America we will labour only for the common good and every night sleep on God's earth beneath the stars.'

She had to admit he spoke impressively. If only Netherlea's new parson could fill his hour-long sermon with such rousing notions. True, she felt a prickle of scepticism, yet who was she to begrudge these hopefuls a life of freedom? She hated to be a hypocrite and saw well enough that Nat's and her own happy situation was a product of good fortune. For the first time in her life she had everything she had ever desired: a secure home, comfort, and most of all Nat, an adoring husband. Who was she to stop these ragged folk from seeking their own dreams of happiness?

Suddenly the preacher began to falter. 'Fetch my chair!' he commanded. She was surprised by this show of weakness. Yet the murmurs of the company revealed not dismay but excited anticipation. Two youths dragged a high-backed chair towards him and Gunn slumped wearily down onto it. 'I feel the sleep of God descending upon me,' he murmured and was answered by a collective sigh. A moment later his head slumped against the chair back and his eyelids fluttered and closed. She shared a questioning glance with Nat. All fell silent save for the quivering cry of an owl hunting above the canopy of the forest. Nobody moved or appeared to breathe.

The voice that broke the silence was different to that which had delivered the sermon; it was a reedy but insinuating whisper. Goose pimples rose on Tabitha's skin. Gunn appeared to be fast asleep while some other, invisible presence used the air from his lungs to expel words.

'It is the spirit,' she heard someone whisper. She found herself craning forwards to hear more clearly. Though to all intents asleep, the voice inhabiting Gunn's body was speaking.

'Hear my confession,' he intoned, and was met by encouraging murmurs. 'Once I walked in a great city. A city of sin and poverty, more wicked even than Sodom or Gomorrah. I was the worst of sinners. I was a gambler, a drunkard, a wretch of a man. And I was unchaste.' The company fell as silent as the grave. 'I never could resist the pull and power of the fairer sex. I cared not if they were low and unclean. A woman for sale promises so much – and that so easily possessed. Besides, I saw that the flesh trade attracted not only the filthiest but also the loveliest of women.'

Tabitha listened, uneasy to hear this description of her own former mode of living. Hunger and desperation had forced her to sell her body when she was nineteen, back in the terrible winter of 1750. As soon as she had coin to provide for her mother and newborn half-sister Bess, she had fled to London. Alone in the capital, she had clawed her way up the ranks of bawdry, from a kept girl in a brothel to an admired lady of the town tumbling in gold sovereigns. Damn the man, she did not care to be given a lecture by such as Mr Gunn.

'I know you wish to forget such encounters,' the voice insinuated. 'I know that those who have earned the grubby coins of shame are still troubled by the sins that you – and yes, I – have committed. I confess it, I too have enjoyed nights of carnality that burn hot in my memory even now.'

Oh, Venus and Cupid, she too had lived such nights, the rogue had the truth of it there.

'Yet you have come here tonight. You, who have been humiliated, used, treated like a dumb carcass by rakes who care not a jot for you. Yes, you . . .'

Tabitha stiffened and sat up. The voice was playing tricks on her.

'I know all. I saw you. Yes, you,' the voice insisted. 'And now you believe yourself unworthy of God's Providence.'

She could not keep her eyes from his face; he was almost unbearably fine to look at, like a blind seer in a court of kings. Though his eyelids were closed, his eyes moved as if watching visions from some other lofty kingdom.

'The moment you came here, I knew you,' he told her. Where she had felt hot, she now felt a clammy chill. Nat knew well enough how she had lived in London, for he had admired her from a distance with the eye of a pleasure-seeking rake. When they had finally met in Netherlea they had been drawn together like the moon and earth until both could no longer resist the attraction. Yet somehow this curious prophet knew her even better.

In the firelight Baptist Gunn was a red-tinged demon of a man, his hair wild, his throat bare, and still his words spilled into the night like tongues of flame.

'I can help you,' he said. 'Only I can save you.' Around her Baptist's followers cried, 'Thank God!' and 'We are saved.'

Stupid people, Tabitha thought. He wasn't speaking to them at all. He was speaking only to her, speaking slowly and with great gravity. She listened for what might have been a minute or an hour, as his words glowed in her mind, incandescent and marvellous, yet as fleeting as fireworks. He told them that a baby would be born this year at Midsummer. A saviour. There would be signs. The king of the forest was one. Another was the spilling of blood.

Even as she nodded drowsily, the questioning part of her wondered. Was Gunn talking about her and Nat's baby? With a great effort she looked up into Nat's lean face and found that he too was transfixed. She nudged him and they shared expressions of anxious concern. She did not like this gathering of portents; her carefree joy felt tainted. Nat reached out with his fingers to touch her. Together they clasped hands across the rounded flesh that housed their coming child.

It was over and the company were dispersing. Lanterns were fetched and Nat led her forward to say their farewells to Mister Gunn. Before her stood the prophet himself – and he was merely an ordinary man. Then his gaze met hers and it was as if he had yanked her to him. Gunn leaned down, his breath hot in her ear.

'We will speak again. Alone.' In a rapid movement his wet lips brushed her earlobe. She flinched back from his touch. Nat had seen nothing. Remounted on her grey mare, Tabitha watched her companions move forward like wraiths into the darkness. Though she rubbed at the tip of her ear it continued to burn, as if hot pincers had nipped her skin.

In time the Mondrem Oak towered above them, grey and silver in the moonlight. It was then that Tom gave a shout and pointed. The black silhouette of a man was standing over the heap of foliage where the dead girl had lain.

'Don't move. Who are you?' Nat challenged, pointing his pistol.

The man showed no surprise. 'Me? I am Private Jacob Hollingsworth of the Twenty-Second Chester Foot. On home leave from Ireland, sir.'

He was a bear of a man, broad shouldered in a muddy red coat. But beneath his battered tricorne his face bore deep lines of hard labour.

'What is your business here?'

'Visiting my mother, Widow Hollingsworth. She lives over by the mere.'

Tabitha recognized the name of the woman as a friend of her mother. Widow Hollingsworth was a foreigner but clever and well-respected.

'And your business here, beneath the oak?'

'I wondered why such a pile of stuff had been gathered and left here. It were not here when I passed before.'

'And that was when exactly?'

'Yesterday.'

Tabitha broke into the conversation. 'And did you see a young woman of about eighteen years old hereabouts?'

The soldier turned to her and bowed. 'No, I never seen any young woman about the place—'

Nat interrupted. 'She was found savagely murdered here today. What d'you know of that?'

'I know nowt at all, sir,' the soldier replied, his voice suddenly tight with evasion.

'It is late now. Tomorrow you must be questioned at Bold Hall. Come at noon. Do you understand?'

'I do, sir. Twelve noon sharp.' He lifted his hand in a salute, touching his misshapen hat.

Tabitha called out as they turned to leave. 'Have you seen an old wolfhound today? Answers to the name of "Hector"?'

Now she caught the gleam of his eyes meeting hers in the moonlight. 'No, my lady. I ain't seen him.' Only this time Tabitha would have hazarded the soldier was finally telling the truth.

FOUR

13 May 1753

Doctor Caldwell was a shambling man of five and thirty; unkempt in his person, with a greasy old cauliflower wig, and the protruding eyes of an overbred pug dog. According to Nat he was an excellent physician, but his manner left Tabitha feeling like a brood mare being assessed for market. Firstly, he inspected her urine in a glass, holding it to the light, then sniffing it, and – rather disgustingly – tasting a few drops on the ends of his fingers. Next, he approached her in her chair and inspected her eyes, her tongue, and her fingers. Finally, he picked up her wrist and produced his pocketwatch. Close up, she was forced to turn her nose from great wafts of his onion-breath.

To her relief, he moved away to the centre of the room and then began the scolding she anticipated. 'I can scarcely credit that you touched a murdered corpse. Did you not consider how you put your child's life at appalling risk? The terror felt by you, the mother, is powerfully transmittable to your child; it might create a dreadful malformity.'

'But I felt no terror,' Tabitha said calmly. She had passed the night comfortably and now drew on her mother's wisdom from years of midwifery. 'Besides, I am not convinced by the argument. A vegetable may have blemishes for no reason, yet if a child has a birthmark or a hare-lip, it must be the mother's fault for eating strawberries or being crossed by a hare or some other nonsense.'

The doctor addressed her in his most pompous tone. 'You carry a grave responsibility, Mrs De Vallory. Not only to your husband, but to Sir John himself. I shall have no more long rides on horseback or scrambling after horrors. And certainly no conjugal visits from your husband. You must think of the child as a bird on a particularly fragile perch. Any shock or violent movement may dislodge it. Do you understand?'

'Very well.'

He eyed her with suspicion. 'Your pulse is somewhat acceler-
ated. You are in a highly nervous condition at present. Very well.
I have some interesting news. I have become acquainted with a
young woman willing to assist you with the child. She would
make an ideal wet nurse to suckle the infant as well as a useful
attendant in your confinement.'

Tabitha listened warily, convinced that Caldwell wanted to set
a spy upon her.

'Mrs Adams is also in the breeding condition; in fact, her dates
are remarkably close to yours. She is sober, clean and strong and
has experience of childbed, unlike yourself. And she is happy to
lodge here, so you need not send your own child away to be
nursed.'

Ever since Doctor Caldwell had asserted that ladies of rank
did not suckle their own children, she had been dreading his
choice of wet nurse. Now, though she scoured her brain for an
excuse to reject the woman, she could find none. Begrudgingly,
she agreed to see the woman the next day.

Ordered back to bed, Tabitha watched her sour-faced maid,
Grisell, clumsily set a tray down on her lap. The cup of vanilla-
scented chocolate had sloshed over half the sugared cakes but
today she would not tempt the maid's black looks. After
dismissing Grisell she spooned frothy chocolate into her mouth
as her mind drifted back to Baptist Gunn. That sensitive spot
on her ear where his lips had brushed her – surely she could
still feel it tingle? Go and see him, indeed. The man was
welcome to romp with his followers so long as she never set
eyes on him again. Thank the Lord he would soon be on his
way and with luck would never return.

Nat came into her room, looking rather more careworn than
usual, wearing his ancient shagreen coat, his hair hanging loose.
Poor darling, she still could not stop herself smiling like a fool
each time she saw him and reminded herself that he was her
husband. Still, she must keep him close and well away from that
preacher.

'You are on official business today? Perhaps a dark coat would
suit better?' she said.

He sat on the edge of the bed and helped himself to a biscuit. 'Please don't fuss. I shall do my best to put this matter of the dead woman to rest, my love. And then with luck I can return to my books this afternoon. Under the circumstances we needn't attend church.'

'Good. Any news of Hector?'

He shook his head. 'Father is wretched. I've sent Tom and a few of the stable boys out to search again. I only pray the dear old creature isn't harmed.'

She shook her head in sympathy.

'What did you make of Baptist Gunn?' he asked. 'Those prophecies? Did you catch his meaning?'

She took a long time spooning more chocolate between her lips. 'There was some nonsense about a baby. It was all mummery, I'm sure.'

'The coming of a saviour this very year. All told in biblical phrases, of course. Do you think "the king of the forest" might be another name for the Mondrem Oak?'

'Perhaps. Though Gunn may be a charlatan,' she said firmly. 'He is a clever preacher and his followers look for miracles. Their aim is to breed a great many children so of course he speaks of an infant saviour. He fancies himself quite the ladies' man. Apparently, he is father to at least seven of those children.' Remembering the wetness of his lips, she felt a flush of unwelcome heat.

Nat laughed. 'A pleasant occupation if you can find it.'

She batted him away.

'I don't care for this notion of spilled blood,' Nat said thoughtfully.

'Please Nat, give him no credence.' She tried to soften her words by stroking his cheek with her fingers. He had been shaved that morning but had since smeared ink beside his nose. She wiped it away and they kissed briefly. Last night they had forgotten their usual goodnight kiss. It was a shame, the very first time of forgetting.

Still he praised the man. 'There was a power to his speech. I've read of these sleeping prophets attracting vast crowds in Germany and France but never thought I'd see a demonstration over here. He has read David Hume, Linnaeus, even Voltaire.

It's such a relief to talk of ideas. Not like our neighbours who study only the hunting calendar.'

She listened, recognizing within herself an entirely unjust resentment against the books Nat and Gunn had both read. Her husband often disappeared for long hours down to his basement room. It was a hateful place, a sinister laboratory, and yet Nat had turned it into his study. He had ambitions of writing one of these new-fangled novels, as well as poetry and erudite papers. Yet no finished works had yet emerged from his hours of solitude. When she had questioned him, he had replied, 'A gentleman must keep his mind occupied.' Am I not enough? she thought. But marriage was turning her circumspect and she did not utter such carpings out loud.

Instead she responded with her old habit of coquetry. 'That camp is quite given over to wantonness,' she teased. 'Though heaven knows, I should never choose to abolish marriage.' She flexed her fingers and admired her own diamond ring. 'I am so much in love with you, Nat.'

He grinned and slid his hand down the curves of her body. 'How went it with Caldwell?'

'He scolded me. But thankfully did not leech me or inflict some other gory torture.' Nat's open palm settled on her stomach; his smile was strained. 'But you do feel well? Yesterday was far too—'

'Yesterday I behaved like the young healthy woman I am,' she replied sweetly.

'Good, good. I forgot to say. Caldwell will examine the dead woman after dinner. I've had her moved to the old chapel. His report will be necessary for the inquest.'

She sighed. 'The truth is, since I first saw her, I felt I knew her. From where, I don't know.'

Nat got up and paced to the window. When he turned back to her he looked abstracted.

'I have been very good today,' she continued, hoping to cheer him up. 'I have agreed to meet Doctor Caldwell's choice of the baby's wet nurse. He recommends a woman of such virtue and sobriety she is sure to report back to him on my behaviour. She can board here so I suppose I shall never be free of her.'

'Why, that is excellent news. I am glad someone will keep a

stern eye on you. And think, sweetheart, this way we can keep our dear child close at hand and not have to visit some remote cottage. With our own child to observe I can mark its progress and maybe even write a paper on the infant's progress. Now will you rest? Take dinner up here. You should not ignore the doctor's counsel.'

She cast him a wry smile. 'Very well, I shall obey, dear husband.' And after kissing her cheek he tucked her sheets high beneath her chin.

FIVE

Where the king of the forest for centuries stood,
He will come amid death and hot-spilled blood.

The New Prophet of the Forest

A distant bell chimed two, signalling that Nat and the doctor must be settling down to dinner. Rising from her bed Tabitha found her riding jacket and looked inside the pocket. There it was – a wilting posy of spring flowers. The primroses and lady's smock still stood firm but the bluebells had collapsed and grown tacky. It was a commonplace of poets to compare a young woman to a flower, for both possessed a loveliness that was fragile and fleeting. And now, she reflected, nothing could revive either. She found two scraps of blotting paper and arranged the blooms before pressing them between the sheets. Then she fetched her mother's box and slipped the papers inside a prayer book. Was that all the memorial the dead girl deserved? Why? Because she had doubtless been poor and desperate and the victim of some man's frenzied fury.

Donning a loose morning gown and soft-soled shoes, she made her way along the crooked passage to the rear quarters of the manor house. Inside Bold Hall the walls and floors leaned at odd angles, the oak frame having twisted and shifted over centuries like the insides of an ancient ship. She was still learning her way around her new home, recognizing little landmarks as she walked. Here was a faded image of the Virgin on one landing, and a plasterwork Wheel of Fortune on the next. It was a queer, crooked labyrinth of a house, but to Tabitha it was a fortress of comfort and security. She found what she was searching for: a spiral stone staircase that she descended very slowly, balancing carefully against the wall.

She emerged near a decayed wooden door studded with nails. She stepped inside, beneath the high ceiling; the atmosphere was musty and cold. Bold Hall's chapel had been empty for many years, the later De Vallorys choosing to worship in the parish church of Netherlea. Ancient monuments covered the walls, bearing crude memorials now blistered and bleached by damp air. The nave was empty save for the woman's body laid on a table and draped in a sheet. Tabitha lifted the covering from the top half of the corpse. The girl's flesh had acquired a greenish-grey hue and released an odour of decay that forced Tabitha's hand upwards to cover her nose. Though the girl's features were now less easy to read, she again tried to picture that pert sparrow-like face when it had been animated by life. She looked older; the last few years had left furrows of worry across her brow. Tabitha's gaze moved over the thin body and snagged on her rounded breasts. A pink rash? No, the reddish streaks were a sign of something more familiar.

The sound of people approaching made her hastily replace the sheet. She crossed to a twisting wooden staircase that led up near the chapel's roof. Clambering up, she reached an ancient gallery and pulled the dusty velvet curtain along the rail leaving only the smallest gap to spy through.

Below, Doctor Caldwell, Nat and Joshua entered the nave. Behind them came the doctor's clerk bearing cloths and aprons, tools and spirit bottles. Soon the man was busy decking the room with fragrant herbs and setting the doctor's tools out on a clean cloth. Meanwhile Nat and the doctor conversed in low voices.

'A damned nuisance about Coroner Crouch. How long will the inquest be delayed?' Nat asked peevishly.

Caldwell shook his head. 'It's a bad fracture to his wrist but I've set the bone securely. What in damnation a great boulder was doing in the middle of the forest highway, God only knows. The carriage axle was shattered quite in half. I'd say that a fortnight or so should suffice if it mends well and his clerk attends to all the papers.'

After sniffing the air with distaste, the doctor turned to Joshua. 'Constable, I should be obliged if you could assemble the jurors and have them inspect the victim's body at the first opportunity. Even placed in an ice house or in a lead coffin the remains will soon putrefy.'

Joshua agreed to oversee the body's viewing. 'I never cared

for that part of the forest,' he grumbled. 'All those tales of ghosts said to haunt the Old Saxon road. 'Tis but a means to keep the gamekeepers and watchmen from catching scoundrels. The woods hide many a manner of thief.'

'Well said indeed, Constable. When the coroner's men returned to retrieve the carriage they found it stripped of a number of valuable furnishings.'

Silence fell as the doctor lifted the sheet and commenced to poke and prod the girl's naked body. He bent over her distended belly where the black gash of the wound was leaking yellow fluid.

'*Striae gravidarum*,' the doctor announced. 'If I'm not mistaken, these ugly stripes on the breasts and belly are a sign this was a double murder. Mark my words, I'll find the remains of a foetus in there.'

Tabitha leaned forward, her elbow catching a hymnal that clattered loudly to the floor. Not daring to breathe, she sat very still. So, the stomach had not bloated after the wounding but contained a child in embryo.

Joshua stared up towards the gallery. 'Could be a trapped bird,' she heard him say. 'I'll go up and get rid of it.'

Tabitha backed away from the curtain wondering where the devil she could hide.

'How advanced is the foetus?' she heard Nat ask.

'Difficult to say. The assailant struck her perhaps a dozen times in the abdomen. One might call it a diabolic attack. Wait, Constable. There is something you should see. A peculiar mark.'

Breathing again, Tabitha peeked through the gap in the curtain. The doctor was bending over the dead girl and now parted her legs as carelessly as a butcher handling a side of beef. 'What do you call that, gentlemen?' he asked.

Joshua's face was plum-red. Poor fellow, he had been a widower these five years and a naked quim was clearly a mortifying sight to him. Tabitha could make nothing of the supposed mark save for a dark blotch on the discoloured thigh.

Doctor Caldwell was triumphant. 'It is a capital "L". Branded into the tissue. Rarely have I seen such a mark before and then only on slaves. It is a sign of a pound sterling, gentlemen. The value of this female to her pimp or keeper. As to the cause of death, I'm afraid it is writ here as plain as day. I shall inform the coroner of the absence of a wedding ring, the presence of a child in the uterus, and the mark of a common *prostibulae* on her flesh. There is no mystery here. It was a dispute between a man and his trull, no doubt over her being with child.'

Tabitha railed silently. It was unlikely that such a fresh 'pullet', as this girl would have been called in the trade, would be destroyed by those who lived upon her earnings. She waited for Joshua or Nat to challenge the doctor's glib assertion. Joshua was nodding his head.

Nat, though, looked uncomfortable and challenged the doctor. 'Surely that was a mighty violent reaction to such an ordinary occurrence?'

'She was their property and labelled so.'

Nat folded his arms and stared at the floor. 'Why leave her beneath the Mondrem Oak? And then cover her body in leaves and flowers? I never saw such a sight in my life before.'

Doctor Caldwell shrugged. 'You poets look for complications where there are none, De Vallory. It is common enough for a villain to lead a girl in the family way to a secluded spot and then deprive her of both her own and the infant's life. And was she not found by children? They no doubt played a game with her, in all their innocence. I'll report what I've discovered to the coroner. Without even a name, or any witnesses, I doubt he will waste much time upon it.'

What he actually meant, Tabitha raged, was that without a name the girl would have no family or friends to fight for justice. Her gaze returned to the victim, who was so much like her former self – much the same age, with the same undignified experience of the flesh trade and even the same state of pregnancy. Yet she had been murdered as a chattel while Tabitha's every wish had come true. To her surprise she felt a burning lump constricting her throat.

Doctor Caldwell had moved to inspect his shining metal instruments. He picked up a short sharp knife. 'First, I must confirm what remains of the foetus.'

Soon she heard Joshua groaning and hurrying away. Then Nat muttered his apologies as he retreated from the chapel. Tabitha sank her head into her hands, praying that the examination would end quickly.

SIX

Back in her bedchamber, dozens of thoughts chased the prospect of sleep from Tabitha's mind. The identity of the dead girl was one matter. She tried again to picture where they had met. The memory was misty and old, from before the time when Tabitha lived in London. Closing her eyes, she caught a fleeting image of the heart-shaped face very much alive, making a wry grimace and laughing. No, her name was now obliterated in the horror of her brutal death.

Grisell returned, bringing Tabitha's half-sister, Bess. Both bobbed a curtsey and the maidservant grumbled, 'She's been mithering for you all morning.'

'Come here, little chick.' Tabitha patted the bed beside her. Bess bounded towards her, and athletically pulled herself on to the high mattress. She pulled her little sister close, stroking her straw-coloured curls. 'Leave her here for an hour, Grisell.'

The woman gave a toothless smile of pleasure. 'If I might go visiting for a short spell?'

She gave the woman leave, and once they were alone Bess announced, 'I don't like Grisell. She always says, "Be still and no singing." Grisell is a grumpy baggage.'

Tabitha stifled a burst of laughter. If Grisell was a sourpuss, she had found her match in forthright young Bess. Tabitha twisted her half-sister's flaxen hair into ringlets. Her own father had been a steady countryman, contentedly married to her mother until his early death. Bess, on the other hand, had been unlawfully fathered by Sir John's brother; it was a criminal act against her mother that still left a foul stain on Tabitha's memory. Privately, she considered it a blessing that Bess's father had died in prison, for he had delved deep in the occult arts and deserved no part in the life of her lovely sister.

'You must not speak so of Grisell. Remember when we read your *Pretty Little Pocket Book*? You must learn to be a little lady.

Be kind to those who wait on you. Young ladies must show charity.'

Bess gave a dramatic sigh, then quickly grinned and started to sing 'Baa baa black sheep' with more enthusiasm than melodic pitch. Then she lay down beside Tabitha and commanded her to 'Go to sleep.'

Tabitha closed her eyes and made a gentle snoring sound. Bess giggled, reached down and kissed her cheek with two soft lips and demanded that she 'Wake up.' Again and again, Tabitha had to pretend to sleep and upon being kissed, wake up and look around herself as if astonished.

Suddenly Bess changed the game. 'Baby,' she chattered, caressing Tabitha's stomach. 'Baby, wake up.'

Tabitha stiffened. Bess leaned down and pressed her lips against her stomach. She waited but nothing happened. Bess's tiny hands patted her flesh. Again, she demanded, 'Baby. Wake up.'

In reply, something fluttered inside her womb. The baby was moving. She held her breath, feeling the unmistakable quiver of a separate being moving inside her.

'How did you do that?' Tabitha whispered.

Bess raised a single finger to her lips to shush her. 'Baby loves me, Tabby.' The little girl's face was bright with certainty. No wonder the servants found her an odd little girl. Tabitha felt safe again; the baby loved Bess. Content, the little girl splayed her warm body against her sister's, until their breathing rose and fell in unison and they both fell fast asleep.

SEVEN

That evening, Tabitha and Nat were eating a supper of cold meat and pickles in the parlour with Sir John. The gathering was dismal, for each few minutes Sir John reached down with his one good arm in search of Hector, who had for years sat like a sentinel beside his master's chair. Whenever his hand grasped air the old man gave a little bleat of disappointment. Since his attack of apoplexy the old man was trapped and twisted inside his broken body. The last year had brought many blows. First, he had lost his son Francis, slaughtered in the harvest corn. His wife, Lady Daphne, was now confined in a genteel private house near Cambridge under the care of an enlightened doctor, her mind so disordered that she could no longer live in society. Yet in a twist of fate, he had learned that Nat Starling, sired on his young serving maid, was his misbegotten son. Gratefully, Sir John had acknowledged him and welcomed Nat and Tabitha to Bold Hall. Now Sir John looked hard at his son, his watery eyes begging him to explain the dog's absence. Nat repeated the news again, though he had told his father a dozen times. Today's search had again brought no luck.

A sudden pounding on the stair brought Higgott, their steward, bursting into the room, sweating hard. 'Sirs, Madam. That soldier fellow who called on Mister De Vallory has struck young Tom. We've locked him in the scullery.'

Nat stood abruptly and reached for his coat. 'Dammit. I clean forgot to question him. God knows there was no need to cause an affray.'

Tabitha also rose. Her husband had many virtues: he knew by heart all of Isaac Newton's thoughts on time and its passing, and the universe and suchlike, yet he rarely turned up anywhere at the correct time.

'Let's talk to him together,' she said, then kissed her father-in-law goodnight and bade Grisell put him to bed. Down in the kitchen wing they found Tom very shaken from having taken the soldier's fist against his jaw. He raised a swollen face that showed one less tooth and a great deal of damaged pride. 'He's your killer,' he muttered after spitting a gobbet of blood. 'He has black murder in his heart, that one.'

Tabitha strode to the scullery and observed their captive through the grille in the door. He was hunched over the stone table, his great cannonball head sunk deep in his hands.

Two brawny lads led Jacob Hollingsworth out into the anteroom. Tonight, the angry lines carved into his face lent him a frightening aspect. 'You cannot keep an innocent man prisoner. Let me on my way.'

'That's for me to decide,' Nat retorted. 'Tom, what happened?'

Tom gave a rambling account of how the soldier had arrived at noon and turned wild by the afternoon, threatening to walk out without seeing the master.

Nat asked the captive. 'And what do you say?'

'I need to go.'

'So you tell me. But that's no reason to strike a loyal servant of mine.'

With a pained sigh the soldier bowed to Nat and grudgingly said he was sorry. Nat continued to eye him coldly. 'The girl beneath the tree. What was she to you?'

'I never seen her. You can't go blaming me when I never seen her before.'

Nat shook his head. 'And what of Baptist Gunn and his followers? Did you ever see her with them?'

'I told you, I never seen her. You go arrest Gunn and that mob in the treehouse before you blame me. Heathens, they are. Won't take the sacrament, nor marry in church as God commanded. If you break one commandment, why not the lot of them? They struck my mother. Every springtime she's picked her simples in the hedgerows but now those devils claim the whole crop for themselves. There be one young jade, called herself Repentance, or some such cant. She cursed at my mother, a venerable lady of seventy years. And then she struck her.'

'The girl you speak of, was she young, slender, five foot tall, considered pretty?' asked Nat.

'No, that i'nt her. The hussy I'm speaking of had the pit-marks of the pox all over her face.'

'Will you swear on the Bible that you never saw that young woman by the Mondrem Oak?'

Hollingsworth's angry eyes slid furtively away from Nat. He took his time, adjusting the buckle at his waist. 'I will swear,' he said at last.

'Were you in the forest on May Eve?' Tabitha broke in. 'Perhaps you went a-Maying to find a girl?'

The soldier cast her a sheepish glance. 'No. I would have naught to do with the doxies round here. I am a clean-living man, my lady. The army brings discipline to a man's life.'

Nat broke in. 'And an observant eye, I reckon. When you go about the forest perhaps you've seen more than most?'

Hollingsworth considered hard before he spoke up. 'Sir, you should know that come nightfall that forest is thick with poachers. Where they come from I cannot say. And it's not just venison, Your Honour. Game birds, fish, conies. They all fetch a good price at the Chester market.'

'You have names?' Higgott stepped forward.

'They was always in disguise when I seen them. They darken their faces with black stuff and wear slouch hats and black cloaks.'

'But you can tell us more?' Nat challenged.

The soldier lifted his large chin and considered. 'I will not be called a rat. There's a great crowd of them and but one of me.'

'We won't repeat what you tell us,' Nat said quickly.

'Well, I seen them congregate in that drinking place. At the sign of the bush on the Old Coach Road. They come together on moonless nights with their sticks and their dogs and their snares, just like the ballads do say.'

When the gathering had dispersed Tabitha and Nat climbed the great carved staircase to their separate chambers. 'He lied when I asked him about meeting a girl,' Tabitha said.

'Aye. The man could not give a straight answer. But I'm glad to know of these raids upon our game.'

She was tired out but roused herself to warn him. 'Remember, only the western portion of the forest belongs to Sir John. If these poachers are taking Lord Langley's venison, let them be.'

He guided her gently. 'If Langley finds out we knew of it but did nothing he will bear a hard grudge. Next time they meet I'll follow them. The new moon isn't long now, the first night of June.'

Nat's candle sent golden beams of light along the walls of the corridor. Here were paintings of Nat's forebears, a long line of noble De Vallorys reaching back to the days of doublets and farthingales. What would they have done to protect their game? she wondered.

'Nat, I don't like you hunting poachers alone. Tell Joshua to call the sheriff in.'

'And turn all the men of the forest against me? I'll take a quiet look at what's afoot. I too can track quarry through a moonless night.'

Nat paused before a portrait of a stout child of two years or so, clutching a feathered hat. A wolfhound puppy pranced at the hem of the child's damask gown.

'My father,' Nat said with amusement in his voice. 'See the coral at his belt.' It was a pretty stick of orange-red coral set in a silver rattle hung with bells. 'Earlier, my father gave it to me. He wants our child to use it.'

Seeing the De Vallory crest stamped into the silver rattle, Tabitha's spirits rose. It confirmed what she could scarcely grasp: that the child she carried would be born to honour, wealth and rank. Yet there was no portrait of Nat in damask and lace in this gallery. His family had lived in a hovel in the poorest part of Netherlea, though he had later been raised in a noble house in Cambridgeshire where his mother was housekeeper.

'I am sorry you were not tutored as a child to take on your position,' she said gently.

'Yes, but I am here now,' he replied. 'I should like to think my experience of the world is all the broader for it.'

'For sure your experience is agreeably broad. And yet you leave me here all alone,' she teased, as they reached her chamber. He held her fast against the door, a hand on either side of her, body to body. Her tiredness fell away and she murmured in his ear, 'I am here now, sir, if you want company.'

He kissed her and broke free. 'I wish for nothing more. But Doctor Caldwell will disapprove. And we must be strong, my love. The pleasures of the marriage bed will be all the sweeter for a little more denial.'

EIGHT

14 May 1753

Mrs Sukey Adams presented herself in the drawing room the next afternoon. Tabitha's first impression was of a flaxen-haired countrywoman whose natural bloom had been blighted by misfortune. Her pink cheeks were smooth but her faded eyes were weary. The pronounced swelling of her stomach was hidden modestly behind a voluminous white apron. She carried her pregnancy well and high and showed strong arms and work-reddened hands. Tabitha privately laughed at her own folly in imagining a hard-faced, crafty spy sent by Doctor Caldwell.

Mrs Adams spoke in a pleasant voice though she blushed when speaking of her circumstances. 'I am lodging in Chester with my little boy, Davey. And looking about for a position as a nurse, my lady. I am well able, having brought up my own son and my sister's children. My little Davey will of course stop with my sister till my time comes. I suppose I must tell you . . .' Steeling herself, she turned her face aside before attempting to continue. 'I am sorry to say that my husband, a journeyman who travelled much between Chester and Ireland in the linen trade has – well, he has discarded me.' Tears welled in her eyes.

'Sit, sit,' Tabitha insisted. Then she fetched the woman a glass of cordial, studying her all the while. There were clear signs of the hard times Mrs Adams had faced. Though she wore a blue linsey-wolsey gown over a white shift, her cap and costume were in dire need of a washtub and hot iron. Her shoes were cheap and mud-caked, as if she had walked the river-path from Chester.

'So you see,' Mrs Adams continued after taking a thirsty draught from the glass, 'I am afraid I must throw myself upon the charity of the world to support me and Davey. But I am a most willing worker, well used to childbed and my little boy was always a greedy eater, yet I had a flow of milk enough for two. As for the coming weeks, I am a good needlewoman and won a church prize for my delicate stitchwork. I do so like to sew childbed cloths.'

'And when will your own confinement be?' Tabitha asked.

A glow of expectation lit the nurse's colourless eyes. 'About Midsummer's Day, I reckon. But as I say, I can manage the two little infants at once.'

'But what if your child is later than mine? Your milk will not yet be ready.'

'In that case I have a most nutritious receipt for goats' milk mixed with a little arrowroot. I have seen children grow heartily on the mixture and it shall not be for long. And I am entirely at your disposal.'

The woman's eagerness to please was a pleasant contrast to the occasional surliness of Grisell and the other Bold Hall servants. Devil take them, she had been lucky to have her great-aunt Sarah as an ally in the servants' hall. 'I shall do my best to keep the worst of them in line,' she had promised Tabitha upon her promotion as housekeeper. This prospective nursemaid appeared to be cut from more sensitive cloth altogether.

'You must have been heartbroken to find yourself alone at such a time,' Tabitha said gently.

Mrs Adams eyes shone with sorrow. 'Oh, I am, my lady. But I have plenty of love to give your little one. Please, my lady. You shall not find a more devoted nurse.'

The woman's simple appeal convinced Tabitha. There were so many careless creatures left in charge of nursing infants. She recalled a nurse at Netherlea who had swaddled a collection of babies and hung them on hooks on the wall while she went off to market. And there had been worse tales, of infants scalded, dropped and accidentally poisoned.

'Very well. I shall give you a trial, Mrs Adams.'

'Do call me Sukey, won't you, my lady?'

'I will. You may board and lodge here till my confinement. I shall give you ten shillings for the two months remaining and the first month of confinement. What say you?'

Mrs Adams stood up and bobbed low, patches of crimson flaring at her throat and cheeks. 'Thank you. You have such a good heart, my lady. I only ask a half-day's leave to visit Davey each week. Just till you are confined, that is.'

'And until you are also brought to childbed,' Tabitha recalled. 'See my housekeeper for what will suit her, but naturally I have no objection to you visiting your little boy. Now, Sukey, do you need to arrange for your box to be fetched? How soon can you begin?'

Sukey Adams curtsied again. 'Why, I shall start this very minute if that suits. Times are hard, my lady. I carry all I own upon my back.'

NINE

17 May 1753

A few days later, the casement of Tabitha's parlour stood open to a radiant view of soft summer sunlight and high billowing clouds. For more than an hour Sukey had been planning the baby's clothes and a great pile of fabrics had been fingered and discarded.

'These rough linens will only do for the baby's clouts,' Sukey declared. 'And there is little enough time left to order muslins and silks for your little one. You must have gowns and caps and mantles, as well as all the swaddling bands and bed-stuffs.'

It was too late in the day to visit Chester so Tabitha wrote a list in preparation to buy the best that the city's linen drapers could provide. Pricked with the notion that she might have been lax in her preparations, she asked Sukey, 'Do not milliners and suchlike sell sets of baby clothes?'

'Oh, you shouldn't want that common stuff, my lady. I have in mind such lordly little clothes with ribbons and holy point patterns. I shall make every stitch with love,' she added complacently. Then, after considering, the nurse asked, 'Forgive me asking, but did you not sew any linens in preparation of your marriage?'

Tabitha laughed at the notion. 'I did not. I was rather distracted at the time. My husband and I were married rather suddenly. Now, what do you say to us getting outside in this fine weather? We still have time to visit Jennet Saxton and her father the constable.'

Sukey looked longingly at the pile of cloths. 'Perhaps I could make a start on some hemming.'

'No,' announced Tabitha. 'The housemaids will help you with that. Save your needle for the fancy work.'

Sukey looked with trepidation towards the window. 'The sun is so strong. Is it wise for us to risk it?'

Lord, if Tabitha had known the woman would be such a stick-at-home she might have bought a wooden dummy board for her fireside. 'I shall lend you a hat. Besides, I like the notion of us two mothers-in-waiting going out for some air. Doctor Caldwell will no doubt incarcerate me once the baby is born.'

Tabitha sent down to the stable men to ready the gig and asked for an older groom, Glover, to drive instead of young Tom. After tying two wide straw hats beneath their chins with ribbons, the two women were soon moving sedately along the drive to the hall's gilded gates. Tabitha described the estate with some pride, having admired it all her life from the humble vantage of her mother's cottage. There was the garden, designed in the old-fashioned manner of knots and box hedges, then the fishpond and dovecote, and the physic and herb gardens in the distance belonging to the dower house. Out on Netherlea High Street they glided past the bakers, the inn and the smart estate office. Outside the blacksmith's yard, Zusanna, the blacksmith's wife scowled up at them and Tabitha felt a moment of sweet pleasure that she must no longer meet the village harridan face-to-face. She pointed out the village lock-up and the wooden pillory beside it. Thereafter the street diminished to ill-patched cottages that were little more than hovels. Soon they came to the grey stone church and parsonage by the church green, and then they were rocking gently on the track into Netherlea woods.

The chimney of her mother's former cottage peeped up through the trees, but the nursemaid's presence prevented Tabitha from calling there for old times' sake. Instead, they headed straight for The Grange, a former monastic building given to Joshua as one of the sheriff's loyal men. On such a bright day it looked its most picturesque, a quaint medieval building with arrowslits for windows, over which a profusion of yellow honeysuckle spread. Jennet ran out to meet them, her face falling to see Glover at the reins.

'Have you not brought Tom?'

'That is not a polite greeting, Jennet. Come along, help Mrs Adams and myself down. And two glasses of your father's sugar beer would not go amiss.'

Inside the dark parlour there were some welcome improvements since her last visit. At last, Joshua had removed his deceased wife Mary's spinning wheel, which had always seemed to cast a disapproving shadow across the room. And someone had procured a few cushions for the oak settle and hard benches on which she and Sukey eased themselves down.

Jennet returned from the kitchen with the moping aspect common to many a girl of fifteen. 'I cannot see why you have all turned against me,' she complained. 'My father says Tom is only a footman and won't let him call on me. And now you choose Glover to drive you.'

'I like Tom,' Tabitha said, stretching the truth a little, for the lad was at times a great blockhead. 'But I agree with your father. You are too young for him to be seriously courting you. Where is Joshua, by the way?'

'He's out the back. But listen, Tabitha. Can I not come home with you and dine at Bold Hall?'

And here is the crux of it, Tabitha thought. She and Jennet were old friends, but if the girl married Tom she would become the lower footman's wife. The remaining servants would not be happy if they had to wait on Jennet at dinner. Yet was she herself behaving too proud to quibble like this? Tush, sometimes this 'being a lady' was such an awkward business.

'Jennet, Tom is on duty tonight so cannot leave his post. And your father will not like it.'

Suddenly the girl slammed down a jug, spilling a deal of its contents over the table. With a cry of, 'And it has all turned out so well for you!' Jennet turned tail and disappeared from the room.

'Goodness,' murmured Sukey.

Tabitha shook her head in half-amused exasperation. 'Young folk think us fools, but we know them to be so. Come along, let's go outside.'

The garden stood apple green in the motionless air and the sun on Tabitha's back felt like welcome balm. They walked together admiring the good crop of runner beans growing amongst the wallflowers and heartsease. Joshua was in his outhouse surrounded by firewood, whittling a spoon with his knife, alone and at ease in his stained work shirt. Tabitha thought he looked strong and well.

Flustered, he bowed to them both. 'I'm right glad you've come, Tabitha. And you, ma'am.'

Tabitha studied his workbench that lay scattered with half-carved objects, numbering a tobacco pipe and a tiny bird. 'These are charming. Could you make me a little figure of a baby to bring me luck? Small and plain, like those poppets the village women used to have?'

A smile broke across his broad face. 'You still dabbling in them old superstitions? Aye well, I reckon it will do no harm.'

At that moment Sukey curtseyed to Joshua, eyeing the wooden objects with equal delight.

'And you, Sukey. Should you like one for yourself?'

'You are too kind, madam.'

'It will be a pleasure,' Joshua said with some gallantry. 'Now wait in the garden if you will and I'll get myself decent.'

They sat outside in a shady arbour, listening to the soporific drone of the bees. 'Do you think we are heathens?' Tabitha asked her companion.

Sukey raised her eyes from a piece of darning she had smuggled inside her pocket. 'No,' she said with clear-eyed frankness. 'I think when the danger is great we must call on any comfort. Madam, if you have a liking for the old lore, I can share many secret ways. Looking at the way you carry the child all around and not so high, I'd wager it's a boy. But we might try that old charm with your wedding ring if you like.'

Tabitha nodded, knowing the custom well. Maybe Sukey was not such a dummy board after all.

Joshua joined them, respectably dressed in a mustard coat and clean shirt, carrying yet more cool beer and some welcome seed cake. 'I see you didn't bring Tom Seagoes along with you. I must thank you for that. I will not have my daughter simpering over some lad who is free with his fists.'

'I have hopes he will grow out of it,' Tabitha murmured.

'Until he does he is too young to marry. And so is Jennet.'

'She has huffed away and left us but I don't want to hurt her, Joshua. I shall ask her to help stitch the baby's clothes. But when she comes I'll be sure Tom is working elsewhere. Now, have you had any news from Jane?'

Joshua pulled an exasperated face. 'Her father lingers on at death's door. God knows if she will ever come home. And now their landlord has her working at his mill.'

Joshua and Jane, Bold Hall's confectionery maid, had been on the very edge of coming to an understanding only a few weeks earlier, before the urgent summons to attend to her father had arrived. Now as he regaled her with a list of frustrations, Joshua wore the look of a sorrowing boy. Tabitha could not help but care about him; he had been her childhood companion, her once-upon-a-time sweetheart but never, thank heavens, her lover. His pain afflicted her, just as Nat's hurts did. She was not certain that was a good thing, but it was true.

Now she noticed Joshua glance warily towards Sukey. The nursemaid appeared entirely rapt in the making of her stitches.

'What did you make of Jacob Hollingsworth?' she asked softly.

Joshua looked away over pale green fields half-mown of hay. 'Private Hollingsworth is twice the man of that gawkie boy. I made enquiries at the barracks and he is well regarded by his commander. A rough cove but a good soldier.'

It was not the first time that Tabitha did not agree with Joshua. 'Did you not think his testimony that he saw nothing of interest in the forest was false?'

Joshua shook his head. 'Was it false?'

She shrugged an answer; she could not prove it.

'I am seeing the sheriff tomorrow and need more proof of his misconduct than a womanish notion. It is a boon at least that the inquest is delayed. I questioned everyone I could find but discovered nothing. I reckon that Gunn fellow is a sly one, protesting he knows nothing. 'Tis said there is no worse rogue than a holy one. As yet no witnesses have come forward. We found a weapon, mind you. There was a large bone-handled knife a few dozen paces away in the shallows of Maidens Mere. It's a common enough instrument, more's the pity.'

'And still no name for the poor girl who died?' Tabitha said.

'Just that trinket. 'Tis a pity half is missing.'

'What trinket is that?'

'Oh yes, I forgot, you wasn't there when I found it. It was on that girl's stiff finger. I have it here.' Joshua reached into his coat and produced a small object inside a wrap of cloth and handed it to her. She held it high up to the light. It was one half of a ring of the type called a gimmel, or twin ring. But at some previous time, this half had been separated from the twin band that fitted above it and the joining pin removed. Yet even what remained was a lovely object. It was a hoop of flattened gold that bore a perfect tiny hand covered in flesh-coloured enamel with a small, heart-shaped ruby set beneath those protective curling fingers. Tabitha guessed that when the missing upper ring was slipped above it, an absent second hand would clasp the first. Carrying it to the bright light at the open door, she inspected the engraving on the inside of the hoop. It read:

I A

GUST

35

So breaks my heart

Tabitha fingered the smooth gold where the lettering had been etched. 'May I borrow this?'

'No. You lose that and I'll have naught to show the sheriff.'

So it was decided that Tabitha should make a copy with pen and ink, which she did with some excitement. For since the moment that Joshua had produced the pretty token she had got an excellent notion of where to find the other half.

TEN

18 May 1753

Chester's Blue Coat Hospital was situated by the city's ancient gateway at Upper Northgate. It was a grand modern structure of brick with two impressive wings, fronted by iron railings and a handsome gate. Tabitha had passed the building many times without curiosity, for it was a charitable institution founded by a former bishop to house and educate poor children and as such it had seemed a place of somewhat grim sanctimony. Yet she remembered how, during her time in London, its sister foundation of the Foundling Hospital in Bloomsbury had been notorious for taking in misbegotten children, so that its fame led her friend Poll to threaten to abandon her own wretched child at its gates. When especially low-spirited, Poll had wailed that her child would at least get three meals a day and a dry bed while she worked the streets supporting a drunken sot of a husband. In the event, Poll had never ventured there, for behind the curses she was a fond mother. And Tabitha had doubted her chance of success, for such disorderly crowds mobbed the gates that a ballot had been started up and only those who drew a rare white ball from a linen bag might have their child considered.

Tabitha and Sukey were met by a dour manservant who informed them that the matron was engaged by a committee. Tabitha assumed her proudest air of hauteur. 'I have a mind to make a subscription for these unfortunates. But first I must look about the place and also speak to the matron. How long will she be?'

The servant eyed her flowered silk robe and glittering jewels. This time he managed a small bow and invited them into a sparse anteroom while he went in search of assistance.

Both women looked about the room, at the pious mottos and plaques. From behind the wall they could hear a schoolmaster giving a lesson in arithmetic, while the sound of childish singing reached them faintly from the chapel. Sukey spoke first. 'How generous you are, my lady, to think of the poor.'

Tabitha pressed her lips tight together to hide her amusement. 'Oh, I am sure they deserve a few pounds. Now listen, whatever little tale I tell the matron, you will oblige me by staying silent, won't you?' Uncertainly, the nurse nodded in agreement.

A housemistress arrived to take them on a tour of the building until the matron might be free. Tabitha observed a placid band of blue-coated boys learning to reckon accounts, while others worked in the yard making fishing nets or dressing hemp. She was shown the long tables in the dining room and nodded pleasantly to hear the children would that day dine on the boiled mutton she could smell stewing. In the chapel she followed the words of a hymn being practised at the order of the music master:

> *In guilt each part was formed*
> *Of all this sinful frame;*
> *In guilt I was conceived and born*
> *The heir of sin and shame.*

For a while she rested in a pew, enjoying the boys' treble voices as she considered the merits of the place. In London it had sickened her that unwanted children were abandoned in ditches, or thrown in the Thames, as casually as unwanted kittens. She had never before had the opportunity to offer charity to any living soul and these young persons were well deserving of an education and a decent start in life. Yet still there was something she disliked about the place.

'Might we see the girls, now?' she asked the housemistress. They were led across the chapel yard into a less impressive building. Here a dozen or so girls between five and ten years old were spinning flax while an older woman tested their knowledge of the catechism: 'Do you believe that you are a sinner?' she asked.

'Yes, I believe it. I am a sinner,' the girls replied in flat, monotonous tones.

'What have you deserved from God because of your sins?'

'His wrath and displeasure, temporal death, and eternal damnation . . .'

Like the boys, these little scholars wore the mark of the charity's blue coat: a short cape-like collar and blue bindings to their indoor caps. A great list of rules dominated the wall: the children were not to stroll or ramble about the town, must pray for their benefactors each morning, meal-time and evening, and learn by heart the holy scriptures concerning obedience to their masters. The final rule was that they must not pursue any learning that might set them above the condition of servants.

The schoolmistress drew the two women over to a table of goods for sale comprising knitted purses and garters. Tabitha bought a few items and tried to make jests with the children, but their glum expressions convinced her that they had been trained to stifle any childish merriment.

'Do you have any infants here?' she asked the housemistress.

'Just one or two. We don't generally keep infants here, my lady. Most are sent out to wet nurses to be suckled. We fetch them back into the school when they reach five or six years old.'

'Might I see those you have?'

They were led to a room where they found a fat nurse with a stout infant dribbling and snuffling at her enormous breast. The nurse looked up, as sleepy and happy as the baby.

'This little fellow came into the infirmary when his widowed mother died of the mortification. A noble lady in his parish kindly paid ten pounds to place him here.'

'Why is he not properly swaddled?' asked Sukey.

'All tight swaddling is forbidden,' the housemistress answered. 'Every child has just one loose flannel gown and petticoat and one cap for its head. No bandages, no stays, tight wrappers or shoes. The doctor says the child will learn to walk far sooner if his body is at liberty.'

'Goodness,' murmured Sukey. 'Yet our good Lord was swaddled in his manger.'

'And do the infants thrive under such a regime?' Tabitha asked.

The housemistress nodded defiantly. 'Oh yes, our only trouble is with the nurses. They roll and pin their charges a dozen times around with bandages so they lie all day in their filth.'

At this moment a miserable wailing emerged from behind a drawn curtain. 'Do you have another child here?' asked Tabitha, striding towards the sound. 'If I am to subscribe to this institution, I need to see—' She pulled the curtain back. A single cradle lay in the recess of the room. Inside it an infant was crying like a feeble cat. Tabitha stopped in her tracks. The tiny face was as wrinkled as a walnut and blotched with red marks. A disgusting stink filled her nostrils.

'That one has not long left upon this earth,' the woman was saying. 'The pox will infect whoever gives suck to her.' Tabitha hurriedly retreated from the blighted child and tried not to breathe. Scarlet eruptions scarred the tiny, puckered face; the baby's eyes and nose were weeping with noxious fluid. She knew the signs of the pox better than many: the pustules, ulcers and poisoned blood. Amongst her former profession it was considered a boon if such infants were stillborn or, like this scrap of misery, passed rapidly to a better place.

'What can be done for her?' Tabitha's voice sounded shaky even to her own ears.

'We will try to feed her a pap of bread and a little wine. If she were older the governors would pay for the mercury cure, but there's no hope, my lady. It is better such children go to God in innocence than grow into such infamous wretches as their own parents must be. It is always the child that pays for the sins of the mother.'

Tabitha watched as tiny fingers stretched towards her as if craving human touch. There was life still in the infant's tiny veins; desperate, hopeless life. Again, Tabitha's throat burned. What was this damned tender-heartedness that came upon her these days?

'A gift of money? For whatever she needs.' She hated to hear the tremor in her voice. Finding a sovereign in her skirt pocket, she cast it on the table.

'We shall see she has prayers and a Christian burial.'

Tabitha headed for the door pulling Sukey by the arm, so desperate was she for clean air.

ELEVEN

'Mrs De Vallory.' The matron was a buxom, upstanding woman of forty wearing a military-style black gown with a plain crucifix at her throat. She made a small bob to Tabitha and nodded at Sukey, keenly interested in both of the women's expectant condition. Tea was brought into her modest office and they settled around a comfortable table. 'Now, how may I serve you?' the matron asked.

Tabitha was glad that she had prepared a little speech, giving out the pretence that she was a friend of the dead girl's mother, for why else would the matron confide the facts of the case? 'I am representing a lady who is unable to publicly visit you, if you understand my meaning?'

The matron nodded, soberly.

'Some years ago she left a child in your care and with it half a token. I understand you use these as a means of identifying any claimants who come forward for a child?'

The matron put down her dish of tea and nodded. 'It is not the Blue Coat Hospital's primary purpose to take in children from wealthy benefactors, but on occasion we do so. We keep most comprehensive records of admission.'

Tabitha laid the rough sketch of the ring upon the table. 'It is half of a gimmel ring with a very particular engraving in the band. Do you recognize it?'

The matron studied the sketch, her eyes widening in alarm. 'I do,' she said, touching her crucifix. 'It was a complicated case.'

Complicated for whom? The matron recognized the ring, proving the connection to this place. Though groping in the dark, Tabitha made a direct sally. 'Today the original of this half-ring goes into the possession of Chester's high sheriff. I am here to keep any enquiry discreet.'

Relief blazed on the matron's thread-veined cheeks. 'Discretion, yes. I am most grateful to you. What wickedness has the girl committed now?'

'I am afraid the wickedness was not committed by your pupil, but upon her. She is dead.'

The matron made a little bleating sound. 'We did our best. The child was not tractable. We cannot be blamed for her depravities. You will ask the sheriff to keep silent about our part in this?'

Tabitha decided to risk her imposture a little further. 'It would be best if you tell me all. The lady who is her . . . close connection . . . is most anxious to learn what befell her. You said you hold her history in the record book?'

She waited as the matron clearly struggled with conscience or fear, she could not say which. 'Do you recall the year of admission?' she asked at last.

Tabitha nodded and gestured towards her sketch of the ring.

The previous day, as soon as she had returned from Joshua's, Tabitha had eagerly tackled the enigma of the token. Settling down in her favourite chair, she had puzzled over her sketch of the letters and numbers on the inside of the ring:

I A

GUST

35

So breaks my heart

The topmost fragment was too short to be explicable, but the second was most likely '*AUGUST*'. Therefore, the next part of the date was likely '*1735*'. The final portion no doubt referred to a separation. Though it might be a gift from a lover, Tabitha also pondered it being inscribed by a mother to her child. Just as the two parts of the ring had been separated, so the couplet no doubt reinforced that parting, speaking of their being '*sadly apart*' or some such rhyming couplet.

'It was 1735,' Tabitha declared, glancing down at the drawing.

The matron went to her bureau and withdrew a leather-bound book. But where she opened the pages only the rough torn edge of the book remained.

'In my surprise I forgot how she left us. This vandalism was the girl's work. But I can give you her history. She came to us at a few weeks old with the half of a ring and a donation of one hundred pounds. The money was to nurse her, to school her, and raise her to be a useful citizen. It is a great deal of money, but I warrant this institution earned its fee in trouble.' The matron said this with a jerk of her chin that revealed a well of bitterness.

'When she grew to girlhood she was the oddest character: unfriendly, sulky and intractable. She first ran away from us at only seven years of age, after she returned from her nurse in the country. It seems she had grown attached to the woman. She was punished, but the following year tried the same trick again. She fooled many in this institution, but not me. I long suspected her discontent stemmed from the wrong-headed notion that she deserved a superior position in life. Somehow, she learned of the hundred pounds benefice and claimed she was being kept here against her will. Then at twelve years old the governors arranged for her to be settled as an apprentice at a wire-making factory. Again, she ran away. She soon came back to fetch the two guineas we always settle upon our girls when we dispose of them. And then we discovered the truth. While in the town she had been debauched and had carnal knowledge with a grown man. She was dismissed from this place. But not before she broke into this office with a stolen chisel, smashed the lock upon the bureau, tore the pages from this book and stole the half-ring deposited by her parent.'

Tabitha used her utmost powers not to look appalled at the governors' callous treatment of the child. It was a common enough tale – a love-starved child cast on the town who made easy prey for unscrupulous men. Well, this at least confirmed how the dead girl had obtained her own half of the ring. Yet who had deposited that half-trinket when she was left as a newborn baby?

'Did you attempt to contact her mother?'

'You must know the answer to that. No, we did not. The child had tarnished our reputation. The last I heard she was living as a common prostitute.'

Tabitha scoured her wits for another means to obtain the mother's name. 'May I see the record?'

The matron leaned over and showed her. There was nothing left save the paper receipt for the hundred pounds, but no name.

'Did her mother ever visit her?'

'I don't believe so. Though many a wealthy benefactress comes

to watch the Sunday service. It is my suspicion that the ladies
most attached to this charity may have disposed of their misbegotten
offspring with us in the past.'

'But you would have recognized the mother's name?'

'No, not at all. Such was the secrecy surrounding the whole
affair that even I never learned it. And I prefer not to know it.'

Tabitha gave a little bleat of frustration. It was like unlocking
a treasure chest only to find another iron casket locked inside it.

The matron asked fervently, 'Must the hospital repay the
balance of the hundred pounds? Though I cannot see why it
should. Every effort was made to guide her in a Christian life.
To think she died in sin. How did she bring that upon herself?'

'She carries no blame. She was murdered. My husband and I
found her slaughtered in the forest.' Tabitha shook her head
wearily. 'No. It seems to me you carried out your duty.'
Damnation, she still knew almost nothing of the dead girl's
background. 'And if we set up a memorial, what name should
we give her?'

'Why, Maria, of course.'

Of course, Tabitha thought, remembering the '*I A*' engraved
on the ring. 'And what surname did she bear?'

'St John.'

At last she had a name. She rattled through everyone with the
name St John that she knew and found none. 'That was her given
name?'

'No. It is the tradition of this institution to give a bastard child
a respectable name. Did you not notice to whom the chapel is
dedicated? St John is our beloved saint.'

Tabitha recalled the guilt-laden hymn she had heard in the
chapel with its taunts of sin and shame. Nat had been born to a
fifteen-year-old serving girl – by the charity school's reckoning,
he was not respectable either. Nor was her little half-sister, Bess.
As she hurried away from the hospital with Sukey Adams at her
side, it seemed to her that Saint John had granted his namesake
only the most grudging of earthly protection.

TWELVE

Nat's spirits lifted as he took an early morning ride across his father's land. He breathed in the sweet air of a May morning as Jupiter's hooves flung up dewy diamonds from the meadows. One day all of these pastures, farms, heaths and copses would be his. Then, just as absolute time flowed into the future, it would pass to his and Tabitha's children and then their children in turn. Suddenly, as he walked his horse over the crown of a bridge, a skinny youth stepped out and hailed him. The scab-faced lad barred his way.

'Your name De Vallory?' he taunted, pounding a stout wooden staff against his palm. Suspecting robbery, Nat was glad of Jupiter's imposing height. Reining the horse back, Nat nodded. The youth dropped a sealed letter on the parapet and then darted away into the trees.

Pocketing it, he saw it was from that remarkable fellow, Baptist Gunn. Later, in the cellar of the Dower House, he pushed aside the dull accounts and invoices his steward Higgott had pressed upon him. Instead he read the letter carefully:

Honourable Sir,

I write to beg your help in a most pressing matter. In short, myself and my followers are being harried off your land by armed men who have twice attacked us in the night. First, they attempted to beat my followers with clubs, and the next night fired half a dozen musket shots in the air and threatened to set our roof alight.

Nat cast down the letter in irritation. Dammit, he had no notion of who might be harrying Gunn. First the murder, then the poachers, and now this. He was finding his new life had plenty of irksome duties to counter his new pleasures. What had he done to deserve such trouble on his doorstep? He picked up the letter again.

Good sir, we would depart most readily, save that we wait in this place for a most particular reason. Such is our danger that I must tell you more of our future destiny. In brief, I have had a dream of such extraordinary power that to keep you ignorant seems a most serious wrong. Here is a true account of my premonition.

Some nights ago, after preaching to my loyal band, I sank into a heavy sleep. In the darkest deeps of the night I was woken by the touch of a moonlit hand reaching inside my bed curtain. I started up and found a man's shape beside me, like to an angel, and he was crowned with light and composed of ever-shifting glimmerings in the darkness.
Next, I felt a flame of knowledge leap inside my head. Letters as bright as the sun's rays spelled words in my brain. I rose and found a candle, pen and paper, and began to write as if scribing words by clockwork. Ever since that night I have received these visitations and fallen in a trance. I am told I spoke something of these very same portents the night we met. Here is a fuller account of my prophecy, though I had no knowledge of its meaning at the time:

> *I say that in 1753,*
> *A second saviour will descend to thee,*
> *These signs will appear by the prophet foretold,*
> *Come Midsummer's Day in the world of old.*
> *Where the king of the forest for centuries stood,*
> *He will come amid strife and hot-spilled blood,*
> *And though the shade-giver never did roam,*
> *He will bear Him o'er waters to His new home.*

There is more, my friend, but it is this verse that concerns me most urgently. You, I am sure, will at once comprehend why it is that we must remain in the exact place where you found us.

And so I beg that you give orders that we be allowed to stay in the forest a while longer. Then, when this prophecy has come to pass, we will soberly go on our way, over the waters to live in glory with our Saviour.

Now you may choose to scorn my message as that of a

*charlatan, or even a lunatic. But I would remind you that
God will often communicate with mortals, coming in 'a
dream, in a vision of the night, when deep sleep falleth upon
men, in slumberings upon the bed, then He opens the ears
of men and seals their instruction.' (Job 33, 15)*

*And now I have set forth my plea and beg your charity
and mercy,*

I should be obliged to remain,
Your humble servant,
Baptist Gunn

With renewed interest Nat pondered the prophetic verse. In earlier
days he had written enigmatic doggerel for a few shillings and
thereby indulged his liking for wordplay. He re-read the verse
again, deciphering its crude symbols. It wasn't difficult. In suit-
ably biblical terms it spoke of a vague saviour, but what the
people would be saved from it didn't specify. Nat recalled a
common chapbook riddle and pulled a volume from his bookshelf.
Yes, he had guessed correctly what had been in the so-called
prophet's mind as he wrote:

An Enigma
Two hundred years I once did live,
And stalk-capped fruits I oft did give,
Yet all that time I ne'er did roam,
So much as half a mile from home,
My days were spent devoid of strife,
Until an axe struck down my life.
And since my death – I pray give ear,
I oft have sailed far and near.

As he had guessed, the solution was an oak tree and the location
in the prophecy was the famous Mondrem Oak. As for 'bearing
Him over the waters', it took no great wit to understand this
must refer to the group's imminent voyage to America in a ship
made of oak.

Nat's uneasiness grew. Why was Gunn hammering home his
message like this? Dammit, he disliked these peculiar goings-on
concerning a newborn child just as Tabitha was preparing to give

birth. Neither did he care for 'hot-spilled blood', not on De Vallory land. Did the blood refer to the young woman already murdered? Or might there be a serious risk to Tabitha and the baby? He bit his thumb and gave the letter grave consideration. He had liked Gunn and enjoyed his conversation. But this sounded like trouble, and he heartily wished he had never made this new acquaintance.

A notion sprang up in his mind. Might he investigate these prophecies on his own terms, without worrying Tabitha? He had recently been handed the perfect stratagem to look into Gunn's motives. At twenty-six years old, Nat was the youngest member of the Cestrian Natural Philosophy Society and had been cornered by the president at the last meeting. 'And what of you, Mister De Vallory?' Mister Foreman had demanded. 'You have told us how all things must be investigated and tested before they are proved. With your reputation a paper on a new scientific topic should give you little trouble. What d'you say, sir?'

Nat had bowed his head to the president. 'Sir, I shall put my brains to work and inform you before the evening is out.'

'Good, good.' How Mister Foreman had pounced on his words. 'Here. I have set your name down for the Michaelmas meeting. Remember, that falls in September, not October, now the calendar is adjusted. Very well, sirs. The next item . . .'

Devil take the man, Nat had meant only to think on the matter and the old duffer had snared him. He had cudgelled his brain for his paper's subject ever since. He needed a topic that would shock those codgers awake; an experiment that would give a prodigious result. And perhaps now he had found one.

He might tell Gunn he was seeking scientific proof of whether or not the future could be predicted. That would flatter Gunn and also be a worthy experiment. For past millennia humankind had consulted seers and oracles, from the soothsayers of Ancient Rome and Druidical priests, to spell-casting witches and today's medical men who devised their cures by casting a horoscope. Could it all be balderdash? Since Gunn's sermon in the forest Nat had been intrigued by this phenomenon of sleeping prophecies. And now here was Gunn's vision arriving in the post like a thunderbolt. One might almost call the timing uncanny.

He tapped his quill on his inkstand. Was the destroyed foetus a candidate for this saviour figure? Yet there were other rivals for the putative crown. Many of the women at the camp appeared to be with child, and apparently a large number were Gunn's offspring. However, they were not his main concern; his thoughts were fixed upon Tabitha and their own child.

Should he share Gunn's letter with Tabitha? The prospect of alarming her made him uneasy. Tabitha was about to bear their first child. She was beautiful, clever, his whole heart's desire, but why in God's name had she touched the corpse beneath the tree? It now seemed to offer a gruesome connection to the prophecy. And even after he had asked her to stay in bed, he knew she had secretly risen and watched the examination of the corpse. He had not confronted her about it, though he had heard her moving about in the chapel gallery. He had even vouchsafed her absence from her chamber by questioning her servant Grisell in return for a silver sixpence. And today, after he had begged her to rest, she had set off for Chester, though at least she had taken that sober nursemaid with her. Truly, her waywardness troubled him. If he showed her Gunn's letter she might throw herself even further into this dark affair. No, it would be better to keep these developments to himself and pursue his inquiries in private.

Hell's teeth, it was another secret to add to his first. He had not yet told Tabitha he had been acquainted with the murdered girl. The girl he knew as Maria. True, it had been damned awkward to speak up at the time of her discovery, with Tom and Jennet standing over them. Since then, he had pictured unburdening himself to his wife a dozen times, only to stop himself in a fit of self-loathing. The truth was, he had hoped the whole affair would be forgotten by now. By rights the inquest should have been over and done with but instead he was left waiting in agony, like Damocles cowering beneath a sword dangling on a horse's hair.

He started at the sound of the door latch at the top of the stairs. Guiltily, he pushed Gunn's letter into a box and locked it away. Rising, he found Tabitha descending from the hall and sprang up to help her down the steep stairs.

THIRTEEN

'**S** it down, my love.' He coaxed her to a grandiose carved chair.

'I have been to the linen drapers for baby stuffs. And I bought you these.'

She handed him a parcel containing two ruffled muslin neck-cloths of a type favoured by the gentry. He thanked and kissed her but felt only the briefest return of pressure. Pulling back, he saw she was unhappy. The testy thoughts of a minute ago vanished in her presence. 'Talk to me, sweetheart,' he urged. He had never before cared for another person as he did for her. Now that he looked on her lovely face, his wife's distress communicated itself directly to his own heart.

'I have news of the dead girl. Her name was Maria.'

To hear Maria's name uttered out loud pained him. And now he had to listen grave-faced to an account of Tabitha's visit to the Blue Coat Hospital and the information she had gathered. Ah, so that was it – the half-ring had been a portion of a found-ling token and not the lover's keepsake he had imagined. His wife truly was as sharp as a nail. According to her calculations, if Maria had been born in 1735 she was no more than seventeen when she died.

'Is it not pitiful?' Tabitha said. 'And of all frustrations, when she left the charity school she tore out the page from the admis-sions book. I still don't know who deposited her there. She was provided with a hundred pounds, a good sum. Who might have left her there?'

She reached for his hand, but he felt suddenly clammy and drew back. No, he had not realized Maria was so young.

'And I have remembered where I once saw her,' she rattled on. 'Down by the Kaleyard Gate where the street girls ply their trade.'

He nodded mutely, remembering the place all too well; the high Roman wall behind the cathedral that sheltered women who waited like moths in its shadow. Here was his chance. If he opened his mouth and said, 'Ah yes, why of course you remind me. That was the girl, I knew her too.' But he was in no wise steady enough for the inquisition that would follow. Tabitha was still talking serenely.

'I know the hospital does good,' she was saying, 'but by Christ, I too would have run away. Those children are bred on guilt and shame. It left me sad. I was glad to have Sukey with me.'

'Good, good,' he muttered.

'So what ails you, Nat?' She suddenly returned to her quizzical self, her eyes as bright as her jewels.

'Sometimes I am wearied by estate business.'

'No,' she said quietly. 'You drew away from me just now.'

He stood up smartly and paced to the wall, his hand settling on the orrery his uncle had installed. It was a model of the sun and planets fashioned from brass and precious stones that moved by means of cogs and wheels. God-like, he pushed the blue earth so it rotated on its daily orbit around the brass globe of the sun. If only it were that easy to turn back time and alter the events of last year.

He tried, clumsily, to distract her. 'The inquest date is still not set. When it is, I won't have you attending such a rowdy gathering. I forbid your attendance, absolutely.'

'That is a rough speech in return for my gift. I am not your slave to be ordered here and there.' She spoke coldly and started to gather up the cloths to leave him.

No, this was not how they should part. Suddenly he reached for her and pulled her into his arms and kissed her, caressing her neck, her shoulder and throat.

'Forgive me. I am out of sorts,' he mumbled into her neck.

She pulled back and studied his face. 'Why, what has happened?'

He longed to confide in her. But then a strange memory presented itself. It was an odd sensation that Gunn's sermon had spoken directly to himself and accused him of being a whoremonger. The preacher had described his own callous sins as if he knew exactly what Nat had done.

He looked up and found Tabitha regarding him with worried sympathy. Now was not the time to make a confession; he needed to prepare himself before he told her about Maria.

He began haltingly. 'My new position here at Bold Hall is

sometimes a heavy one. With my father sick and all this dreary correspondence, I swear, sometimes, I had rather be a nobody again, with responsibility to no one. When we first met, I wrote my poetry and lived freely as a pen-to-hire. True, I've been the luckiest devil in the world, but it doesn't always feel that way.'

Tabitha was watching him narrowly. 'Yes, it is hard. It does not help that we still have no visiting cards from our neighbours. Our only new friends are those faith-mongers in the woods.'

'Yes, well. They will be gone a few days after the solstice.' He glanced down at the orrery, picturing that moment when the daylight hours would be at their longest and Midsummer celebrated.

'Do you honestly believe Gunn did not know Maria?' she asked. 'According to the matron at the Blue Coat Hospital Maria was a harlot from when she was little more than a child. Gunn spoke so very warmly of sin, Nat. You cannot deny he is as much a libertine as any Covent Garden rake. Can you not order him off your land?'

Nat considered for a moment. Tabitha was right, of course, but now he had a plan bubbling in his mind, to scientifically test this sleeping prophet. He was reluctant to give up the notion. He kissed her brow and spoke softly. 'All those women and young children. I should let them sleep in safety a while longer. I don't want to be callous like the great lords hereabouts. But if he's not gone by Midsummer I will send them packing.'

She was watching him closely and he suspected her bright eyes had detected his evasion. Then he felt her hot fingers squeezing his.

'What is it, my love?' he murmured.

'Maria was so like to me. Young, alone, and now cruelly slaughtered. There must be gentlemen aplenty who will not risk their reputations to speak up for her. Men who left their wives untouched to entertain a pretty harlot.'

Nat's heart punched his ribs. He swallowed and clumsily changed the subject. 'The baby is well? There was no contagion at the hospital?'

It was her turn to mumble. 'There was a sick child at the hospital. But all is well.'

'I beg you, take care. Rest, make ready for the birth. Your safety is all to me.'

Tabitha looked more softly upon him. 'I miss you by my side at night,' she murmured. 'I detest Doctor Caldwell and his rules.'

Nat cursed himself. In his first swell of fatherly pride it was he who had asked the doctor to forbid Tabitha any activities that might put the child at risk. It was his fault that they had lost their best solace, forgetting how any disagreement melted away when they were entwined in the act of love. It was not even the sating of lust that he needed most; he longed only for them both to be restored to their former selves. Now, Nat felt their separation as a punishment; one that – in some dreadful way – he deserved.

FOURTEEN

Tabitha had always had a fancy to attend Netherlea church dressed in the highest fashion. That Sunday morning her costume was indeed glorious, stitched of pale yellow silk, much flounced and embroidered with a pattern of flowers and scrolled leaves. She had needed to let out her bodice laces to accommodate her condition but, nonetheless, in a smart *capuchin* cloak and an elegant feathered hat, she enjoyed the curious stares of the villagers as Nat led her up the aisle.

Seated inside the De Vallory pew she took out her new fan – a pretty article decorated with classical dancers – and cooled her face. Behind her back the villagers chattered in loud voices. From above the hubbub a snippet concerning herself reached her ears: '. . . marrying her, an' her so big with a child of Beelzebub's bower . . .'

She fluttered her fan even faster. Thank the Lord that Nat had not heard the insult, for the new minister, Parson Hope, was leaning over the pew-end declaiming in a loud monotone. And Bess was muttering in a soft sing-song voice to a wooden dolly carved for her by Joshua. Beelzebub's bower, indeed. She would gladly swear on the great church Bible that she had known no other man than Nat since returning to Netherlea. What vipers those women were. Turning her head, she fixed a black look upon Mistress Dainty and her two crone-like companions, their jaws clacking away.

Parson Hope at last stepped up to the pulpit. In keeping with the feast of Rogation Sunday, his theme was the land and its division. She listened with renewed interest, for the notion of land had meant nothing to her before she married Nat.

'*It is the Lord that maketh the poor, and He maketh the rich; He that can lift up the poor personage, to sit with princes and have the seat of glory.*'

Truly the Lord had raised Nat and herself, not quite to the seat of glory but certainly in that direction. Their child would by rights own much of the green land hereabouts. Well, if he were male, that was. And now, thanks to Sukey, she had news on that subject, if a sign from the otherworld could be trusted. The previous afternoon the nursemaid had enquired if she would like to know if she carried a boy or a girl. Tabitha, who had exchanged her own stitching for a closer study of the London pages of *The Gentleman's Magazine*, said that she would, being long familiar with the harmless ritual. 'The pendulum test is infallible,' said the nurse, and agreed to perform it at once.

A few minutes later Tabitha lay very still on her bed. The air was muggy; looking up at the ceiling a swarm of tiny gnats circled, unaware of the spiders' webs that laced the high wooden beams.

For herself she scarcely minded either way, for a little girl would be a delightful companion for Bess. Yet Tabitha knew a boy would please Sir John, to continue his family line.

Though Sukey's girth was largely hidden by her voluminous apron, Tabitha ventured an opinion. 'Your baby is carried very high, Sukey. And not at all around your rear. She is a girl, I should say.'

The nurse's expression darkened. 'No, I am sure I carry a boy like you.' Then changing her mind, she added, 'What do I care so long as I have my baby safe in my arms? Now, I need your wedding ring.'

Tabitha felt a moment's reluctance at removing the blue-white diamond ring. Nat had slipped it on her finger one glorious starry night when he had requested her hand in marriage and sworn that he would love her till the stars fell. It was her talisman; both a sign of Nat's love and his enduring protection. 'Be careful now. It's worth the world to me.'

Sukey was watching her with a distant expression. 'He thinks mighty highly of you, my lady.'

Tabitha laughed. 'So do I of him. Between you and me, I can scarcely wait till the baby is here and my sweet Nat is back where he belongs in my bed. It truly was a blessing that Doctor Caldwell sent you here, so I will have a little freedom while you care for my infant.'

'It is indeed God's bounty,' the nurse murmured, as she strung the ring on to a long golden chain. 'Lie still, now. And be silent.' Tabitha's eyelids were growing very heavy as she lay motionless, enjoying the slight breeze blowing in through the casement.

'If it swings around in a circle it's a girl. If it swings back and forth, then a boy,' Sukey reminded her. As if she didn't know that herself. The nurse let the ring hang high above the apex of Tabitha's stomach. It rocked gently, the chain hanging from the tip of Sukey's forefinger. Nothing happened; the ring rocked, neither circling nor swinging. Tabitha wondered which direction the nurse would send it.

Then, as if collecting momentum, the ring began to move. Tabitha glanced up at Sukey's intense face and then down to the ring as it swung back and forth from the direction of her feet towards her head and then back again. The gem in the ring cast rainbow reflections across the whitewashed walls. The nurse was smiling warmly down upon her mistress. 'It will be a boy.'

Naturally you would say that, she thought. 'Thank you, Sukey. And shall I test you, now?'

'No.' Sukey unthreaded the ring. 'I'll wait and see. I have Davey so this one will be a surprise.'

Tabitha's thoughts returned to the present as Parson Hope announced the next hymn: 'The Lord my pasture shall prepare . . .' She smiled to hear Nat's tuneless voice. Singing was not one of Nat's many talents. She was surrounded by her little family, her darling Nat and sister Bess. Perhaps, she told herself, there was nothing to fret over. Yet she had not felt easy since the day in the forest. Baptist Gunn takes an interest in you, she warned herself. As a girl she had learned that the Eye of God was forever fixed upon the sinner below; and even now she felt a telltale trace of Gunn's invisible eye watching over her.

FIFTEEN

A procession of Netherlea folk formed in a ragged mass and began their annual Rogation walk around the parish's boundaries. Nat felt the novelty of the occasion as he reined in Jupiter to a slow walk just behind the parson and churchwardens. For the first time he had a part to play in what had always seemed a quaint ritual, for this time the ritual traced the path of his own future inheritance. At each ancient stone, broken cross or prominent tree, the parson enquired of the parish's elder members whether this was a true marker of Netherlea land. Only when the parish clerk had made a mark on his paper, and any restoration made by carving a symbolic cross, or white-washing the stones ever brighter, did the procession move on.

By afternoon the score or so persons had entered the forest. Behind them Joshua drove the gig at a walking pace, bearing Tabitha, Bess, Jennet and Grisell. Here at the long avenue of birch trees known as the Twelve Apostles was the final boundary of the parish of Netherlea, lying coterminous with the De Vallory estate. Perspiring and weary, the parson led the prayer for the last time: 'Bless this good earth, and make it fruitful, consider the old ancient bounds and limits . . .'

Finally, a young lad was called forward, to be lifted up and bumped upside down to a chorus of shrieks and laughter. Thus the parish duty was almost done; to stake out a map using the brains of the most ancient villagers and impress it into the pliable minds of the lads and lasses who would one day take their places.

It must have been the loud racket that brought two mounted men bearing down upon them. Nat walked Jupiter a few steps towards them, as if guarding his flock. He spotted pistols at the men's belts. 'Who are you? What is your business here?'

The stouter of the two men, a slab-faced brute, reined back his horse. 'My name is Mullock. I am Lord Langley's head keeper and this good man assists me. I am here to tell you all to shift yourselves off Lord Langley's estate.'

Nat leaned forward in the saddle. 'As you can see, we are beating the bounds this very day and I assure you this is Netherlea land.'

Mullock shook his head in slow denial. 'You got that all wrong, young fellow.'

'It is Mister De Vallory of Bold Hall, to you. This row of birches – known as the Twelve Apostles – forms the boundary between our land and His Lordship's estate. I swear it was so in Gaffer Furlow's memory ever since he was a lad. And so it is today.'

The old greybeard tottered forward. 'Aye, I beat the bounds since the Great Frost of 1684, when the trees exploded like cannon fire and birds dropped down dead from the skies. Since then I watched these trees a-growing an' they was allus' Netherlea trees.' He feebly waved at the men with his twiggy arms.

Mullock snorted. 'What does Lord Langley care for the ramblings of such noddle-heads? His Lordship has had the whole forest surveyed for improvements to his park. This avenue will make a fine approach to Langley Hall.'

Nat bristled. 'No. This is Sir John De Vallory's land.'

Mullock's companion, a handsome, black-browed fellow, smirked and whispered that his father was 'cracked in the head'.

Nat had to restrain himself from striking the man. The need to keep a hold of this tract of forest suddenly overwhelmed him. It was his father's earth and he carried his father's blood in his veins. He dismounted and spread his map across a tree stump. The two keepers swaggered across to inspect it. 'That's a mighty old map, sir. You will find His Lordship has taken the measure of this whole forest. He is extending his park—'

'You will find he is not,' Nat interrupted. 'The Twelve Apostles are the boundary to our estate.'

'No use looking backward, young fellow. His Lordship and his gentlemen friends are enclosing all this common land that currently falls into waste.'

Nat was aware of shifting and muttering among the men and boys behind him. 'I shall call in our lawyers tomorrow.'

Then to everyone's surprise, Tabitha's voice broke in. She stepped down from the gig and began to speak in a ringing voice. 'You are wrong, sirs. This is no waste. Our villagers have rights upon this common land, to glean and to gather. Their pigs have rights of pannage, their cattle have rights of pasture. And come winter, our people are free to hunt small game, gather fruits and winter fuel. Your master cannot take that from them.'

Mullock tipped his hat at Tabitha but his lips curled. 'I wouldn't wager on that continuing much longer. T'int worth bothering your pretty head with, I should say.'

It was Tom who sprang forward first, swinging his fists. 'How dare you speak to Her Ladyship so brazenly. You always was grasping, you Langley folk. You must fight us here and now if you want it!'

The keeper laughed but did take a step backwards. 'I wouldn't say no to a few rounds with a bunch of striplings and dodderers. But we'll let the masters meet at law first. Talking of which, we have orders to send those ranting squatters on their way.'

Nat swung around, contemptuous. 'You mean Baptist Gunn's camp?'

'We don't bother with no names. But His Lordship won't tolerate squatting hereabouts.'

Nat's endurance snapped. Taking his own pistol out of his belt, he strode to within two paces of Mullock, and though he did not point it at the man, he set his finger at the trigger. 'Go speak to your master. This is De Vallory land and will stay that way to my dying breath. Do you hear me?' Footfalls moved behind him as a ring of Netherlea men gathered at his shoulders. He was glad of it. 'And if I see you, or any other of Lord Langley's men on this side of the Apostles, I will not be responsible for the consequences.'

Again, the scoundrel tipped his hat. Then without a word the pair of keepers disappeared into the trees.

'Come now. Get along,' Nat called to the crowd. 'We'll not be cowed by bullyboys.'

The procession continued behind the parson, though now Nat found his gaze drifting into the forest as if it were enemy territory. As soon as the final marker, a towering yew, had been celebrated with a feast of oranges, the villagers made off for home. Nat halted his horse by Tabitha where she sat in the gig. 'We must go ahead and warn Gunn. The way is too narrow for the gig but if you take my arm we can walk.'

'Please do not go there,' Tabitha said, too quietly for the others to hear. 'His camp is so close to where Maria was found.'

Nat's blood was still pumping hard with righteous fury. 'I will not let Langley dictate what happens on my father's land. I said Gunn's camp can stay till Midsummer and so they shall. Come along. Take my arm.'

Tabitha stubbornly stayed seated, so he was glad when Jennet spoke up on his part. 'You should take a drink in this heat, Tabitha. You can rest awhile at the camp. I for one admire their piety.'

'I am surprised at you, Jennet,' Tabitha snapped. 'There are rumours enough in the village about Gunn. Talk of midnight gatherings at which his followers dance in wanton fashion. You should stay well away.'

'Sweetheart, you should rest. Ten minutes. No more,' Nat coaxed.

Tabitha nodded and sighed and he helped her down, noting that she winced as she reached the ground. Perturbed by her discomfort, Nat instantly forgave their momentary disagreement. Lord, his poor pet. He was learning what pains women must endure to continue the human race.

SIXTEEN

I f Tabitha had been reluctant to visit the camp the first time, on this occasion she felt a physical dread. Upon their arrival at the treehouse Baptist Gunn seemed to detect a cooling in their manner and strove to return to their friendly ease. To Tabitha's irritation, Jennet and Grisell at once settled easily around the rough table, nodding and smiling at the young people who brought jugs and tankards of nettle beer. If only she had followed Sukey's wise counsel and stayed at home, peacefully sewing in the shade. The nursemaid had complained of breathlessness in the heat and now she felt the same affliction after walking for only a few minutes.

When Nat was persuaded to sit, Tabitha had no option but to follow him. Gunn's herbal woman appeared at her elbow and urged a cooling cordial upon her. When the woman had left her, Tabitha studied the cup. The last time she had drunk this stuff she had slept long and dreamed such dreams that she had scarcely felt in possession of her own will. When Nat and Gunn turned to study Nat's map, she tipped the cup's contents on to the grass. Helping herself to Jennet's beer, she listened to the various conversations. Nat was carelessly explaining his map of the De Vallory estate to Gunn, apparently unaware of how many men might covet another man's bounty. Two camp women were telling Jennet and Grisell tales of what they would find in America: that it was fair and fertile and free of all the sins of old Europe. Bess had meanwhile boldly stepped up to join the two ragged girls who had led them to Maria's corpse and were noisily playing a game by the forest edge. They were shrieking and laughing so hard that Tabitha comprehended it would be awkward to call her sister back at once.

She rose from her seat and went in search of the outdoor kitchen, hoping to overhear a morsel or two of gossip. This time the camp women were not singing psalms and were more wary of her presence. She did her best to divert their attention. 'I wonder, do you know of this so-called wise woman, Anna Hollingsworth?'

'That old witch,' the pox-faced young woman sneered. 'She thinks she can forbid us from picking the herbs hereabouts. Ask yourself. Why should she need them?'

'You know why, Repentance. To keep that filthy fumbler of a son under control,' another said to a chorus of sniggers. Repentance? So that was the woman's name.

'Is he a danger, then?' Tabitha asked.

Repentance screwed up her face. 'He is one of them that likes a look but don't have the courage to touch. A few of us spotted him peering through the branches. You know the sort.'

Tabitha did indeed know of men who took a deal more pleasure through their eyes than their fingers. To indulge such clients, peepholes were at times created in bawdy houses for their private delectation. The notion struck her that Jacob Hollingsworth might have spied on Maria and killed her in terror of being found out. She had a shrewd idea that his mother would know. That was it – she might take this opportunity to escape the camp and visit the widow and her son this afternoon. First she had only to ask a few more questions. 'Do you think the soldier could have killed that young woman we found?'

The response was curiously unbalanced: Repentance agreed he probably had done so, with such enthusiasm that Tabitha suspected her of overacting. The plump woman who was somewhat comically named Abstinence, appeared not to care.

'I have discovered more about that poor dead girl,' Tabitha continued. She noted a few sly – or were they alarmed? – glances. 'Her name was Maria and she was only seventeen years old. It seems she was reared at the Blue Coat charity school in Chester.' She watched them all carefully.

Repentance shrugged. 'What else do you know? Why was she even here in the forest in the first place?'

'That remains to be discovered. Unless any of you care to tell me,' she said firmly. The fire crackled and the contents of the pot bubbled but no one spoke.

In the silence a heavy hand unexpectedly fell on Tabitha's shoulder. She swung around to face its owner. Baptist Gunn held her fast by the arm. His glibly handsome face was intent upon her.

'Fetch more beer and food, you women,' he said, standing so close to Tabitha that she felt the force of his person like a hot iron. 'And you come with me,' he said only to her, before directing her so rapidly that she had no time to resist. He took a path she had never seen, and in a moment they were surrounded by a dense wall of shrubbery. Gunn swung around, confronting her.

'I have been waiting. You never came to see me.'

Startled, she replied in a brittle voice, 'Why ever should I come and see you?'

'Because I can help you. Because I know who you are,' he murmured. He leaned towards her and his wide eyes were an invasion. One hand still dug into her arm, pulling her towards his heat and masculine scent. He spoke softly. 'I have learned what will become of you. Your only way to avoid disaster is to trust me, Tabitha. Trust me and all will be well.'

She shook her head, trying to break contact with the black points of his eyes. 'I will not,' she said, though her mouth was almost too dry to speak.

'I know it is hard for you. All this leisure to reflect on your past acts. And your present so tedious.'

'Enough!'

'No. If you wish to be free. If you choose not to waste away here. To wither away . . .' His fingers slid to her bare wrist and gently coaxed her forward. His voice grew low and confiding. 'You know how I feel. That I would sink to my knees and kiss the hem of your skirt. From the first time I saw you I have thought of little else. I need you by my side. And in my bed,' he added, moving his rough finger ends to her bare palm.

At once, she pictured it. Oh, before she was married . . . maybe, yes. There was something thrillingly carnal about the rogue. Unwillingly her gaze returned to his unruly hair, his expectant smile, his well-formed lips. No, she had given her heart to Nat. She recalled her husband's heartfelt smile when she had joined him at the altar to be married, and her conviction that this was the man she was put on earth to share her life with.

Gunn's hand ran up her arm to her face. His stubby finger caressed her lips. His steady gaze was all lust; his fingertip breached her parted lips.

She broke away and spat his briney taste on to the ground. 'And you a sainted preacher?' she protested.

'Oh no. I am a sinner. The truth is I love to sin. And with you, God himself will forgive me.'

'You are a crazed fool. I'm leaving.'

'No, Tabitha. You are the fool. I shall have you. I have seen it in a vision. You cannot—'

'Tabby! Come see.' Bess's girlish voice broke her trance like a rock thrown at an enchanted mirror. Tabitha grasped her sister's small hand and without looking backwards broke away from Gunn and hurried to where the children played. I must never, she vowed to herself, ever be alone with that man again.

When she returned to the clearing, she found Gunn had beaten her to Nat's side. She hesitated awkwardly while Bess skipped back to her new friends. Then spotting Joshua at the edge of the clearing she joined him where he waited like a sentinel. Pretending it was of little matter, she asked him how distant Anna Hollingsworth's cottage was.

'A quarter-hour or so from where you left the gig.'

'Would you drive me there?' she asked. 'I don't care for the company here.'

Joshua nodded and then cast his eyes over to the benches and beer jugs. 'Neither do I. And I have a few questions myself for Private Hollingsworth.'

After instructing Grisell to keep a close eye on Bess and Jennet, Tabitha called over to a perplexed Nat that she would be back in an hour's time. 'We are not too far from my mother's old friend. It may be the last opportunity I have to visit her.' Gunn himself did not even raise his head but she was certain he was listening hard.

Leaning on Joshua's arm, Tabitha entered the dark tunnel of thorns that ran between the sunny forest glade and the topsy-turvy ways of the camp. 'That man, Gunn,' she asked him. 'Might he not be wanted for some crime? I feel he is capable of any wicked act.'

'For that I need his true name. All these followers of his bear new Bible names for it's a condition of their joining. Baptist don't sound like a commonplace name to me.'

'True. Baptist, Repentance, Abundance. There is something of painted sepulchres to all this, Joshua.'

'Aye. I shall look into him and his raggle-taggle band. Have you thought, Tabitha, how folk will reckon you and Nat are involved in all this prophecy claptrap?' He jerked his head towards where the baby pushed out the front of her gown.

'Then they are idiots.'

'If I were you, I would stay well away from here. That rogue Gunn is already feeding your husband by hand.'

Annoyed, Tabitha worried over the likely truth of this in silence.

'On the other hand,' Joshua said, 'we did find Hollingsworth under the oak tree that night.'

Reluctantly, Tabitha told her childhood friend of the women's complaint that he had ogled them in the forest. 'You done well. And she were a good-looking young woman.'

'Yet she was with child. And stabbed in the belly. These peeping Toms are not generally of a violent nature. Their great pleasure comes from watching.'

Joshua looked sour. 'There are times, Tabitha, when I wish you would not make such worldly observations.'

'The trouble is,' she remarked tartly, 'I find too much make-believe and nice manners rarely uncover the truth. Oh, I forgot myself. I want to hang the poppet you made for me on the Mondrem Oak. It won't take a moment.'

They took the short side path to the ancient oak. There they looked up into the tree's great limbs, which twisted aloft as if they had been born in torment, echoing the fervour of those who had hung offerings and desperate prayers upon them for ages past. It occurred to Tabitha that the tree was a timeless entity, each year renewing its own form in leaves, buds, and acorns. She pulled the carved figure of the baby from her pocket and hung it on a low branch.

'May the Man o' the Oak bless your child,' Joshua murmured. She smiled back at him. The tree spirit had been a part of their village games, called Puck by some, or Robin Goodfellow by others. He was easy to believe in here, beneath the creaking branches and rustling canopy of leaves.

Remembering Sukey's offering, she pulled that out too and hung it on a separate branch.

'Be that your nursemaid's poppet? Fancy giving her own little 'un such a flouncy rig-out. Got notions of grandeur, has she?'

Tabitha looked more closely at the small figure dressed gorgeously in scraps of lace. Certainly Sukey's offering was dressed like royalty beside her plain little bumpkin. 'She's a better seamstress than me, that's all.'

'Well, she's helped herself to your finest lace, I reckon.'

Tabitha didn't even know if that was true.

'When her own babe's born, she'll put one piece of cake in your child's mouth and two in her own.'

'What is a scrap of lace to me? She's a good woman.'

'So you say.' Then he reached his fingertips to brush the gigantic trunk of the tree and muttered into the dark ridges of the bark, 'Touch wood, may all come good.'

A moment later Tabitha repeated his words and gesture, which she surmised had been performed as long as even the oak had lived, as a protection against future ill-luck.

SEVENTEEN

D rooping faces seemed to leer back from the shadows and lidless eyes shone where the sun glinted among the leaves. Tabitha was no longer easy in her own skin; her entire being felt polluted by Gunn's advances. How glad she was of Joshua's burly stature and wary good sense as the gig rocked along a narrow track to the widow's home. She thought of Maria wandering through the forest alone. It was an easy place in which to get lost and stumble on to the wrong path. And she remembered Hector, who had vanished so quickly he might have dropped into a bottomless well.

Widow Hollingsworth's house was a dwelling of the strangest type, its bowed frame originating in two great whale ribs brought home from the Grand Tour by a local nobleman and erected as an archway on the banks of a mere. Many years earlier, the widow had arrived in the forest after long travels from her home in Germany; taking a great fancy to the greenwood she had begged leave to settle there. She had constructed walls of turf around the whale ribs and thatched the roof with furze and hazel twigs. Over time, when the loyal donkey that had borne all her possessions had died, she spread the creature's skin across the roof to keep out the rain. Charitable visitors had contributed to her one-room dwelling: there was a little leaded casement, a chimney pot, some simple fencing for her garden, and a low dwarfish door.

The widow was a tiny, crook-backed woman with the face of an eager but wrinkled child. Tabitha introduced herself and the dame made much of remembering her mother. On finding that her son was absent somewhere in the vicinity, Joshua set out in search of him. It was just as well, for, after dipping beneath the low lintel, there was little space for even Tabitha to squeeze inside the room in her hooped skirts. On a stone hearth the widow was boiling up soapwort in her cauldron. The heat was stifling and smoke and steam filled the room in search of the miniature chimney pot.

As the widow pulled the frill of her white cap from her eyes Tabitha saw a black-crusted gash across her brow, surrounded by an ugly plum-coloured bruise. Where the mark extended over her eye socket the lid was swollen and the eye itself peered out bloodshot and sticky.

It seemed only polite to offer to help the widow in the familiar task of soap-making before raising the question of her injury, so Tabitha set to work cramming the pounded leaves of the plant into the cauldron of boiling water. The widow began to speak of Tabitha's mother in the accent of her faraway home, as a healer rich in compassion and wise in book learning. Listening, Tabitha felt a shift inside herself. On her own life's path, she had drifted far from her mother's ideal of healing others. Perhaps as the squire's daughter-in-law she could find her way back again.

'She was blessed to have you as a daughter,' the widow concluded.

'I am afraid she deserved a more dutiful daughter.'

'No. Even here I heard how you helped your mother.' Her eyes glittered knowingly beneath unruly white eyebrows. 'Do not judge yourself by the idle chatter of the ignorant. Besides, De Vallory's son has chosen you. And now God has blessed you with a child. Your mother must be smiling down from heaven.'

Tabitha looked away, suddenly stung by emotion. She rubbed a leaf and inhaled the familiar astringent scent before forcing a brave smile. Together they began to strain the mixture into a row of muslin-covered crocks. 'Did you know I found the murdered young woman beneath the Mondrem Oak? And that I touched her corpse?'

The old woman continued measuring and pouring the liquid by eye. 'Is that why you are troubled?'

It was easier to talk while they concentrated on their task. 'My doctor tells me I've put the child in danger. Yet my mother never blamed a baby's mother for any chance misfortune.'

She nodded slowly in agreement. 'Call me Anna, *liebling*. Do not be anxious. I have a gift for you. To replace your mother's blessing.'

The widow shuffled to the tiny patchwork bed and returned with a leather pouch. 'Here. It is an eagle-stone to keep you and the child safe.' She shook it on to Tabitha's palm. It was a lump of bumpy yellowish rock clasped in a mount of tarnished silver.

Tabitha shook it and it rattled like a nut in a shell. Recognizing the charm, she clasped it tight against her heart.

The widow fixed her bright eyes upon Tabitha's face. 'It comes from an eagle's nest and holds strong power. The stone has bred an infant stone in its own womb, as you can hear. Remember, it will keep your baby safe inside your body so long as you keep it close against your skin. When the birthing pangs begin it will show great virtue.'

'Thank you. I am most comforted.' She opened her bodice and slid it inside her stays where it felt warm between her breasts.

'Only return it after your confinement. I lend it to those who are in need.'

Tabitha smiled and agreed, then finally asked, 'How was it you got that wound?'

'I stood up to those hoydenish women from the preacher's camp.'

The little woman's foolhardy courage prompted Tabitha to go to her and put her arm around her childlike shoulders. Her heart winced in sympathy, for the widow's skull was as fragile as an eggshell. Gently, Tabitha asked, 'Baptist Gunn and his camp. What do you think of them?'

'I know it is a stupid goose that flocks to the fox's sermon.'

'And Mister Gunn himself?'

The widow looked up at Tabitha full in the face. 'Tell me, *liebling*. What is that man to you?' Then she reached for another crock and began attentively to ladle the liquid.

Tabitha shook her head as if she might shake the memory of Gunn probing her mouth with his finger. 'He disgusts me.'

'He has a wife, does he not?'

She had a sudden vision of herself in his arms, of those lips on her mouth, of the muscular weight of him. 'No, it isn't that sort of . . . fascination. He has his pick of any woman in his camp. I loathe him.'

Anna placed fingers as fragile as a bird's bones over Tabitha's hand. 'Mister Gunn has a talent but not a worthy one. Such persons are – I only know what name I was taught in Saxony – an *Aufhocker*, an evil that changes shape to make harm. He can enter the mind through the eyes and ears, he can invade dreams, conjure hope or despair. You will think me an odd one, but I swear I heard of his coming in the birds' calls. You know that in the ancient days we could speak the language of animals? Ah, now all that is lost. Yet even now, if we listen long and stand as still as a mossy stone, we can hear the temper of our animal kin, if not understand each word. And they speak of this: the forest hearkens to an enemy. It is collecting its memories through its long questing roots and is watching from its high, whispering leaves.'

'So what will happen?'

The old lady stoppered the first of her crocks with a dab of wax and a round pebble. 'There is ill-will brewing hereabouts, in the strange lights that move at night and the wraiths who linger at the crossroads. My son Jacob sees them, too. He goes out at peculiar hours taking his spyglass with him. I shall be glad when his regiment is recalled.'

'You worry for his mind?'

'*Ja*, I never heard him talk so. In the old days I was so proud of him. Look at this.'

Anna reached into a bundle and pulled out a small brass acorn. 'Jacob helped the king himself when his horse bolted at the Battle of Dettingen. His regiment kept him safe beneath an oak tree. The king said such bravery deserved to be remembered.'

Tabitha handled the small symbol. A brass acorn and two leaves. How strange that she had first seen him in his tattered red coat at the Mondrem Oak.

'Now,' Anna lamented, 'he talks of ghosts. This is an ancient, unforgetting land. Rich in burial holes, ancient boulders, holy wells, just as in Saxony. If Jacob claimed to see such ancient spirits of the land I should not doubt him. But it is not those he sees.' Anna appeared to crumple, the vitality draining from her body. 'Though he swears he never met her when alive, Jacob has watched her in the forest. Day and night, he waits for her to visit him. I fear she is wandering the same paths in death as she did in life; that he is love-struck for the very same girl. That corpse still walks, that one you found slaughtered beneath the Mondrem Oak. And I have pondered this – why can she not show herself in the sunlight like an ordinary mortal?'

EIGHTEEN

There was no opportunity for Tabitha to speak to Nat until that afternoon, when she went to his chamber with the intention of warning him away from visiting the camp again. She found him sorting through a heap of stable-hands' grubby clothes beside his pier glass.

'I borrowed these so I might pass as a poacher on Friday night. What d'you think?'

'Lord, they smell of horses.'

Nat tried on a greasy round hat and pulled it low over his brow. 'Good news. At last I have the subject for my paper at the Cestrian Society.'

Tabitha clapped her hands with pleasure. 'I am happy for you.'

He changed the first hat for a workman's leather cap. Tabitha shook her head and he removed it. 'My subject is this: Can humankind predict the future? What do you say? I have begun a study of prophecy. In every part of the world, in every generation since the days of the Etruscans, divination has been used to guide mankind. The building of the Parthenon, the great naval battles of the Greeks – these all depended on the readings made by *haruspices*.'

'What are they?'

'Forgive me, it is rather gruesome. A *haruspex* was an expert in the interpretation of animal entrails. Even Cicero complained that in his day everyone was stark mad about entrails.'

'How delightful,' she said dryly.

He sorted through the threadbare shirts and chose one, then pulled off his coat. She admired his body as he undressed, tracing his shoulders where the skin was boyishly smooth above muscle and bone. She wondered what Doctor Caldwell would make of her unmatronly thoughts. No doubt he would warn her that physical desire would cause some ghastly deformity to her child.

'I intend to test these beliefs. Then I will present my findings at the Michaelmas meeting.'

Her spirits had sunk a little on hearing the subject of his research. 'Surely you are a sceptic, Nat. You will reject any hocus-pocus?'

He lifted her fingers to his grinning lips and kissed them. 'Says she, who today offered a pagan gift to a tree spirit. Joshua told me.'

Feeling oddly shy, she slid her hand over the warmth of his shoulder. A delightful tingle moved through her body. She wished he would stop talking and hold her tight. Instead, he broke free and slid the grubby linen shirt over his head.

'Leaving an offering at a tree is nothing but old country lore.'

'So you do not believe it will help you, even a little?'

It was true, she had hidden a pang of annoyance when Joshua remarked on how much finer Sukey's poppet was than hers. Momentarily, she had feared that her own baby might suffer ill-luck beside the good fortune attracted to Sukey's baby.

'Tell me,' he reassured her. 'I am not mocking you.'

'Yes, I do believe it, with some simpler part of my nature. It does no harm. Nat, if you wish to learn of prophecy, you should speak to Private Hollingsworth's mother, Anna. She also mistrusts Gunn. She knows about the earth and the forest in ways the preacher never could. And she told me her son Jacob believes Maria's ghost haunts the forest. I do wonder, is there not a supernatural law whereby the murdered victim haunts their destroyer?'

He nodded, and half-heartedly said he would look into it. Then she told him all about the pendulum test in as entertaining a fashion as she could muster. 'So, according to the spirit in my wedding ring – or perhaps the notions directing Sukey's finger – we shall have a boy.'

Nat shook his head cheerfully. 'I am afraid that is not much of an experiment. The mathematical odds mean the test will always be correct half of the time, which gives a mightily favourable outcome. Yet, if it is true, a boy will please my father.' He pecked her briefly on the cheek. 'Now, how can this waistcoat be made tighter?' She stepped around him and tightened the laces at the back.

Standing before the pier glass he surveyed his homespun jacket, spotted neckerchief and leather breeches. His gold-flecked eyes shone in the mirror and his hair fell down free to his shoulders. 'Will I do?'

'Oh yes, you look a proper country buck. A man to tumble in a hedge with.' She ruffled his hair. 'If Doctor Caldwell would allow it, I might even pay you for a night in a hay barn.'

He grinned like a cat. 'Oh, as it's you, I shouldn't want too large a fee.'

'You conceited rogue.' Suddenly, she couldn't resist a little jibe. 'Well, at least Gunn does not slice open animals – save for Lord Langley's venison. So when is Gunn leaving?'

'Not yet.'

'Why not?'

'Because I want him to stay. I intend to prove him either a true prophet or a false one.'

She tried to disguise her dismay. 'Truly, my love, I should rather you did not study him. Anna believes he is dangerous. He exerts a powerful influence over others. Those women follow him like sheep.'

'Many men would pay for that secret,' he teased.

'Be serious. Even if Gunn himself did not kill Maria it is doubtless someone from his camp.'

'They will be on their way to America soon,' he argued. 'This is my best chance to observe him close at hand in case he is dangerous. And to observe a sleeping prophet and test his prophecies.' Seeing her silent exasperation, he continued more severely. 'Be reasonable. I cannot bear thinking only of corn prices or bills of account. I must keep my mind stimulated, Tabitha. You knew that when we married.'

She felt his criticism like a lash and could not resist hitting back. 'Are you truly so uncertain of yourself,' she demanded, 'that you must look to a penny-catching prophet to foretell your future?'

Before she could change her mind, she hurried away to her chamber without even wishing him goodnight.

NINETEEN

That night a cloud of loneliness settled over Tabitha. She went to bed and pulled a bolster into her arms and imagined it was Nat's solid back, lying beside her, breathing gently. She was still clutching it when the first gobbets of hard rain rattled on the window and woke her in pitchy darkness. Then raised voices reached her. Befuddled, she sat up, recognizing Bess's childish tones. Pulling on a wrapper she went next door and found Sukey holding a candle over Bess who was weeping in her little bed.

'She had a bad dream, my lady.'

'Tabby!' Bess was a portrait of sorrow, her arms open to her sister, desperate to be held. Tabitha sank down beside her and caressed her heaving back.

'You shout at me,' Bess suddenly cried, pointing to Sukey.

''Tis only because I will not indulge her.'

Tabitha yawned. 'Leave the candle and get some sleep, Sukey. My sister has a powerful fancy.'

When they were alone Tabitha stroked the damp strands of her sister's flaxen curls. She was grizzling now, her little body still hot as her sobs slowed down.

'What was it frightened you?' she whispered into the darkness. She could see the shine of Bess's eyes staring at nothing.

'Yesterday, we played a game. We sang a "Go to the woods" song.'

Tabitha recalled Bess warbling a song all the way home:

'Let us go to the woods, says Richard to Robin,
Let us go to the woods, says Robin to Bobbin . . .'

Bess searched her elder sister's face. 'We played a ghost game with aprons on our faces. I waited at the big tree. Then a big girl jumped up from being dead. We screamed.'

'Yes, I heard you all screaming, little one. And laughing, too.'

'Tabby.' Bess's voice faltered. 'I dreamed I waited at the big tree. Then a ghost came. With a big knife. Then gown all red and . . . baby all chopped up. It frightened me so!'

Tabitha fought through the fog of sleep. Had the children in the camp been playing a game about Maria? If so, this was proof, of a sort, that they knew about her murder.

She felt the little girl's hot brow. 'The dream is all gone now. I shall stay with you, poor chick.' Tabitha settled on the bedclothes and comforted her sister. Then she stared up at the blackness of the ceiling, pondering. More talk of ghosts. She had a country-woman's respect for such appearances, for that was generally all that a ghost was – a harmless vision of the dead. Yet Bess had seen more than that. A big knife. The baby chopped up. How did Bess know of such horrors? She lay awake until the birds clattered across the roof at dawn, fretting over the sleeping form of her precious little sister.

'I heard you were up from your bed last night.' Nat raised a concerned face at the breakfast table next morning.

'I was only in Bess's room. She had a nightmare.' Tabitha sat down beside him, hopeful of a truce after the previous night's foolishness. 'She needed comforting. And so did I.'

He at once reached across and kissed her cheek. 'I apologize for my sharpness.'

'As do I.'

They toasted their reconciliation with bowls of chocolate and buttered rolls and began to look cheerfully at the morning's post. Tabitha picked up a vellum sheet addressed to them both, closed by a large red wax seal. 'Oh my stars,' she murmured. 'At last. An invitation.'

'Who from?'

'Lord and Lady Langley. Listen to this. A Whitsun Ball to be held at Langley Hall with hunting the next day. Nat, that is scarcely a fortnight. What on earth can I wear?'

'That is a very lovely gown you are wearing now.'

'This? No, I must call on the dressmaker at once.'

Nat set down his knife. 'Tabitha, hold your horses. We needn't jump to their command.'

'Oh, please can we go? I will be indoors for at least a month after the baby is born.'

She studied the beautifully engraved card decorated with dancing figures and musical instruments. Lady Langley had even signed the invitation in her own scrawling hand. Nat walked to the window where sunlight glinted through the diamond leaded panes. His back was rigid and she wondered if she had annoyed him. Yet he looked composed when he turned back around to face her. 'We can always go the next time we get an invitation. Your confinement is an excellent excuse this time.'

Disappointment twisted Tabitha's spirits. Among all her worries she longed for some carefree entertainment. 'What is it, Nat?'

He looked like a guilty boy as he shrugged and looked away. 'I should have preferred to get the land matter settled before visiting Langley Hall. My father never liked them. You know Langley's lawyer is still throwing pettifogging objections at our claim. And what about you, Tabitha? Would you honestly be comfortable hobnobbing with those haughty old countesses?'

'I can converse with anyone. I dined at palaces in London.'

He watched her for a long moment, considering.

'Please,' she begged.

The corner of his lips twitched upwards. 'Very well.'

'I shall reply at once,' she said, her face bright with pleasure as she went in search of pen and paper.

TWENTY

31 May 1753
The Feast of Ascension

At last Coroner Crouch was recovered sufficiently to inquire into Maria's death. To Nat's dismay the inquest was to be held at Netherlea's tavern on the High Street. It was an uncomfortably warm day; after pushing through the press of villagers in the hallway, Nat was directed to a private back room where he was obliged to wait. He learned that the matron of the Blue Coat Hospital was being questioned first. The other witnesses waiting alongside him were Doctor Caldwell and Joshua. Both were silent and grave, so Nat merely nodded and retreated into his own thoughts.

He was desperate to be done with the whole affair. The last few weeks had destroyed his peace of mind, so plagued was he by guilt and uneasiness. As for Tabitha's continual digging around Maria's history – sweet God, he could bear no more of it. He was even secretly grateful they no longer shared a bed, for if they had done so Tabitha would at once have noticed his fits of wakefulness. Whenever his poor darling reached out to him with expressions of tenderness he was forced to recoil. He loathed himself. He did not deserve her natural affection.

Through the walls he could hear Coroner Crouch's voice hectoring the matron like a schoolmaster. He ran over his strategy. When he was questioned he must show fortitude and composure. He must not shame his father and his new position by showing himself unworthy. Neither must he say anything that might distress Tabitha, most especially since Caldwell had instilled in him that any upset might injure her or her baby. Neither must he show himself to be a loose libertine or, even worse, a suspect to the murder. The inescapable facts must remain hidden: he had known Maria and had carnal knowledge of her. Maria had been murdered upon his own father's land. He had been the first to discover Maria's butchered body. Those facts alone might raise the coroner's justified suspicion.

And then there was his stupidity the night before the murder. His first wrong step had been to take a different way to the Cestrian Society, descending from the city walls into the stone alley by the Kaleyards. There, beneath the genteel promenade encircling Chester, the harlots lingered beside the crumbling Roman gateway. He had covertly studied their faces as he walked: the girls and women parading in tawdry gowns, their crude paint exaggerating knowing leers. Maria had not been one of them. To his irritation, a bold nymph had clutched his sleeve.

'You after some company, sir? Anyways you like it, all for a shilling.' He shook her off and heard a chorus of catcalls. 'Hold your horses, pretty fellow. Me and my pal will share you for two bob.' He had escaped, bounding up the steps to where the cathedral bell was chiming seven in the evening.

It had been the same night that Foreman had commandeered him into presenting his Michaelmas paper. When the meeting began another fellow had stood, nervously dropped a sheaf of papers, and had begun to discourse upon canals. Not canals again, Nat groaned silently. Instead of listening, Nat's thoughts drifted back to the sisters of carnality in the alley. No doubt Maria had been upstairs in that ratty little tavern. He had a vague sensation of conscience interrupting his thoughts, but he pushed the irksome killjoy aside. No, he really should call upon Maria and inquire into her health. He still felt a pang of guilt at missing their last assignation without sending a message of apology. It would be a polite call, nothing significant that he need discuss with Tabitha. He persuaded himself that his search for the pretty harlot sprang entirely from his better nature. Later, he wondered if the May-tide sunshine was to blame, and the ribald songs of the season, and his own weakness as Nature's sap revived in his veins.

When the Cestrian meeting finally dispersed it was still a fine evening and the air felt pleasantly warm on his face. Above the cathedral tower peachy clouds gathered, as the great golden ball of the sun sank behind Chester's rooftops. It would do no harm to take a further quick look down in the alley. This time it stood empty. He found the tavern, its entrance no more than a low black lintel. Maria was not in the smoke-filled parlour, so he started to climb the rickety stairs. He was halfway up when a stranger bumbled into view above his head, clearly a harlot's cull, judging from his disarrayed dress and swaying gait. Nat retreated on to a small side landing but the man had taken note of him. While Nat courteously stood aside, the stranger drew level, then halted and silently confronted him, leaning forward and studying him with malice in his bulbous eyes. Nat stared back; he did not recognize the round, meaty face and fat neck bulging above a lace-trimmed stock. A moment later the stranger turned and clambered down the stairs.

The incident forgotten, Nat reached the poky attic room he remembered so well. Looking inside, he found Nancy with her petticoats raised to her thighs, wearily washing herself with a little sponge above a wash bowl. He caught a stimulating glimpse of her grotto of Venus and then asked in a friendly fashion, 'Seen Maria of late?'

Nancy lifted a face magically free of her previous fatigue. 'What you wanting with her? She flitted off with them strangers without even a proper fare-thee-well.'

'Who did she leave with?'

Nancy shrugged coquettishly. 'I don't recall no names. Come along in, Nat. Share a bottle with your old friend Nance.' She was certainly enticing; her hair tumbled loose and her pert face was pink from exertion. A year ago he would have lost the night in sweet debauch, waking up so addle-headed that his own name would have been a brandy-blurred memory. This time he came to his senses as the reek of another man's sweat entered his nostrils and he eyed the stained mattress. What a dolt he was. His wastrel days were ended. Tabitha awaited him back at Bold Hall. He had won the prize of his life and need never prowl around such places again.

'Not tonight, Nance. Take good care of yourself.' He flung a silver florin towards her and nimbly, she caught it.

Today it was crucial he maintain his sangfroid. If he gave the coroner the slightest suspicion he had not only bedded and befriended Maria, but also searched for her the night before her murder – as coincidences went, it was the devil of a hangman's knot and he did not trust Coroner Crouch to untangle it.

Nat's reflections were interrupted by the clerk calling for the

doctor to give his report. Caldwell was led away by a clerk into
the largest of the tavern's parlours. As the doors opened there
came an eruption of raucous chatter from those inside. 'Is it you
or I next?' he asked the constable.

'Me. It won't take long. Mark my word, 'twill be a verdict of
unlawful death. With no suspect to charge, that will be an end
to it.'

Within minutes, Joshua had disappeared to face the coroner.
Nat called for the tapster to fetch him a restorative of brandy
and drained the glass fast. He mopped his brow until the clerk's
footfalls rang out again and he was called. He made a composed
entrance into the rancid-smelling room. Coroner Vicesimus
Crouch was sitting like a grizzled hawk, showing every sign of
frustration. His broken wrist was awkwardly strapped to his chest
while his free hand was balled in a fist that frequently banged
the broad table. Beside him sat a terror-struck clerk frantically
sorting through folders and papers. To the other side sat the score
of jurors, almost all of them known to Nat as local householders.
A rope had been strung across the other half of the room, behind
which a crowd of Netherlea villagers jostled and gawped at the
show. He was led by a clerk to stand before the coroner, where
a cheap Bible was thrust into his hand. Dammit, he had forgotten
he must swear an oath. Nevertheless, he repeated the words from
a printed paper in a steady voice.

The coroner then spoke. 'Mister De Vallory, I and the jury
you see before you are charged to inquire for Our Sovereign
Lord the King how, when, where and in what manner the
deceased woman known as Maria St John came to her death.
I should be obliged if you would give us an account of how
you discovered the deceased and any other circumstances you
believe may assist us.'

Nat gave a careful account of the visit to the forest and their
finding the dead woman beneath the Mondrem Oak.

'We have heard from Constable Saxton how you sent for him.
Now sir, how was it you identified the deceased woman?'

Nat's breakfast suddenly churned uncomfortably in his guts.
'I did not identify her.'

The coroner scowled and riffled through his papers. Not finding
anything useful, he demanded, 'Yet you knew her name?'

Keep your nerve, Nat told himself. 'No, it was my wife who discovered her name.'

'Your wife discovered the name of a common prostitute? I am baffled, sir.' Lord, for a moment Nat profoundly wished the coroner had suffered greater injury than a crack to his wrist.

'My wife inspected the half-ring found upon the victim's finger and knew it for a foundling token. It was she who questioned the matron at the Blue Coat Hospital and in that way identified her.'

'Ah, very good, sir. Did you make any further enquiries concerning the manner in which the deceased came to her death?'

'I did, sir. I questioned all those I met in the forest that day and none would give me her name or any information. I also asked Constable Saxton to call in the surgeon and make wider enquiries.'

'Very well, sir. You may stand down.'

Nat congratulated himself as he took a seat on a chair drawn up for him by the clerk. The interrogation was over and he had not broken down. Pressure lifted from his mind as the coroner spoke to his clerk, no doubt preparing to sum up his findings.

'Call Miss Nancy Blair.' Nat started and looked up. The clerk disappeared and Nat watched, dry-mouthed, as a young woman walked in, her hips rolling, her costume a mélange of tawdry purple stripes. Upon her head was a low-tilted straw hat heaped with artificial flowers and ribbons. Nat discovered her face and that he knew the woman. Hell's teeth. It was Maria's roommate, Nance.

The crowd's murmur of curiosity rose to a jabbering cacophony. Coroner Crouch demanded silence. Nance turned her head to where Nat sat, no more than six feet away from where she stood. Her saucy eyes communicated amusement as they met his own. What the devil was she trying to say? Did she mean to betray him? Nancy swore by oath upon the Bible. Next, she was addressed by the coroner. Could Miss Blair give an account of how she first met Maria St John?

Nat lowered his head and studied the stains on the ancient floor of the tavern. Crouch would certainly ask her about the men who called on Maria. He licked papery lips, desperate to escape the room. No, no, he had to stay. He must have courage and bear the accusation with dignity when it was made against him.

The coroner first asked Nancy to confirm that Maria had followed the trade of a common prostitute, with which she agreed. Next, he asked if Maria had generally been accompanied by a pimp or keeper. Nat raised his head, for he had long considered Maria's destroyer might have been the sly rogue who often loitered outside the inn.

'Aye, she did have a keeper, Your Lordship. A flash young whipster of the name of Dobbs. But it weren't him as finished her. Dobbs tumbled under a set of carriage wheels last autumn and had his brains knocked about. He is since then a mute, kept at the cathedral poorhouse.'

The coroner turned to Joshua. 'Constable. I'd be obliged if you would corroborate those circumstances and have them added to the record.'

Joshua agreed and the coroner continued. 'And who were her particular gentlemen friends? Now remember you are on oath.'

Nancy caught Nat's eye. Her painted lips curled in a mischievous grimace. God save him, he was for it now. He held his breath and studied his hands.

'Well, she did have a good number of gentlemen friends.' Dammit, the minx was tormenting him. 'But I ain't reeling off the names. I were too busy with me own trade to be watching her roistering over me shoulder.' Guffaws and hoots rose from the wilder village men behind the roped enclosure.

'Let me put it this way, Miss Blair. Who do you believe was the father of her unborn child?'

'That I cannot say,' Nancy replied, not at all intimidated. 'If she were breeding she kept it a tight secret.'

'So you witnessed no signs of her being with child?'

'No, Your Lordship. She never said aught, only went on her way when the New Year come in January. Fell in with some persons who told her they'd take care of her. I reckon you must look to that party to find who put the bantling in her belly.'

Nat did a rapid calculation. He had left off seeking comfort with Maria in the middle of last August, as soon as his feelings for Tabitha had been reciprocated. Blockhead that he was, he realized that if he had been the child's father, Maria would have been mighty close to confinement when she died. Recalling her corpse on the slab, his own eyes were witness to some distension of her abdomen but nothing more. That poor destroyed infant was not his. The relief of it made him momentarily close his eyes and thank his lucky stars.

At last the coroner summed up his findings. He introduced the fanciful character of a fellow who had debauched Maria and then enticed her to that lonely spot when she told him of the child. He had then killed her rather than face the shame, or the monetary price, of venal sin. Yet the coroner did not leave Nat's conscience entirely untroubled. Before announcing the verdict he directed his pugnacious gaze to the entire company. 'In the name of the law, if anyone here today did ever make the acquaintance of the deceased, or has any further information concerning the unfortunate victim or her attacker, speak now.'

The question rang out in silence. Nat bent his head and gritted his teeth. It was a supreme effort not to speak up. Finally, after a brief interlude the foreman of the jurors returned with their decision. Coroner Crouch gave the verdict: of unlawful death by murder, by whose hand they knew not, that person being moved and seduced by the instigation of the devil to kill both the former foundling named Maria St John and the child of her body.

Nat rose and hurriedly left, feeling as light-headed as if his body was rapidly draining of blood. He could not face going home. Instead, he took Jupiter out into the cool gloom of the forest. There, alone beneath the Mondrem Oak, he allowed himself to grieve over the girl he had certainly not loved but had liked well enough. He pictured again her wide mouth, pointed chin, the way she had giggled into his neck and the pleasing handfuls of her soft breasts. Christ, what terror she must have known in her final moments.

He dismounted and slipped inside the curious chamber hollowed inside the oak's vast trunk. It was as warm and enclosed as a child's rainy-day den. A bundle of dried fern was heaped by the smooth inner wall, perhaps left by playing children – or maybe not. For the first time he wondered if Maria had been surprised by a stranger stepping suddenly out of this hiding place. Jacob Hollingsworth, for instance. Then he walked around the outside of the tree and stood for a long while over the spot where they had found Maria's body. The golden hour of twilight illuminated a scene of exquisite beauty. The setting sun turned the foxgloves to frilly spires of shining mauve. Time felt slowed down and his life infinitely precious, as if he might never again experience such a breathless moment. In such a crystalline drop of time he no longer felt alone. Tabitha had told him how the soldier had seen a woman's ghost in the forest. Tonight, he could believe it. Maria is still here, he thought, waiting in the consoling warmth of the sun-baked earth and the motes dancing in the glittering air.

TWENTY-ONE

When the day of the inquest arrived, Tabitha found she was mightily provoked to be forbidden by Nat from attending at his side. Blazing with curiosity, she clandestinely instructed her great-aunt Sarah to attend and meet her straight afterwards on a quiet lane. Sarah had given her a most engrossing account of the proceedings. The appearance of a harlot as a witness had surprised all those assembled, and most particularly the men of the village. Fiddlesticks, how Tabitha longed to question that young woman. And why should she not? Wasting not a moment, Tabitha hurried to the stables. Half an hour later she waited in the back of the gig, enjoying the breeze that lifted off the river as it wound beside the track that led from Netherlea to the Chester highway. Glover sat at the reins, trustworthy and silent. By the time the lone figure appeared from the direction of Netherlea, the light was sinking, gilding the solitary walker in a halo of gold. From her great aunt's description this had to be Nancy Blair, walking with a brazen roll of her hips, now slowed by weariness. Twisting around in her seat, Tabitha saw something of her younger self in the pretty trull; in the carefree merriment that masked an undertow of fear and watchfulness. To her surprise, Tabitha found the spectacle uncomfortably affecting.

When Nancy grew level with the gig, Tabitha leaned over and asked, 'Can I take you to the highway?'

Nancy squinted up at her, the paint on her face somewhat greasy with sweat. 'And who are you when you're at home?'

'You don't know me. I sometimes worked down at the Kaleyards in the winter of 1750. I was saving my coin to get away to London.'

Nancy took in the shining black gig and liveried coachman, and then Tabitha's sapphire riding coat and its shining guinea buttons. 'I'd remember you if you'd worn such a rig-out back then.'

Tabitha ventured a smile. 'No. I was all holes and homespun back then. My name is Tabitha.'

'Tabitha what? Who's paying for all this then?'

She reached down a hand to help the girl up and was relieved when Nancy grasped it and sprang into the seat beside her. With a word to Glover, the horses began a slow walk. 'I came back here from London penniless. But, as fate would have it, I fell in love and got married. Listen, I want to ask you about Maria.'

'Married? Who d'you get married to?'

Tabitha tried to hide her impatience. 'I married Nat De Vallory.'

Nancy broke into a ripe guffaw. 'What, 'im who was a poor scribbler and is now so rich he wants for nothing.'

'I shouldn't say he's that rich. Why do you say that?'

'It's widely spoke of round the town.' Nancy could not disguise her envy as she looked Tabitha up and down. 'You done pretty well from it. Did he give you that pretty ring as well?'

Tabitha sighed and decided to start afresh. 'The matter is this. I was with Nat when we found Maria. Someone butchered her along with her unborn child.'

'Aye, don't I know it. I just come from parroting my piece at the inquest.'

'Yes, I heard of it from my . . .' No, she must not enrage this woman by speaking of servants. 'My great aunt was listening at the inquest. I believe the law treats the matter lightly because Maria was a streetwalker. Can you tell me who she was living with after she left the Kaleyards?'

A sneer appeared on Nancy's face. 'Damned if I know. I told His Nibs the Coroner that I never knew who done for her or I should've said my piece.'

Tabitha shook her head sadly. 'Maria did not deserve this. I'm trying to find her family. And I want her killer to be punished.'

The gig moved on a hundred yards or so before Nancy spoke. 'I do recall she was mighty fond of a gentleman who lives over this way.'

'Who?' Glancing up, she saw they had almost reached the junction with the Chester highway. 'Please,' she begged.

Nancy started to laugh, and it wasn't a pleasant sound. 'You truly don't know, do you?'

'No, I don't. I hope you told the coroner.'

Nancy shrugged and pulled an ugly smirk.

'Tell me his name and I'll let the constable know.'

Nancy let out a shriek of laughter. 'The constable. What a lark! Drop me here. Look, the wagon is waiting for me.'

Tabitha was so frustrated that she considered telling Glover to hurry the horses on. The wagoner, however, hailed the young woman and Nancy leapt down and sprinted towards him. Tabitha was soon alone with the driver again, musing over her dislike of Nancy and wondering who Maria's gentleman had been from Netherlea way.

TWENTY-TWO

1 June 1753
New Moon

The great milk moon that had overseen May-tide waned away to nothing, so on the first of June the night sky was as black as a crow's wing. Setting out to observe in secret what mischief the poachers might be carrying out on his father's land, Nat forsook Jupiter for a steady and less conspicuous mount, aptly named Dormouse. Leaving the lights of Bold Hall behind, man and horse entered a dizzying void of darkness. The road was merely a patch of lesser darkness when he passed into the forest, aware of the waft of vegetation and then the muddy stink of a mere. Beyond scent and movement, the nightscape was empty save for the jangle of harness and clop of hooves.

For a long spell Nat brooded over his narrow escape from exposure at the inquest. Such was his giddy sense of elation at escaping any public shame he had in the end told Tabitha only a much-excised account of his ordeal. If she had still been fretful, or even quarrelsome, he might have been tempted to confess the full facts to her. In the event, the prospect of the Langley Ball meant she had greeted him in a light-hearted temper. Let her have her moment of happiness he told himself. He persuaded himself that to upset her now would be callous, if not dangerous to her health.

Each hoofbeat brought them deeper into the forest. He was not a natural woodsman and an occasional stray branch snagged him with sharp claws. A breeze lifted the leaves and then larger branches rocked with an almost human moan. Or was it a ghostly cry? A sudden suspicion made him draw rein and listen hard. He heard the shrieks and scampering of small creatures and something else, too. From his right-hand side he heard a footfall far heavier than a roaming deer or badger. No, two sets of footsteps. Now he heard low whispering.

Eerily, a word or two reached him in a woman's urgent tones. 'Hard to get away . . .' and 'I love thee so . . .' and 'T'will all be as I said . . .' The man whom she entreated replied in too quiet a voice to comprehend; a measured tenor with no distinct words. These were no phantoms; more likely an all-too fleshy pair of lovers from a nearby village. Still Nat could not see them, and it struck him that they might soon settle down to the proper purpose of a clandestine meeting. He shook the mare's reins and set off again, glad of her steady walk that carried him along a track she could follow far better than he. Soon he knew as well as a blind man, that he and his horse were again alone.

A while later the faint glow of lamplight emerged out of the darkness. He turned the mare towards a stand of trees and dismounted before hitching her reins to a branch. Very quietly, he crept towards the building which looked to be no more than a wooden hovel. A lantern shone on a leafy bunch of boughs fixed by the doorway, forming the proverbial sign of a bush tavern of the lowest type. The night-hunters had not yet arrived. He pulled down his hat and went around the corner to lean against the hovel's outer wall and wait. Choosing not to carry a valuable timepiece, he studied the night sky and calculated from the Pleiades that the time was still an hour to midnight.

He had good notice of the men's approach and used that time to retreat behind a tree and wait unseen. The darkness hid them, save for the few final seconds when they drew level with the tavern's lantern. For a moment faces sprang out in the golden light, revealing a mixture of strangers alongside Netherlea men. There was black-bearded Cam the blacksmith, and Williams the insolent landlord of the Netherlea Inn. He was glad he had come alone; if he had raised the constable's men they might have wanted to arrest a good many of his tenants. The matter of poaching, Nat was beginning to understand, might not be a simple one.

Once they had all passed inside, he crept back to the building and perched beside a wooden bench beneath the unglazed window. At first the poachers took care to speak in low voices, but as the ale flowed the men's passions rose. One booming voice complained of his gaoled brother's troubles.

'Still a six-month left in gaol and 'is young 'uns is near to starving. A brace of hares or birds would fill their bellies.'

Such modest desire for game was soon overridden. A chorus of grumbles arose. 'Come on, lads. What d'you say to bigger sport? I seen a herd of young harts over by The Pale. The wind's to the east. We could chance a few shots before they scent us.'

Nat recognized this voice as belonging to Cam, the fearless but slow-witted husband of his old admirer, Zusanna. Uncertainty broke out in a flurry of questions and doubts. 'Stow that! Under't Black Act shooting deer be a swinging offence,' argued a weedy-sounding fellow. His companions agreed. 'Remember old Dick Feather? Transported across the ocean to work like a slave in Virginia for seven years. All for selling a haunch of venison to a waggoner.'

'Aye, and 'e were reckoned lucky. Them others danced on a rope at the Broughton gallows.'

'Damn that whoreson Langley,' thundered Cam. 'Raise your cups, lads. God save the poor! And God damn the rich with their hearts as cold as Old Nick himself.'

Nat was straining hard to listen at the loose shutter, unnerved by the seething discontent between those who upheld the Black Act and these common men who risked the gallows for a pot full of meat. He was so intent he almost missed the sound of running footsteps approaching from the track. Casting around to hide he was forced to crouch in an unmanly fashion beneath the bench. Devil curse him, if these fellows found him – Sir John's son, hiding like a craven – they would never let him forget it. You numbskull, he silently berated himself.

The new arrival was almost upon him from the sound of his gasping breath. To Nat's vast relief the newcomer opened the door in a blaze of light and disappeared inside to a volley of loud greetings. Though a stranger to Nat he was welcomed as a friend named Billy. It was hard to catch every word as Billy delivered his news in breathless gasps. '. . . First of the Twelve Apostles,' he panted. 'Found him swinging by the neck. Cut 'im down and loosed the rope. P'raps still lingering in this world. The best friend I ever knowed.'

Crouching in the darkness, Nat held his breath.

'I know who done it,' growled Cam. ''Tis that raggoty bezzler Mullock's work. If I come across him or any other damned gentry folk out in the dark tonight, I swear he'll never see another sunrise.'

TWENTY-THREE

Nat retraced his way to his horse and slid back into the saddle. By continuing along the Old Coach Road he could circle back to the Apostles. As he moved through the darkness, he did his damnedest to make sense of Billy's announcement. Why hadn't the man sent for the constable? For sure the men were poachers, but nevertheless . . . Slowly, as the mare trotted along, he guessed the rather different story. If keepers like Mullock had any sense they knew to stay within the law and not string up poachers however often they threatened to; their job was to deliver them to the sheriff. But they did have the right to kill any dog who was trained for, or engaged in, poaching. That was if they were not first 'lawed' and the dog's three foreclaws lopped off, leaving the creature too lame to ever again give chase. It was a damnable business, Nat decided, feeling rather more natural sympathy for hungry cottagers than Langley and his ilk.

After a long spell he approached a row of pale trees he hoped were the silver birches of the Apostles. Nat dug his heels into the mare's flanks and hurried alongside the row of trees. He slowed at the final giant. It was as tall as a tower, pale and silent, and tonight seemed peculiarly alien to mortal man. He dismounted and searched around its mottled trunk.

The dog lay in a pool of darkness on the ground, its long body stretched in a grotesque parody of a malefactor cut down from the gallows. Nat touched a silky paw and it was as cold as stone. Exploring the furry body, his fingertips hesitated over a patch of heat. Yes, there was the slow rise and fall of the creature's laboured ribcage. A cut length of hemp still lay around its neck.

'Come on, boy. D'you still live?' Crouching, Nat murmured softly. He still had a lonely child's love of man's best companion, a bond as old as the forests and the stars themselves. Dammit, he had no choice; he would carry the dog in his arms all the way to Netherlea.

Before he could make an attempt, a shout of challenge reached him from the road. 'You there! What you doing with that there dog?'

Nat could see nothing, but recognized the voice as Cam's. The poachers must have taken a faster shortcut along a forest path. Cam's threat still rang in his ears that he would kill any solitary gentleman he found wandering in the dark. Well, he would not hide or try to run. There was nothing for it but to show himself.

'I am Nat De Vallory of Netherlea. Is that you, Cam? I was riding past and saw this poor creature close to death. I was about to carry him to the animal leech.'

This at least enticed the poachers into view and Nat saw they had darkened their faces and pulled on black clothes and hats to prevent being recognized at their night's sport. Surrounding him, they made a demonic sight as they noisily assessed the dog's condition. Agreement was reached to fetch a handcart to carry the dog home.

Attention returned to Nat himself. 'So what you doing here at dead of night, De Vallory?' Cam demanded. The blacksmith opened the little door of a dark lantern and held it aloft to study Nat's costume. 'And all rigged out in working men's clothes? I hope you in't spying upon our business?'

Nat scrabbled in his mind for some credible excuse. 'Can't you guess? I'm making enquiries into that young woman's death. Her killer is still running free. I'm hardly going to chase the killer through the forest in a gold-laced coat.'

Behind the lantern, Cam's bear-like face watched him narrowly.

'You watching that camp where that mock-preacher is gatherin' folk?' asked Billy.

'I may be.'

'Only I reckon I seen that dead girl walking in the woods with that faith-monger calls hisself Baptist or summat.'

'Aye, that one who all them young lasses lift their smocks for,' chortled another.

Nat turned to Billy. 'You are sure of this? When did you see them together?'

Billy could add little to what he'd said, only that he'd glimpsed a young woman with long brown hair walking at Gunn's side some weeks past, in the spring.

'We've got work to do, lads,' Cam interrupted. 'So, Mister De Vallory, you going to snitch on us to the sheriff, or what?'

'It isn't that long since I enjoyed a night's coursing with my own dog, lads. So long as you don't go after my father's stock, I have not seen a soul all this night,' Nat said coolly. 'But I'll tell you now, Lord Langley wants to enclose all this Netherlea land and I intend to fight him at law. Sir John has always been content that you hunt small game here but if Langley gets his way, he'll clear all the woodland to improve his prospect from Langley Hall.'

He was pleased to hear grumbling amongst the men and felt the antipathy lifting from himself on to a common enemy. 'But tell me,' he added, 'have any of you seen my father's wolfhound, Hector? He vanished here three weeks ago. It's broken my father's heart near enough.'

Cam snorted. 'A wolfhound? Sir John can always go buy another dog for a few gold guineas. Why should we care for Sir John?'

Nat stood his ground. 'Because any decent man would wish to spare such loyal creatures from suffering.' Reaching for his horse, he wondered if Cam might try to waylay him. He set his foot in the stirrup and, still unhindered, set Dormouse back on the road to Bold Hall.

TWENTY-FOUR

Though His Mother will be mocked as a sinner & whore
She is modest yet blessed, and rich while poor.

The New Prophet of the Forest

2 June 1753

Tabitha had waited up for Nat's return until nearly two in the morning before sinking into a fractured sleep. At daylight, she padded straight to his chamber and thanked Christ to find him unconscious to the world inside his rumpled bed. She stood awhile watching him breathe, tracing the contours of his pale face in the tangle of dark hair. What was wrong with them both that she loved him most fiercely when he was insensible? She leaned over and kissed his warm brow without waking him. God bless him. He was safely home from his night adventure in the forest and she was happy.

Fortified, she felt able to begin her preparations to move into the solar, the room where from time immemorial the De Vallory heirs had been born. When she had at first protested, Nat sheepishly confirmed the custom. 'Sir John will expect it, sweetheart. It is not the most modern room in the house, but you must endure it for only a month before you are churched.' Now she stood at the centre of the high-beamed chamber with Grisell, Sukey and Jennet, drawing up an account of what was needed. The bed was a high carved tester bed with thick curtains embroidered with faded crewel-work of bizarre creatures – were they griffons or spiders? Disapproving, she surveyed the heavy black furniture carved with ugly mermaids and monsters. The rough plastered walls and creaking wooden floor made the place feel as chill as the depths of a well.

A crude birthing chair leered at her from the room's centre. It was made of worn ebonized wood, nothing but four sturdy legs, a curved back and a horseshoe shaped seat through which the baby might drop. 'Grisell, would you put that horror away until it's needed. It looks like a ducking stool from the days of the Witchfinder General. Pray do not torture me on that.'

Sukey made a soft tutting sound that her mistress was learning meant she had something to say. 'The groaning stool can prove of great benefit, my lady. It will keep your bed free of all the blood and waters voided at the birth.'

'Thank you, Sukey. A delightful reminder. So, we'll need a new-filled featherbed, bolsters, my lace bedlinen – oh, and hangings. That tapestry looks as if it depicts the harrowing of Hell. Find an arras that shows a happy scene please, Grisell. And a good thick carpet underfoot. And a great deal of firewood to warm the air. Don't forget your sleeping place, Sukey. You will need a truckle bed, too, in the anteroom.'

Finally she returned to the window and peered through glass so ancient it bulged and shrunk the view like a pair of warped spectacles. This was the older, less-inhabited wing of the house and there was nothing to see but a row of tall trees. A garden would have been welcome, or a view of meadows.

'What else is needed?' she asked the others, stifling a yawn. Truly, the room must not have been aired since the last heir was born.

Sukey tut-tutted. 'Mister Higgott has got the cleaning of the De Vallory cradle in hand but it must not be carried here yet to prevent bad luck.'

'You see to that and I shall choose some books and pictures,' said Tabitha. 'And as I'm to receive visitors here, we will need good glass and china for tea and cake. Well, ladies, I hope it is no omen of misfortune, but I cannot bear to stay within these cold walls for another moment. Let us take our sewing outside to the gazebo and breathe fresh air.'

Nat's first improvement to the garden had been to build a fashionable summerhouse in which Tabitha might rest while gazing out upon the parterres of the garden. It was a charming circular summerhouse built around eight ancient oak pillars with three wide bays open to the air and a fine prospect across the paths and flowerbeds. The back walls were filled with woven hazel coppice set with two windows glazed with red and green glass.

'It is like a house built by a pixie,' Tabitha had said, laughing when she first gazed up at the newly thatched roof that rose to a point.

Soon the women were busy with their needles, sheltered from the sun by the patterned chintz curtains Tabitha had hung across the open bays. Jennet had expressed a keenness to learn some of Sukey's more esoteric stitches, especially the pinprick designs she called holy work. The two of them were bent over meticulous sketches representing the Annunciation Lily, the Crown of Glory, and the Tree of Life. Meanwhile, Grisell was rapidly hemming the inevitable pile of clouts to wrap around the baby's backside. Little Bess had climbed inside the large rush basket of plain cloths and pretended it was a boat until she fell suddenly asleep. Soon tiring of her needle, Tabitha began leafing through a magazine containing fashion plates fresh from Paris. This Madame Pompadour, the King of France's mistress, truly set the fashions for the whole of Europe. Tabitha marvelled at her confections of lace, flowers, and silk. What to wear to the ball at Langley Hall filled her mind with pleasant visions. Though her grass-green gown was with the seamstress, being altered to the latest style, it was the embellishments that would confer that essential Parisian modishness.

Tabitha stretched her back, glad of the cushioned chair she had installed for her comfort. 'Let the child only come soon and rid me of this heaviness. Ladies, do you have any notions of how to hurry the child along?'

'How soon does the doctor say it will come?' Grisell asked.

'He cannot say. I could have conceived almost any day after the seventh of October last year.' Saying this, she smiled to herself. 'For sure, I was with child in the first month I was ever with Nat, so much did we love each other. By Christmas I knew the signs and we married as soon as we could in January.'

Sukey picked up an almanack and proved to be an excellent mathematician. 'Let me see. As all good Christians know, two hundred and eighty days was the length of the Virgin Mary's pregnancy, from Ascension till Christmas Day. So the babe could arrive as early as the end of this month or the first few weeks of July. But a first child is generally late. So he could be as late as the fourteenth of July.'

'Lord, that is more than a month, perhaps six long weeks. Look, it's the full moon on the fifteenth of July,' Tabitha protested, peering over her elbow into the almanack's pages. 'You know what they say of Midsummer madness: when the moon is full, wits are in the wane.'

'It depends on the day,' Sukey said. 'Sunday is a lucky day so that may counter the bad moon.'

Jennet looked up from her work. 'So, Sukey, what is the most auspicious day to be born on?'

The nursemaid did not even hesitate in her precise stitching. 'Christmas Day, of course.'

'So when will your baby be born?' Jennet asked.

Sukey smiled down into her elaborate holy point patterns. 'Like Mrs De Vallory, I kept no record. Yet I feel sure the mistress is but a few weeks ahead of me.'

'So your husband was still with you in October?' Tabitha asked.

Sukey serenely completed a few more stitches before answering. 'He was, my lady. I confess I miss him like my very heart was cut away.'

'I am sorry, Sukey. I pray he may soon return.' She mused for a moment. 'Strange. The girl who died in the forest was with child, too, but due to give birth a little later I believe.'

'It's said she was a common whore killed by her keeper,' Grisell cut in harshly.

Tabitha protested. 'We do not know who killed her. And all of you who are so enamoured of Mister Gunn, do not forget his camp is right by where she was found.'

Jennet was quick to defend him. 'There is no proof he was involved. Besides, he has such a noble, godly look to him.'

Tabitha laughed. 'You mean he has a handsome face.'

Jennet flung down her needle. 'Mister Gunn is the finest preacher in the country. I for one could listen to him preach night and day.'

'As could I,' added Grisell.

'You cannot blame Mister Gunn for that trull's death,' Sukey added. 'The matron at the charity school said she was the wickedest of girls.'

'Now, Sukey,' Tabitha scolded. 'That is not to be made common gossip.'

Sukey looked up, her cheeks flushed. 'Beg pardon, my lady. I could scarce believe such devilry in one so young.'

Then considering, Tabitha asked, 'What do the people say hereabouts? Who killed Maria?'

Jennet shrugged. 'You know Netherlea folk. Always contrary. There's stories of a man leading her into the forest and killing her, all to have no debt to the parish for the baby.'

'And what have you heard, Sukey?'

'No good Christian could deny it, mistress. She took the road to sin and reaped as she deserved.'

Tabitha shook her head mournfully. 'And you, Grisell?'

'It were not Mister Gunn,' she said sourly. 'He is striving to make a better world, for ordinary folk. It makes a change from being ordered about by those who are no better than you are.'

Tabitha looked away, stung by what could only be a personal jibe. 'If you are not happy here, Grisell, you can always take your chance and sail away with Mister Gunn. Though they do say that if the Cherokee does not shoot you first, the wild animals will devour you.'

'I will not fear those dangers if the Lord is with me,' Grisell announced complacently.

Tabitha had heard enough. 'Good. Then you will not mind packing your bags and crossing the ocean without a written character.' She stood up, ready to leave. 'Come along Jennet, I wish a private word with you.'

Strolling back to the house, Tabitha asked, 'What on earth can I do with Grisell?'

'Let her go to America.' Then Jennet added with a bitter little laugh. 'After all, she is not a very good maid.'

'I think I may. Enough. I must also ask you a favour. I hear you visit the camp to hear Gunn preach. Would you tell me if you hear aught of Maria? No one will answer my questions, but I reckon they trust you.'

Jennet tossed her fair hair. 'I should like to, Tabitha, but it is a long walk home alone in the dark. Can Tom come with me? Surely someone else can attend you at dinner.'

An uncomfortable memory sprang up in Tabitha's mind. 'What about your father? I doubt he would approve.'

'Father? He always finds complaint these days. Why is it that old men must forever be jealous of us young people and our pleasures?'

Tabitha remonstrated. 'Joshua is no old man. And he loves you dearly, you silly maid. Very well. I shall release Tom but you must be discreet. Pretend to ask about an old friend of yours who is Maria's age and appearance but do not mention her name. Do you understand?'

Jennet gave a little skip of joy. 'Thank you, Tabitha. May I go now? I shall just call at the stables and tell Tom.'

TWENTY-FIVE

And His father though born of the lowliest state
Is a most honoured wretch due a glorious fate.

The New Prophet of the Forest

3 June 1753

On Sunday morning Nat came to Tabitha's chamber as she dressed. 'The Mondrem Oak has been attacked. Who would do such a thing? I'm riding over to take a look and won't be home until supper.'

She begged him to let her follow him in the gig, making promises that Glover would drive her slowly and steadily. Truly, she insisted, she was suffering from being so confined with a band of foolish women. Nat reluctantly agreed, though the weather had turned overcast. Out in the pastures the sheep huddled in the corners of fields and once inside the forest a chilly wind lifted the leaves, making a mournful sound. As the gig followed Nat deeper into the trees, she caught sight of others who had heard the news, all heading with grim purpose towards the prodigious tree. By the time she arrived in the forest clearing a great gathering of villagers mingled with folk from the camp. The mighty oak had been stripped of most of its votive offerings: the coloured ribbons, talismans, flower posies, and written prayers lay pell-mell on the ground. Worse, some of the tree's lower branches had been hacked away, then tossed on the ground like mangled limbs. The amputations bore wounds where the creamy flesh was beaded with golden sap. Tabitha looked for her own and Sukey's poppets. There was no sign of her own tiny effigy, though Sukey's poppet was discovered safe on a nearby shrub. She wiped it down and slipped it in her pocket.

'Why would anyone do this?' she asked out loud. Those folk gathered close around her were quick to share their suspicions.

''Tis that villain of a keeper, Mullock, if you asks me,' proffered a passing workman.

'Aye, and behind him will be Langley. Damn his eyes,' added his companion.

Spotting Anna's son poking among the fallen branches, Tabitha moved closer to observe him. 'Good day, Private Hollingsworth,' she called.

The soldier bowed in a civil fashion. 'My lady. Here's good wood broken from that venerable tree. I should rather fashion it into something useful than see it smashed beneath men's boots.' He had a good bundle of the straightest limbs tied over his shoulder.

'Is it for your mother's fire?' She watched him for a moment as he measured by eye a narrow branch. Joshua had called him a respected soldier, yet Gunn's women had called him an ogler. His mother feared he was haunted by a ghost. Tabitha could not reconcile these opinions with the rough-hewn fellow who moved alone through the chattering crowd.

Nat motioned her over to a stand of trees apart from the crowd. He turned to her, looking anxious. 'I suppose I must speak up and calm these people.'

Tabitha glanced over her shoulder and guessed there were now more than fifty persons milling around the tree and the mood was growing fractious. A few youths were waving fists. 'I don't think that would be—' Her eye was caught by the arrival of Gunn. She watched him with fear and – dare she even think it – unwilling fascination. How strange it was that he could plant uplifting notions in her mind and at the same time, disgust her so. The crowd parted to let Gunn stride confidently up to the oak's massive trunk, which he touched with both hands as if his fingers could heal the damage to the injured giant. Before Nat could compose his words and step forward, Gunn took absolute charge.

'Good people of the forest. Behold this shameful act. Remember all our prayers, our hopes, our wishes. Remember all our heartfelt offerings to this venerable great oak. All broken, by those who care not a jot for the common folk.'

Gunn opened his palms in a gesture of appeal and all eyes and ears were his. 'You know Lord Langley that lives in his great hall?'

Mournful replies of 'Aye,' and 'Worse luck,' came in response.

'Langley intends to steal this place, the common people's forest. He wants to take an axe to this holy tree. And why? So that he and his family can make a smooth-lawned park. So that he can impress his idle friends. So that you and your families will be banished from these greenwood groves forever.'

Gunn turned his bright, penetrating gaze towards Nat. 'Is this not Netherlea land? What of your rights and what of Sir John's rights, that were witnessed here only six days past when the Netherlea villagers beat their bounds? If the De Vallorys lose their rights, then so do you. And should you not stand up for young Mister De Vallory and his fair wife, so ripe with child? Should you not stand up for your own rights and those of your children?'

Nat flinched. Tabitha also started, affronted at their own affairs being made the subject of a sermon by no better than a hedge preacher. Yet the situation could not be more awkward, for the man held his listeners rapt.

'Look at where you have to live. Mud floors, draughty doors, empty plates, cold and hungry children. Look at Lord Langley's mansion, as big as a king's castle. The roaring fires, the dogs that eat fine meat, the groaning tables of dainties, the overfed children raised so proud they would as soon kick your children aside as throw them a farthing. Do I tell you lies?'

A chorus of 'No!' and 'Not a word,' erupted from the multitude.

'It is time to stop tipping your caps, time to stop bowing and scraping. There is a better place than this. A better land, a promised land. A green and fertile Eden. On Midsummer's Day I sail for America. We sail on a ship of destiny. Sail with me and be chosen by God to be blessed forever.'

Cheers and roars of approval rang out. Tabitha raised her eyes heavenward. Gunn was turning the villagers' misfortunes into a recruitment call for his American settlement.

Then came cries that Gunn should make a prophecy. 'Let us hear God's word,' they called. As if on his command the wind dropped. The air was still and hushed, darkening to charcoal grey. Gunn called for a lighted torch and at once the crowd fell silent. Next, a chair was fetched for the prophet. Tabitha wondered

how it was they came to be so well prepared – as if they alone
had known the oak would be attacked.

'Shall we leave? Before he tells all our fortunes to entertain
the assembly?' she whispered.

Nat was watching the preacher with a dogged expression. 'No.
I must hear this.'

As before, Gunn quickly fell into what appeared to be a heavy
slumber. A flaming torch was held close to his face, so that
reflected firelight moved across his features in an unearthly
fashion. When he spoke his voice had changed, as before. The
loud and compelling young man was now a whispering, uncanny
presence. Suddenly, though still seeming deep in sleep, Gunn
stood. He uplifted his arms like the crucified Christ. As all fell
silent, he uttered his prophecy.

'I, the instrument of Almighty God do foretell these matters.
And the first sign is this. That a new messiah will be born in the
West, an innocent born of the oak, yet gaining his inheritance
one thousand miles from its roots. And this messiah will bestow
the Lord's blessings upon the new nation.

'And the second sign is this. His mother shall be borne of a
humble home, yet she shall be a lioness. Though some will call
her Jezebel and harlot. And I am told by the Holy Spirit that his
blessed mother is quickening even as I speak.'

Tabitha squirmed. What extraordinary timing. At the moment
he spoke she felt her own child fluttering like a caged canary
inside her. Some would call her strong, a lioness. And most would
call her a harlot.

Others in the crowd also felt the power of Gunn's prophetic
words. A few women fell upon the ground crying thanks to the
Lord for the holy child within them. Tabitha puzzled over how
this young man could seize all their minds in his grasp like a
master puppeteer.

'And the father of this new saviour shall also be raised from
the poor and needful, and called vagabond and knave and yet
also be honoured by the Most High.'

In the deepening dusk she looked to see how Nat took this
new prediction. Nat's family had once been poor enough, and
look at him now, the master of Bold Hall and one day to be a
baronet. What was Gunn saying? That they were this new

messiah's parents? She felt a sickening mix of embarrassment and fear.

Gunn spoke again: 'And a new constellation shall rise in the sky, announcing from the heavens that the child will lead men forth to glory. And the child's name shall be a nation.'

'I have heard enough.' Tabitha grasped Nat's arm and pulled him towards the waiting gig. Halfway there, a hawker thrust a pamphlet into Tabitha's face. The illustration made her halt, stock-still. Giving a small coin to the seller she seized a copy and only shared it with Nat once they reached the horses.

It was a chapbook of the flimsiest style, illustrated by a crude woodcut of a man who looked nothing like Baptist Gunn. However, the title told of the same man who was now speaking to their own motley crowd of tenants and villagers.

Tabitha read the title out loud: '*The New Prophet of the Forest: In Which the Preacher Baptist Gunn Whilst being in a Trance Unfolds the Many Decrees of Fate giving Several Instances wherein his Prophecies have been Fulfilled. Giving also a Most Wonderful Relation of those Strange and Surprising Events that Will Yet Come to Pass.*'

Nat took it from her and riffled the pages with great interest. If only, Tabitha thought, such a wretched little book could indeed tell her what the future might bring.

TWENTY-SIX

7 to 10 June 1753
Whitsuntide

Over the next few days both the villages and forest were aflame with the preacher's call to join him on the voyage to America. Tabitha watched Grisell closely, looking for hints that she would join the exodus. 'Baptist Gunn is brim full of the Holy Spirit,' she overheard her saying. 'Not like that Parson Hope, who dines on rich meats bought with the tithes from other men's labours.'

Tabitha consoled herself that such notions were not only talked of by her own household. Almost everyone seemed to have a story of friends or kin who were sailing to Pennsylvania or Pittsburgh or some other colony of the Americas. It was a better life over there, folk said; a chance to remake humanity in a godly fashion, free of kings and corruption. And free of upstart ladies who were once London whores, she mused to herself, as she watched Grisell bang down her food at every meal.

Alone in her chamber, she took out her mother's box to add the pamphlet containing Gunn's prophecies to its contents. After studying it, she had learned little more of Gunn himself. It was written in the excitable manner of most of those books of wonders sold by pedlars who traipsed the land with their heavy packs. It made much of Gunn being struck on the head while a youth and thereafter being blessed by the miracle of 'speaking the future most true'. The tone was flattering, which made her suspect the prophet himself had taken a hand in writing it, describing himself as owning 'a most noble and arresting appearance'. Well, that certainly sounded like the conceited cunny-hunter. Next were the printed prophecies: of the saviour, the significance of the oak, the saviour's lowborn parents, and the new constellation. Rumours of the De Vallorys connection with the prophecies were spreading further afield, to Chester and beyond. For the first time she wondered if she should go away, to Bath or some other populous place. No, here she had her own servants, Nat at her side and Joshua close by. Yet could they protect her from 'hot-spilled blood' and strife?

Inside her mother's prayer book were the flowers she had collected from Maria's body, now as dry as straw. Tabitha wondered if she had known her killer; if she had tried to protect her unborn child as well as herself when the knife-strokes had begun. The horrific vision of such a death forced her to action, to pace the room and then gather all the items she had collected. She found the drawing of the half-ring and then, though she was not entirely sure why, she added Sukey's poppet to her collection. She stared at each in turn but could not uncover the significance of these oddities. Devil curse it, the Midsummer culmination of the prophecies was creeping ever closer; if she could not solve the mystery soon, she feared that no one ever would.

As Whitsuntide approached Nat gave all his tenants a holiday, hosting them with ale and sweetmeats in the old-fashioned, open-handed manner almost vanished since the Civil War. He threw his heart and soul into playing the young squire, firing a pistol to start the running races on the church green and giving the prize of a piglet to the young lad who first scrambled up the greasy pole. Tabitha once more felt herself to be the village May Queen, wearing her whitework dress embroidered with flowers, her fertility a sign of Nature's blessing upon their marriage. Together with their tenants they celebrated the best of the freedoms of England: the romping and the rivalries, the dancing and drinking, all in honour of the spreading boughs of forest green.

The only ill-note was the presence of the pamphlets concerning Gunn's prophecies. A bow-backed chapman was moving through the throng, his tray slung around his neck displaying the usual ribbons, pins, and almanacks alongside fresh copies of Gunn's prophecies. Tabitha asked Nat if he would send the man away, but her husband confessed that he himself had bought a copy. 'It is best to let it be,' he said, and she stilled her tongue, for the day was too merry for quarrels. After dining in the orchard on a roast hog at a trestle table, Tabitha came indoors to bed. The next day she would need all her strength for the Langleys' ball.

* * *

Tabitha's reworked gown was the prettiest grass-green taffeta with a gay trim of pink fabric roses, ruffles and bows. The seamstress had let out a number of seams and inserted new panels, though even with a lace *fichu* tucked into her low neckline the gown still looked rather provocative. Sukey assisted with her hair, curling it with hot irons, then puffing it into a malleable mass. On her dressing table Tabitha propped a printed picture of Madame Pompadour looking delightfully coquettish in an elaborate gown decorated with flowers. Though her nursemaid had not the skill of a French *coiffeuse*, she tried hard to twist and plait and finally, to puff Tabitha's hair with clouds of starchy white powder.

Tabitha was not entirely sure she suited the greyish pallor of powder, but the clock announced it was too late to wash it out. Next, Tabitha stared hard at the print of France's leader of fashion and tried her damnedest to copy the porcelain paleness of her heroine's skin. Painting a wash of *blanc* over her face and shoulders, she was a little disappointed at the startling effect. Next, she began to build up the *à la mode* circle of rouge on her cheeks. She sat back and anxiously studied the remarkable reflection in her looking glass. She could not tell whether or not her own strong features suited this mask-like repainting. Still seeking the delicacy of La Pompadour, she dressed her hair with a cluster of feathers, then supplemented it with a choker of ruffled satin, a spray of diamonds at her shoulder, two bracelets, and a painted fan. Standing, she inspected herself in the pier glass.

By some delusion of vanity, she had expected to see the reflection of her former slender self, a tall frame that could carry the hoops of a wide-skirted gown with absolute elegance. What she saw in the mirror did not flatter her. She touched her overbrimming bosom and adjusted her *fichu*, which struggled to cover the roundness of her body. Through the weighty silk of her skirts she pressed her hands to either side of her abdomen. In reply, she could feel the child kick in his watery womb. Lord save her, she should not have pressed Nat to accept the invitation.

Her door opened and Nat's face peered inside. She turned to him with self-mocking desperation. 'Nat. Help me. Whatever happened to my elegant style? I had hoped to look fashionably French.'

Nat did his best. He stripped off half of her jewellery and the feathers and rubbed gently at the circles of rouge. Even better, he struggled manfully not to smile too broadly.

'I have no other suitable gown,' she whimpered.

'You are more beautiful than ever,' he said kindly. 'Though the effect of so many frills is somewhat *de trop*.'

She caught a glimpse of her reflection: fussily dressed and unusually flustered. 'Could you send word I am unwell?'

He looked down at her with tender concern. 'My darling, there is this issue of our land. It will be best to speak to Langley in his own home. Come along, sweetling. The horses are restless.'

TWENTY-SEVEN

A flunky with a gilded lantern ushered the De Vallory carriage through the iron gates into Langley Park. There was no sign of the hall, only a serpentine driveway meandering through glorious parkland. Wide cropped meadows opened up around them, scattered with glossy cattle and snow-white sheep, chewing the cud as if in a picture book.

'What the devil can he want more land for?' Nat grumbled.

'Some men can never have enough,' Tabitha replied.

The hall came suddenly into view; a prodigious mass of grey stone fronted by a classical pediment supported by massive fluted pillars. As the carriage stopped a footman approached with a wavering flambeau. She whispered to Nat. 'Thank the gods you will inherit cheery Bold Hall. I should hate to live in such a horrid mausoleum as this.'

Nat took her hand and whispered, 'Well, my dear, it was you who insisted we accept the invitation.'

They were ushered into a room of luxurious ugliness and waited to be announced beside a pair of black marble statues depicting two negro slaves. Tabitha adjusted her lace *fichu* and found that her fingers were slippery.

'Mister and Mrs De Vallory of Bold Hall.' As their names were called Nat winked at Tabitha and they moved into the grand saloon. Her first impression was of walls as crimson as a monster's maw, illuminated by thousands of dripping candles. A crowd of genteel people turned to inspect them. Straightening her back and holding her chin high, Tabitha stepped forward as gracefully as she was able. With growing confidence, she noticed that most of the guests were in their middle years and far less modishly dressed than they were. She glanced up at Nat, proud to be on the arm of the finest-looking man in the room. Tonight he wore his long hair tied back, his new ruffled stock at his neck; his clever, cat-like eyes were not at all cowed by the onslaught of curiosity. 'Let them stare,' he murmured.

For some time they sauntered around the public rooms, admiring items of dazzling modernity and expense: here were life-like Italian paintings, unread books in gilded cages, furniture created from mosaic or marble, or what might even have been solid gold.

A man in the black coat of an upper servant approached them and bowed low. 'Mister De Vallory. Lord Langley begs your attendance in his private study.'

Nat hesitated, turning to Tabitha. But before he could speak the man anticipated Nat's concern. 'I shall escort Mrs De Vallory to Her Ladyship's sitting room.'

Tabitha pushed Nat gently on his way. Here was Nat's chance to clarify Sir John's ownership of the land. A moment later she followed the upper servant to a distant room where a plump woman wearing a great weight of diamonds was holding court to a circle of nodding listeners. Lady Langley was a woman of sixty or thereabouts, with grey hair streaked with yellow and a countenance and neck peppered with large moles. Tabitha hung back at the room's edge where no one greeted her or offered her a chair. Hot and awkward, she was about to return to the public rooms when Lady Langley caught sight of her and uttered a strangled sound. Tabitha stepped forward and, with considerable demands upon her balance, curtsied low. In a voice both screeching and clipped, Her Ladyship complained so that all in the room could hear each word. 'Look! Now the unmannerly brute has invited a former London harlot. Here, to my house.'

As Tabitha rose from her curtsy, she felt a rare heat scorching her skin. She straightened to full height and inclined her head courteously. Then she replied as smart as a whip: 'Your Ladyship. Compared to your own disobliging manner, I assure you that any London harlot is a queen of courtesy.'

Turning on her heels, Tabitha heard a wave of tittering laughter escape from the company. It was a hollow victory, however. Leaving the room, she drifted from chamber to chamber, miserable with regret. Oh Lord, what would Nat say? Might she have ruined his diplomatic strategy by insulting Langley's wife? She found herself in the supper room and disconsolately took a glass or two of champagne and drained them in a couple of gulps. Now she was alone, she experienced the gaze of strangers as a heavy, unsettling pressure. The faint smile fixed upon her face began to ache. And the pain from her tight brocade shoes was no longer dull but threatened to bring stupid tears to her eyes.

'Mister Beaufort Langley at your service. Might I fetch you a little supper?' A young man bowed low before her. She was vastly glad to be rescued, but he was not a prepossessing fellow, for his figure was more than portly and his face gleamed with sweat. Thanking him, she sent him to jostle at the banquet table while she watched her fellow revellers. It was now horribly evident that, never before having attended a ball outside of London, she was wearing entirely the wrong gown. The women gathered here were dressed with an austerity and uniformity that represented an aristocratic simplicity. Pale blue, grey or ivory satin was stretched over wide skirts worn with a simple ribbon at their waists. At their necks and bosoms were dazzling diamond and sapphire brooches and pendants. She felt herself a painted parrot beside pristine doves.

Her companion returned with a plate of cheering dainties, and for a pleasant few minutes she nibbled at game pie, potted cheese and sweetmeats.

'Madam,' her companion said. 'I cannot stay silent. You are the most wonderful creature I ever saw in my life.'

'How long is your life so far, sir, that you have seen so little?'

'I am nineteen next September.' As he spoke a spray of spittle and cake crumbs escaped his thick lips.

'You live here?' she asked, backing away.

'No. I am Lord Langley's nephew and live in Nantwich. And lady, I am smitten.'

Tabitha raised her fan to hide a wry smile. 'From your directness, sir, I assume you know who I am.'

'I do. Though I confess I was expecting more of a Magdalene than a Madonna. Yet I confess I do like the combination of the two.' He took a step back and eyed her with the air of a dilettante. Oh, for a more modest gown, she reproved herself. Over his shoulder she searched for Nat, nodding occasionally as the youth wittered nonsense at her.

'Would you care for a turn around the terrace?' Turning to Langley's nephew, she stifled a yawn. It was ten in the evening and she was used to being abed by now. A breath of air might help her survive another half-hour, she decided. Young Langley took her by the arm and led her through a maze of corridors until they reached a door that opened out on to darkness.

'Let me show you the view,' her companion murmured.

Tabitha frowned and held back from the pitchy night. 'The sun has set—'

'I will keep you safe.' His arm snaked around her shoulder and a moment later pulled her forward. She found herself outside in darkness as black as the devil's boots. Langley reached for her arm and held it fast. No longer a buffoon, he said, 'Your husband wastes his time over that scrap of land. My uncle is determined to have it.'

She attempted a spirited reply. 'That remains to be seen.'

Langley gripped her arm tighter. 'The world your husband strives to join is an exclusive one. He must learn to play by our rules or leave the table.'

'Perhaps he is a more skilful player?'

'No. He will be doomed to fail in any endeavour. But perhaps you are a lady of skill, madam? Might you not stand as his proxy?' His hot breath told all in the silence. With a thump he pushed her hard against a wall of stone. His fingers, as plump as warm slugs, pressed against her shoulder.

'Come, come, madam. Give a fellow a chance.' He clawed at her left breast, then squeezed it very hard. The youth's fat body was surprisingly strong.

'How dare you? I will—'

He covered her mouth with his other hand to silence her. She could not breathe. Then he leaned down and hissed into her ear. 'If your husband wants to keep your forest acres, you and I must be friends. Meet with me each week at a private place. What d'you say?'

Momentarily he loosened his hold of her and she gasped for air.

'Never.'

Her mind raced. On the streets she had been taught to defend herself. Should she kick him hard? No, the angle was wrong.

'Or we could take a quick tumble here and now. As a down payment. What, eh? You owe your darling husband no loyalty.' He laughed unpleasantly. 'Ask him who he was searching for in a certain Chester tavern back in May.'

She barely listened. Her hand snaked into her skirt pocket and found her ivory fan. Yanking it out, she stabbed the pointed end of the handle directly into Beaufort's face. He shrieked and sprang back, his face in his hands.

Wasting no time, Tabitha fumbled the door open and moved as fast as she could along the dimly lit corridor. Turning away from the brilliant chandeliers, she made for emptier rooms and dim backstairs corridors. Her hair was slipping down and her *fichu* had lost its pins, uncovering her half-escaped breast. She climbed a narrow set of stairs. The noise of the assembled guests grew fainter. She tried a modest door and found an empty bedroom. There she tidied herself at the glass where her reflection looked ashen and frightened. She longed to find her bedchamber. Her hand slid inside her satin stays – good, the eagle-stone still sat safe against her heart. She had been an idiot to let Beaufort Langley lead her away from the public area. Being newly married she had fancied herself immune to such approaches. That, and being so far gone with child. Wake up, she upbraided herself. Marriage and imminent motherhood have softened your street-sharp instincts. Do you think to sleepwalk all the rest of your life?

TWENTY-EIGHT

V enturing out along the corridor again, Tabitha came to a long room lined on each side with marble statuary; she thought it ugly stuff: men and wild animals locked in combat, naked boys and leering goat-hooved satyrs. Hearing footsteps approach, she stood back in the shadow of an alcove and waited, spying on a pair of menservants who sauntered along, making sport of their masters. While they passed, she surveyed the paintings displayed where the candle sconces cast a soft glow. There were plenty of thickset Langley men with loose lips and double chins. Setting off again, she studied the women, idly wondering what great trouble it might give a painter to flatter the present viscountess.

She had walked past the modest painting before the impression imprinted upon her eyes reached her mind. Turning back on her heels, she picked up a candle and studied the portrait closely. It was of a woman of middle years, her grey hair escaping from a high lace headdress of an ancient fashion and her bodice trimmed with ermine. She wore no jewels, but a plump hand rested at her waist. On the finger stood a ring bearing two tiny clasped hands. It was identical to Maria's ring. Tabitha saw no hint of Maria in the matron's face yet detected an echo of the Langley features in the round, liquid eyes.

'Hello,' a voice called out behind her and she looked around. Before her stood a small woman of twenty years or so, with a snub nose and dark hair tied up in curling papers. She introduced herself as Sophie Rix. 'I heard you speak to Lady Langley earlier,' she whispered, then bit her lower lip. A contagious smile erupted. 'Lord, you were so brave! It was the best entertainment I've ever had in this ghastly place. I crept up early to bed, but forgiving my disarray, might you come in my room and talk a while?'

Tabitha agreed and followed her into a large chamber in which a great many clothes were untidily scattered. Sophie poured her a glass of brandy and Tabitha downed it gratefully after kicking off her shoes.

'Everyone in the neighbourhood was agog when you won your husband,' Sophie confided. 'You showed such spirit. By the by, my husband is a second cousin removed, or some such, to Her Ladyship. But you must not mind that – we both endure, rather than enjoy, these visits. There are so many unwritten rules here. I am a coward. I never dare let them see my true nature.'

Over another steadying glass of spirits, Tabitha found she liked Sophie sufficiently to confide in her a little. 'Do you know who is portrayed in that painting I was looking at?'

The two women returned to the corridor to take another look. Sophie stared for a long time and then frowned. 'I believe she could be Lord Langley's sister. The ermine suggests she is noble, of course. But it is well before my time.'

Tabitha agreed. 'That cap and gown are of another age. The twenties, perhaps?'

'I believe she's long dead, I'm afraid.'

Tabitha gave a little groan. She had secretly hoped to find this woman sequestered away somewhere in the hundred rooms of Langley Hall, a wrinkled old dame who would eagerly confide of a long-ago dalliance that had bred young Maria. Feeling despondent, she asked, 'Do you know how long ago she died?'

'I'm sorry, no. But we might find out tomorrow. There will be opportunities for private conversation. May I ask why you wish to know?'

'A friend of mine had a gimmel ring exactly like that one. I thought I might have another made for her and should like a model for the jeweller. I wonder where the original is?'

Sophie shook her head.

'Now, I must go and find my husband.'

Sophie's pretty eyes shone bright. 'Mister De Vallory of Bold Hall. You lucky creature. And you with child so quick. My husband is still downstairs. He is a good man but no picture book. I am content with my household but as for the rest . . . Marriage is a lottery. You may draw a thousand blanks before you gain a prize. And it is two years since we married and still we wait for a child.'

Tabitha considered that Sophie was certainly still young. 'There may be ways to help you. And we are neighbours, Sophie. Would you care to call on me?'

Sophie grasped her hand. 'I should be delighted. Well, if my husband will permit me. He finds these large parties a trial. Marcus is happiest with his books.'

'What manner of books?'

'Oh, dusty old tomes that no one else can read save for a few fossilized old fellows.'

'We may find our husbands have more in common than you imagine. Even I struggle greatly to get Nat's nose out of an old book.'

As the gentlemen would take their refreshments in the field the next morning, the two women agreed to meet at nine and take breakfast in each other's company. Tabitha could have kissed her new friend but stopped herself. Until she knew more of these unwritten rules she must watch and listen and keep her natural spirits under check.

Heading out into the corridor again, Tabitha finally came upon a maid servant and was taken to the chamber where she and Nat were to sleep. After Grisell had undressed her and been dismissed, Tabitha reclined on the vast tester bed and tried to sleep. Her eyes were closing when Nat returned, his neck linen loose and his eyes bleary. After throwing off his clothes he climbed in next to her, smelling of spirits and sweat and other men's pipe smoke. She roused herself as he gave a rambling account that showed he was as drunk as an emperor. It appeared that Langley had forged records of a supposed land sale by his father. She could feel the anger radiating off her husband's skin. 'Langley will hang in chains if I have my way. Hang in chains, I say! I am a public spectacle. A mere dupe. My father's land is trussed up in pink legal ribbon.'

She kissed his shoulder, feeling the tendons as tight as wire.

'As for you,' he whispered, dipping his dark head to kiss her. He ran his hands over her body, and she had to stifle a whimper of pain as his fingers trailed over her tender breast. No, she could not tell him of her encounter with Beaufort now, for fear he would want to knock the fellow down. Instead, she pulled away and raised herself on her elbow. She stroked Nat's hair, longing to kiss him but fearful her shift might fall open and he would see the marks on her skin. 'Sleep now,' she whispered. 'It will all look better in the morning.'

He was entirely foxed with brandy and her caress soon slowed his breathing and sent him to sleep. She continued to sit up. What was it people said? The little thieves hang for their crimes while the great ones sit on the bench? The Langleys intended to steal not only from Nat and his father but from their unborn child. The general opinion was that Langley's men had attacked the Mondrem Oak to warn Nat and his tenants they must do as they were told.

She remembered how Nat had once compared a tree to time itself. Each of us chose our branches and those we disdained withered and fell away. What branches were left for her now? Well, there was her marriage that seemed so changed these last weeks, compounded by the natural fears of childbed. Gunn's crude proposition felt like a return to her old life, to be subject to men's calloused hands and soiled bodies. She quailed to think he might ever have any power over her, as he did over the women at the camp. And now Beaufort Langley had tainted her, too. Ever since the day they had discovered Maria's body beneath the Mondrem Oak she had felt a secret force acting against her. She felt it in Maria's murder, in the loss of Hector, in Gunn's peculiarly apt prophecies, in the Langleys' unwarranted hostility. Exhausted as she was, she tried to recall Beaufort Langley's accusation against Nat. What was it? Visiting a Chester tavern? She could make nothing of it. No, her future was entirely unreadable and that was the most frightening notion of all. She had imagined marriage and motherhood at Bold Hall to be an end to all life's uncertainties but instead she sensed a dreadful ordeal lay ahead. She looked down on Nat's peaceful face and was reassured by a tide of love as fierce as that of Venus for bold Mars. By the gods, she prayed, let time only run faster so I can stand and fight against more than suspicions and shadows.

TWENTY-NINE

10 June 1753
Whit Sunday

Through the fog of a thumping thick head, Nat recalled the previous night's humiliation. Pox them all; if only he could have woken a thousand miles away from Langley Hall. Beside him Tabitha slept on, looking smooth and ripe in her nightshift. He longed to retreat into their private world of lovemaking beneath the bed sheets. He touched the warm softness of her cheek. Damn Caldwell, such unnatural rules were made to be broken. Gently, he nuzzled his lips against the hollow at her throat and tentatively licked the warm salt of her.

A loud rap sounded at the door. A voice cried out, 'All gentlemen to saddle up and meet on the forecourt.'

Stoically, he dressed and found a mount waiting for him in the Langley stables and thereafter followed the chief gentry of the county across miles of heathland. Beaufort Langley came cantering to his side, an ungainly lad and damned if only for his connections, but Nat had little choice in his company. The youth jawed on about horses and dogs, mocking Nat for having brought no better horse or a hound of his own. Dammit, he wished he had Jupiter beneath him and could kick up the dirt in the coxcomb's face.

'My uncle has some fine new pups in his kennels,' the youth boasted. 'Look them over if you wish to learn about good blood and fine points.'

As Nat made a barely civil show of considering the suggestion, it struck him that his father might well be cheered by a replacement for dear old Hector. He had only to endure the morning's hare coursing and then take a look.

In the event, the day's sport went badly for many a hare escaped. The sun was rising to noontide when the final course commenced and Nat gave a heartfelt huzzah under his breath when yet another zigzagging hare disappeared into a wooded covert. He headed off unobserved, planning a brief inspection of the pups before returning for Tabitha and making an early break for home.

At the gate to the kennels, Nat was silently inspected by a surly dog keeper before he was ushered inside. For all its fancy brickwork, it was not as well kept as that at Bold Hall; the straw was dirty and the water not much better. He took a quick look at the pups, but they were all foxhounds and of no use to his father. Making to leave, he shook his head in disgust at the sound of dogs frantically barking; one poor creature was even howling to the wind. Nat's head was down, busy inventing an excuse for an early departure, when he noticed a dark shape raised up on its hind legs frantically clawing at the fence. Nat stopped bolt still and then ran a dozen paces. The dog was like a wild beast, scrabbling to leap the barrier. He knew those loyal brown eyes anywhere and reached for the dog's muzzle as a long tongue ferociously lapped his hand. It was Hector, though now he was bone-thin and the poor fellow's grey muzzle had turned stark white. It was his expression, however, that made Nat curse like a soldier. The dog fixed on to him the eyes of an intelligent friend, communicating wild love and a terror of abandonment in equal measure. For an instant Nat considered summoning Langley and charging him with theft. Then his eye fell on an open wound along the dog's flank, crusted black with dried blood. Bitterly, he pictured Lord Langley as he had been the night before: a bully with the chilly eyes and leathery skin of a toad, all primped up in gold satin and diamond buckled shoes. He kept a circle of cronies at his back, to laugh at his feeble quips and applaud his cruelties. No, he could not face making a case for Hector's return, only to be abused by that reptile.

He ran a few steps and vaulted over the barrier, then grasped the squirming dog beneath the belly and heaved him up and over the fence. 'Stay, boy!' Nat spoke in the most commanding of tones and then returned back over himself. Squatting down, he whispered grave commands to the dog, instructing him eyeball to eyeball to do as he was told. Only then, when both man and dog were composed, did he set out for the gate.

The guard at the entrance was no fool. 'Sir, I thought it was a pup you was after. Not that old bag of bones.'

'It's a wolfhound I want,' Nat said smoothly. 'His Lordship said I might borrow this old fellow. Sir John has a dam in heat. He's an old dog but I'm sure he's up to the job. I'll return him in a week.'

Nat remounted his horse and Hector trotted after them to the stables. Finding the De Vallory carriage, he thrust the lively dog up and through its door. Next, he found his groom, Glover, at work in the harness room next door and ordered him to get the horses in harness.

Through the open top half of the door he spotted Beaufort Langley ambling into the yard. Nat grasped Glover's arm and hissed, 'I have found Hector wounded and starving. Don't tell a soul. I will be inside the carriage with him. If anyone asks say you have orders to drive the carriage to the park gates.'

Glover frowned and nodded. Slipping unseen back into the coach house, Nat let himself into the carriage. Pulling down the window blind, he grasped Hector by the collar. Crouching down low, he again addressed the dog. 'For your life's sake, Hector. Not a sound.' The dog whimpered pitifully. Nat raised a stern finger. 'Silence!' The creature began to tremble and dropped to the floor, sinking his head mournfully on to his paws.

'You there.' Nat could hear Beaufort's voice outside the door. 'What's going on here with De Vallory's carriage?' Dammit, Langley had spotted Glover making ready. Nat stopped breathing. Glover, the blessed fellow, gave only a sour grunt in reply. Nat nervously stroked Hector's cheek, compelling his bright liquid eyes to stay calm. The carriage rocked as Glover fixed the harness.

'Anyone in there?' The voice was barely inches from where Nat crouched. He reached up and grasped the inner door handle as tightly as he could. Sure enough, pressure from the outside yanked his wrist hard, but he held it firm.

'Begging your pardon, sir.' Glover's voice from outside was surly. 'Would you kindly stand aside.'

The next moment the harness rattled and the carriage jerked and rolled forward. Nat slunk back against the seat and threw his head back, his eyes closed. How could he collect Tabitha? It was too great a risk to turn around to the house and fetch her.

He had Hector safe and the crucial matter was to return him to Bold Hall. He would send Tabitha a message once they were well on their way. She would not be pleased, he knew that. But nothing else mattered now, save the prospect of reuniting his father with his dear old companion.

THIRTY

Over a breakfast of smoky souchong tea and tiny cakes, Tabitha made enquiries about the Langley family. After an hour of tedious chitchat, she had learned only that Lord Langley's deceased sister had been a spinster named Phyllis with a reputation for nothing more remarkable than a passion for beadwork. Questions regarding her jewellery and its current whereabouts were met with derisive stares. Such an old maid would apparently have owned nothing of great value.

By one in the afternoon Tabitha had almost given up her hunt for information. Many of the other guests were leaving and she grew impatient for Nat's return. Bored, she oversaw the packing of her and Nat's boxes, and then lingered in the corridor, studying Phyllis's portrait. When a matronly cleaning maid asked her if she might attend to her chamber, Tabitha pointed to the picture and asked if she had ever known Miss Phyllis Langley.

'That one? The poor lady died of the dropsy a long way back. It was the year the old king died, I reckon. Twenty-seven. I know it because we was already given our black armbands for mourning the king and then she left the world as well.'

'That's such a pretty gimmel ring on her finger. I had one like it myself and lost it. I wonder where that has got to now?'

The maid squinted at the painting. 'I have a notion Lady Maud got a hold of that ring. But an old-fashioned trifle like that is not what you young ladies wear nowadays.'

By two o'clock Tabitha was still waiting to be collected when Sophie approached to say her farewells.

'Forgive my presumption. Are you acquainted with a Lady Maud?' Tabitha asked quietly.

'I am. She is now Lady Randall-Scott. And the Langleys' daughter, so a distant relative to my husband.'

'Ah. Might it be possible for me to call on her? I know it is rather forward, but I believe she might be grateful for some information regarding her gimmel ring.'

Sophie frowned, clearly startled. Then her habitual cheeriness returned. 'I can but try, Tabitha.' Just then the dark-coated upper servant of the previous night approached and the two women fell silent.

'Mrs De Vallory.' Bowing, he explained that neither her husband nor the carriage could be found.

'Then he must have left a message,' she asserted. As Tabitha took leave of Sophie, inquisitive eyes turned upon her, taking keen pleasure in her discomfiture. Skin him alive, she told herself. How dare Nat abandon her like this?

At the stables she learned that Nat had left hours earlier in a state of impatience. 'He wanted no one to see him go,' the stable boy insisted. And most especially not me, she cursed silently.

THIRTY-ONE

At the Bush Inn, the landlord had not so much as a scrap of paper about the place, nor ink or sealing wax. Back outside, Nat looked up to see smoke rising above the trees. Yes, the preacher must possess a supply of paper, for he had written to him only a few weeks back. It was raining steadily by the time Nat arrived at the camp, and a sad, mud-churned mess the place had become. A group of ramshackle tents had been erected for Gunn's most recent recruits, surrounded by ragged laundry dripping from the trees' branches. Nat made for the treehouse and knocked loudly on the door. A few minutes later he was ensconced with Gunn in a snug little den made of rough-hewn wood as the rain rattled overhead on the thatch. After warily sniffing this strange new habitation, Hector sighed and dropped sphinx-like at Nat's feet.

Gunn had a travelling desk and rapidly supplied Nat with pen and ink. Fearing his message would be opened at Langley Hall, Nat speedily wrote to Tabitha that he would send the carriage back to her directly, all couched in the blandest terms. While a search was made for one of Gunn's lads to take the message, Nat could not resist questioning the preacher.

'This messiah of yours . . . what do you truly believe will happen?' he asked. 'Who do you think will bear the child?'

Gunn folded his arms and assumed a grave expression. 'The answer will be revealed by God when the time is right.'

Nat watched the man carefully. 'Are you the child's father?'

Gunn kept his eyes cast modestly downwards. 'I may be so blessed.'

'And the murdered young woman with the child slashed from her belly. How does she relate to the prophecy?'

Gunn did not even flinch. 'How could I know? I never even knew her.'

Nat smiled amiably as he said, 'A man saw you walking out with her. She was very fine looking and by all accounts a game girl.'

Gunn jerked his handsome head in denial. 'He is a liar. I am well used to accusations from the ignorant.'

Irritated, Nat stood and stepped over to a crude shelf that bore a line of books. Many were familiar, such as Wesley and Bunyan, as well as a few curiosities: a life of Savonarola, and Machiavelli's famed *The Prince*. His fingers trailed over a chapbook of Home Physic and a guide to Pennsylvania, before opening a nameless tome with worn leather bindings. Inside, the author was named as Della Porta. The name meant nothing to Nat.

Still his mind brimmed with questions. 'I can understand that your followers believe in your prophecies. But as one rational man to another – what truly are your odds of success?'

Gunn shook his head derisively. 'You cannot chalk up the odds of prophecy like the score in a game of hazard.'

'Well, let us suppose I was writing a scholarly paper upon the predictive faculty. As you know, there is a long history to the subject of divination. What if I were tempted to describe your feats of foretelling? I would be fair in my arguments – if you were honest with me.'

At last the preacher betrayed a spark of self-interest. 'How fascinating.' He pressed his lips tightly together and nodded slowly. 'I may be able to help you.'

'You would need to make a new prophecy. Given under scientific circumstances.'

Gunn fell silent, steepling his fingers, appearing to turn matters over carefully in his mind. 'What manner of test?'

'A prediction I could measure. Made without your followers present. There could be no outside help, of course.'

'Where?'

'We might agree a place. But not here.'

The preacher was looking up at his low ceiling, apparently calculating. 'Well, my good friend. If I do it, you would agree that one favour deserves another?'

Nat nodded, having guessed already what the preacher might ask.

'I was inspired to offer free passage to America to all those poor souls who need my help. But God has not sent me the coin. Not yet.'

With a sense of weariness, Nat asked, 'How much?'

'Fifty pounds.'

Nat gave a startled laugh so that Hector looked up at him, alert. 'Be sensible, man. I have no such ready sum to give you. How could you make such foolish promises with no funds?'

'Because I trust in God.' He smiled artlessly, 'And in you.'

Nat shook his head. 'It is impossible.' Hector released a low rumble. Nat reached for his collar in preparation to leave.

'There are ways,' Gunn murmured, 'that convey the spirit of prophecy directly into my mind. I need you to propose a question quite unknown to me beforehand. The best would be a question you are truly searching an answer to. Your own need will create the energy, the magnetism if you will, for me to draw the spirit of prophecy into myself.'

Nat considered the question he was desperate to know the answer to: Would Tabitha be confined safely? He said firmly, 'I won't give fifty pounds for some fairground trick.'

'But you will give me something.' Nat did not care for the imperturbable certainty in the man's tone.

'I will think on a fair fee. But I will not be your gull.' Nat stood and beckoned to Hector.

'Give my good wishes to your wife,' Gunn said as he took a friendly leave of his guest. 'Will she be present if I submit to your experiment?'

Whenever they attended fairs or shows, Tabitha found it easy to spot the trick behind a charlatan's patter. Yes, he would like her to be with him.

'Perhaps,' he said.

'Then tell her this,' Gunn said with an annoyingly fond smile. 'Tell her she may also ask me any question of her own choosing.'

THIRTY-TWO

L ife was devilish odd, Nat reflected as the carriage pulled through the welcome gates of Bold Hall. Hector sprang up on his hind legs at the open window, ears alert and nose twitching at the feast of familiar smells. Though Nat was dishevelled and spotted with paw-prints, he took Hector straight up to his father. The old man was asleep in his great crimson bed, but Hector soon woke him with yips of excitement and a cold, questing nose.

Sir John's hand trembled as he patted Hector's brow. Though his speech was not decipherable, Nat knew he mouthed the gentlest endearments. 'I will call the dog man, Father. Your poor hound needs good food and gentle tending.'

Sir John made no more trials at speaking, only reached up and clasped Nat's hand in his own, so that the son felt his father's tremor of joy shake his own bones. Then Nat left the two old companions to the pleasure of each other's company, feeling he had concluded a job well done.

Back in his chamber, Nat ached for a hot bath before Tabitha returned but could find no servants to help him. His valet was still stranded at Langley Hall and it being Whit Sunday and he and Tabitha intending to be absent much of the day, most of the household had taken an afternoon's leave. Searching for help he came upon Sukey Adams stepping out of his wife's chamber. She at once curtsied in her rather pleasing, modest fashion. 'Master, you are home.'

'Yes. Your mistress will be some while yet. Would you find someone to prepare me a bath?'

'I will, sir.'

Back in his chamber, he began casting off his morning costume, noting a bad rip to his favourite riding coat. Yet still, the happiness at reuniting his father with Hector kept his spirits dancing. And there was also the prospect of having a fascinating subject for his society paper. True, he was disappointed at Gunn's request for a large fee, but his investigation would be so much more intriguing if he could describe from start to end this mysterious process of prophecy. Laying down his gold pocketwatch, he noted it was still too early to expect Tabitha. From his dressing room the sound of pouring water reached him and he wandered in wearing only his undershirt. There he found Sukey Adams emptying the heavy water ewer.

'Let me help you. Are there no men to do this?'

'Thank'ee, sir. No, they're all away. I am only just back from Chester myself.' She let him lift the great ewer and empty it into his tub in a cloud of steam.

Considerate of her maternal condition, he dismissed her. Then, throwing off his shirt, he thought of nothing but the pleasure of hot water easing his sore limbs. Naked, he descended into the heat and steam. For a moment he was bothered by the remembrance of Lord Langley's duplicity, but told himself that all would come good again by some means or other. Perhaps Gunn truly could foresee the future and give him some advantage. His body lay luxuriously submerged and his eyes were closed when soft steps sounded behind him. Two gentle hands began to rub his scalp, washing his hair with some pungent-scented liquid. The sensation sent little thrills of pleasure down the length of his nerves.

'You are early, my love,' he said with a sigh.

He broke away and looked behind himself through the steamy atmosphere. God damn, it wasn't his wife at all but that nursemaid, her face glowing prettily pink.

'Let me wash you, sir,' she murmured.

He pulled away, annoyed at having left his valet behind at Langley Hall. 'No need,' he said brusquely. 'I can manage well enough.'

He sank back again to soak himself, but sensed she had not moved from the spot behind him.

Her fingers slid on to his shoulders. ''Tis good to feel the touch of a man's flesh,' she said, so softly he almost doubted his ears. Her wet fingers kneaded his tight muscles pleasurably. The cloth of her apron was warm behind his head. He had a sudden uninvited vision of pale thighs as soft as silk.

She continued to speak in a voice so low he could barely catch

her words. "Tis so long a time now I've been alone. A healthy
woman cannot stifle her longings forever. I am yours to take, sir.'

Guilt paralysed his throat. He swallowed hard. Tabitha might
run upstairs at any moment. If she heard even a whisper of this
encounter, he might lose her entirely. He wanted none of it.
Wasn't he already enduring enough self-torture over Maria?

'Go away,' he croaked. 'And don't ever try that trick again.'

She grazed his back again with her finger ends and her long,
lazy strokes ignited the gunpowder of pleasure. Lord, he would
not be the first to be tempted. Many a man talked of how the
serving maid was as good as any lady in the dark.

'I mean no harm to my mistress,' she murmured. 'No
one need ever know. It will be a secret never spoken of.'

'No one need ever know,' chimed in his mind. By God, he
had starved himself of the vital act these last few months. She
reached over his shoulders. Her fingers soaped his chest then
drifted down towards his stomach. With his eyelids fluttering he
stifled a groan, sinking into irresistible pleasure.

'My lips are sealed. But my body is entirely open to you,' she
breathed into his ear.

He was aware of her stepping away and the rustle of her skirts.
Watching her through the haze of steam, she turned her back to
him and lifted her petticoat. He discerned white stockings with
blue ribboned garters, plump thighs and a round pale rump. His
body tensed, ready to take her, quickly and eagerly.

'All is safe,' she reassured him through the damp steam. 'With
the child on its way there can be no unlucky consequences.'

The words dragged his wits back to life. He felt a wince of
surprise that a woman with child should be such a wanton. His
child's own nursemaid. He stared at the pleasing apparition of a
willing woman for a painful few seconds, his base instincts
driving him to pleasure but his mind calculating the cost of being
discovered. 'Leave me,' he said at last.

She turned solemnly back to confront him, her skirts falling.
She was blushing, he thought. Or was her high colour the fury
of rejection? 'I don't understand,' she said, and he heard her
contempt. 'No one will ever know.' She was staring at him very
hard with those round, washed-out eyes. Damn it, there was
something decidedly off-colour about the woman.

Nat reached for a towel and wiped his wet face. 'You are wrong. I will know. Why not remarry, Mrs Adams, if a chaste life is so galling to you? If you must stay here, mend your ways or I shall see you in the pillory. Understand?'

With her head bowed, the nursemaid retreated and disappeared. Nat submerged himself again, but no soap could wash away the encounter. He had come mighty close to surrendering to Mrs Adams's will. Tabitha would have turned hellhound if she ever found out. And then, as the water grew cold and grey around him, he wondered if he had been too lax and should have sent the hussy packing. No, if he dismissed her now it would be a devilish nuisance to replace the woman. The child's birth was so close now, it would be unfair to burden Tabitha with yet more worry. But he was damned if he would allow Mrs Adams to stay longer than a month after Tabitha's confinement.

THIRTY-THREE

For the whole journey home Tabitha had struggled to hide her mounting fury from the servants as she rehearsed the roasting she would give her thoughtless husband. She looked for him upstairs and down before finding him at his father's bedside. Seeing Hector safely returned gave her pause. Yes, she was mightily pleased that Nat had rescued the dear hound and told him as much. But it was impossible to forgive Nat so easily. 'But what of me?' she demanded. 'How could you leave me behind with those people?' She could hear her voice rising, alarming Sir John, who watched her with confusion clouding his rheumy eyes.

Nat kept his head down, fondling Hector's ears. 'Shall we speak in the library?' he asked softly. Lord, his voice was very quiet after hers.

She followed him, still seething like a kettle. Closing the library door behind them, Nat turned to face her. 'I am sorry. But as you can see, Hector was injured. I had the smallest chance of rescuing him while the other men were at their sport.'

'Yes. That's good.' She felt her lungs working hard against the whalebone of her stays. A flurry of blue stars flashed at the edges of her vision.

'Tabitha. Take a seat. You are overwrought.'

She lowered herself into a chair and blinked the annoying sparks away. 'Naturally I am overwrought. Do you even care about me? Last night that cockroach Beaufort Langley propositioned me.'

He was instantly at her side. 'Why didn't you tell me?'

'Because you were drunk. He proposed that I visit him privately. And he told me some story about you searching for someone in a Chester tavern. What was that?'

Nat opened his mouth to reply but suddenly closed it again and turned away. There was a long pause before he said, 'For God's sake, Tabitha.'

'Why would he say that?'

Nat turned around looking alarmed and very pale. 'I cannot say.'

'Glover said that you called on that Gunn fellow.'

'Yes! To get paper and ink to send a message to you.'

'Don't shout at me.'

'This is not the time to make a drama, Tabitha. I am out of sorts about my father's land. We are being cheated by the Langleys. And father is so frail, and you so close to lying-in. It was not an easy task to rescue Hector and I came home filthy and covered in the dog's slobber—'

'Yes. Sukey told me all about it.'

'What? What did she say?'

Tabitha shook her head in disbelief. 'Sukey? What does she ever talk of but how virtuous she is? At least she is biddable. Not like Grisell. She is welcome to sail to America any day she chooses. Sukey I can at least trust.'

The room fell silent. Nat had his hand pressed hard to his brow, as if in deep pain.

'I forgot to say,' Tabitha said in a more appeasing manner. 'I have found out more about Maria. Well, about the gimmel ring at any rate. It came from Langley Hall.'

'Forget Maria, will you! The whole affair is over. The coroner gave the verdict. She is dead and gone.' Seeing his wife's stricken face, he at once regretted his loose tongue.

'No,' she said quietly. 'I will not forget Maria. I said I would find out her name and her killer and now I am getting closer. And you don't want me to, do you?'

The question rang out unanswered. Nat looked very tired – tired of her perhaps?

He sighed heavily. 'Come and sit here beside me, sweetheart. I have no mind to quarrel.'

His sudden surrender took her by surprise. She joined him on the sofa. His hand reached for hers and stroked it gently. 'This matter of my father's land makes me so ashamed. And your ill-treatment by that execrable Beaufort Langley. How dare he insult you like that? We were both treated intolerably but we must not strike out at each other.'

'You are right,' she said in little voice. She felt a rush of warmth towards him; he was her darling Nat, after all. 'When we look back with hindsight, I am sure time will have healed all these problems.'

He glanced up with a new light in his gilt-flecked eyes. 'Yes. Yes, indeed. Listen, there is one other matter I must tell you,' he said. 'You recall I have to submit the subject of my scientific paper. I have proposed a trial of Gunn's prophetic skills.' He began to speak of the matter with boyish enthusiasm but instead of calming her, she felt a boiling reflux of anger. She listened incredulously to his plan to invite the preacher to perform for them. 'What do you think? You can ask a question, too. It will be entertaining to inquire into the future.'

'Here. At Bold Hall?'

'Yes.'

She did strive to compose a civil reply but failed. Her voice shook. 'Do you not see what he is doing? Our lives have been overshadowed since ever he first came here. What does he want in return?'

Nat looked away. 'Well, he wants a fee.'

'What a surprise. He will certainly trick you for money. He also wants some dreadful influence over you. How many times must I tell you? I fear that man. If you must give him money give it only on condition that he leaves this very day.'

Instinctively Nat recoiled from her tirade. 'No. I think you are—' he began.

She interrupted him. 'It is not me!' she cried. 'You cannot always blame me. It is us. What has happened to us, Nat?'

Then not wishing to hear his reply, she hurried away to her chamber, feeling dizzy with grief, her thoughts fractured into a thousand sorry pieces.

THIRTY-FOUR

13 June 1753
Ember Week

A few quiet days passed in which Tabitha continued to be chilly towards Nat whenever they unavoidably met. She was still feeling mournful as she sat outside in the gazebo where the women were completing the childbed sewing with a new urgency. Grisell bent over her pile of hemming, sending her needle back and forth like a shuttle on a loom. Jennet and Sukey shared the tricky final stages of a length of holy point lace. Bess was playing on the rug with offcuts of fabric, chattering to herself as she tried to embellish her doll's gown. Only Tabitha dawdled at her work, breaking off to stare abstractedly into the distant rose beds, or leaning back to close her sore eyes. The others were wary of her, for she slept badly, and the little cleft of a frown had formed between her eyes. Finally, she sat up and looked about herself impatiently. 'Jennet. If you could be told what would happen in your future life, what would you wish to know?'

The maiden's large grey eyes shone mischievously. 'I should like to know when I will marry.'

The older women smiled indulgently.

'That is indeed the greatest conundrum for most maidens,' Tabitha said. 'For all your plucking flower petals and chanting old rhymes I think you still have no firm answer.'

'Aye, one old charm tells me I go to my wedding in a golden carriage, and the next predicts a dustcart.' They all laughed.

'Have you used the customary days to enquire who the lucky fellow will be?' Sukey suggested. 'On Midsummer's Eve, if you walk seven times around the church sowing hempseed, you will be sure to see your future bridegroom.'

'Tabitha and I did once try to divine our husbands. But such charms do not always send the answer you wish for. I did wonder,'

Jennet asked Tabitha, 'whether you wished for Nat as your husband that night we set a charm upon your mother's wedding ring?'

Tabitha gazed down into her lap. 'Yes. I did.'

'Then your wish came true. For now, you have him.'

Tabitha smiled tightly. 'I have a pretty ring,' she said, extending her fingers to admire the brilliant gemstone. 'And a child on the way. But whether I have all the man I wished for, I am no longer sure.'

Grisell raised her head to mumble, 'Aye, there is more to marriage than four naked legs in a bed.'

'And not even that consolation at present,' Tabitha added sorrowfully. Suddenly she flung her work aside and turned to Jennet. 'You must take mortal care of who you marry, Jennet. Men!'

Sukey raised watchful eyes. 'Goodness, mistress, that is only the mother's melancholy talking. You will soon be eased of your burden. Then you and the master will be blessed with many more children.'

Tabitha studied Sukey for any trace of impertinence, but found only the usual complacency in her round cheeks and faded prettiness. 'Perhaps.'

'I know what I should ask.' Sukey kept her eyes on her needle-work and gave a little smile. 'I want only to be sure of my baby's blessed delivery.' She raised her head and regarded the others boldly.

Tabitha gave an approving nod. 'You, Sukey, no doubt know all the best means to be sure of a safe delivery.'

'I have tried to learn them, madam. For instance, it is good to sew, my lady, but we must not spin. You know what they say; a spinner may spin a rope to hang her own child by the neck.'

'How cheering you are, Sukey. Amongst all these dreadful warnings – of having no shocks, of not dancing or riding, of avoiding, in fact, any happy frolics at all – does Dame Nature give any encouraging advice on how to deliver a happy, healthy child?'

Truly the woman had forgotten how to laugh, for she gave a long dull account of how her mistress must eat whatever she took a fancy to. 'Some women get a fancy for a peck of dirt or charcoal and that can be indulged. But remember, not too many sweet-stuffs, for they will make your child a girl, while a nice sour dish will be sure to produce a boy.'

'Oh, and there was me longing for an apricot tart.'

Sukey was startled into confusion. 'Well, madam. Perhaps if you should like it, it might do you good?'

Tabitha buttoned down a grin. 'I am sure the child's sex is long decided. I doubt a piece of apricot tart will geld my little fellow on the instant.'

Bess appeared at her side. 'Tabby. Dolly's lace is falling off.'

She smiled at the child. 'Oh dear. Sukey, would you make a few stitches to hold it?'

The nursemaid reluctantly laid her lace aside to tack the slip of lace on to the doll's gown. Tabitha just heard her mutter, 'Wasting good lace on a child's dolly.'

Well, Joshua had warned her that Sukey would take what she could for her own child.

'Sukey. Bess may have what lace she wishes,' Tabitha said sharply.

The nursemaid stiffened; her lips pressed tight together. For pity's sake, Tabitha thought crossly, she'd not take orders from her own nursemaid.

Rattled, Tabitha finally questioned Grisell. 'So, what would you wish for if you could see the future?'

Grisell harrumphed and laid down her sewing. 'I should want to know when I will ever be free. I've been in service all my days from ten years old and I'm bone weary of it.'

Tabitha tried to choose her words carefully. 'I am sorry for that, Grisell. I will talk to Mister Higgott about you working shorter days.'

Grisell cast her an insolent look. 'Hold your breath, madam. I may not want to stay on.'

Tabitha felt not only stung but upset. Yet instead of unleashing her tongue, she only said, 'If so, you must give me proper notice. You shall have no letter of character otherwise.'

The ensuing silence was thick with mutual resentments. Suddenly Grisell cast a furious glance at her mistress and said, 'Letter of character! It is your character that is talked of from here to Chester. You being born as low as any and now mysteriously raised so high.'

This was too much. 'Grisell. Get out of my sight.' Tabitha spoke very quietly but with a distinct chill to her voice. 'And stay out of my sight until I decide what to do with you.'

With a great deal of huffing and banging, Grisell left them. Shortly afterwards, Tabitha rose from her chair and called to Jennet to accompany her.

The two friends crossed the lawn. As soon as they passed out of hearing of the others, Tabitha said, 'I am reluctant to put an old woman out on the road but devil take her, she tries me!'

Jennet did her best to commiserate; they talked of an alms house if a place could be found.

Finally, Tabitha turned to other matters. 'And you, have you any news from the camp?'

Jennet shook her head. 'Not much, I'm afraid. I made no mention of Maria, only asked if a certain lost friend of mine had ever stayed with them. Then I described the young woman we saw under the tree. No one had seen her.'

'Or pretended not to.'

Tabitha picked at a few rose petals and, frowning, let them tumble to the ground. 'Maybe I am wrong to send you there. Maria may well have been killed by Gunn and his followers.'

'Mister Gunn would never commit a sin like that.'

'So you still find him as saintly as ever?'

Jennet grew indignant. 'I never met a preacher like him. Though as for saintliness I did hear he was married once and put his wife aside as she was barren.'

'That is not very saintly. Who was she?'

'Salvation was her name.'

'And her true name?'

'Oh, no one uses their old names at the camp.'

'And did you ask who or what Trinity is?'

'I did. I pretended my friend spoke of it. No one would say a word. And they looked suspicious.' She began to play nervously with her long flaxen hair. 'I should like to hear him preach again tonight. Might you give leave to Tom to accompany me?'

Tabitha considered only for a moment. Her need for information before Gunn's visit made her reckless. 'Very well. Listen, tonight I want you to find out if Mister Gunn has any money. Enough for this voyage. Can you do that?'

Jennet eagerly agreed. 'And Tom?'

Without a second thought, Tabitha gave him leave to accompany her.

THIRTY-FIVE

And though the shade-giver never can roam,
He will bear Him o'er waters to His new home.

The New Prophet of the Forest

T he first time Jennet had gone with Tom to hear Baptist
Gunn preach she had felt a peace settle upon her unlike
any she had ever known before. The preacher had stood
before the crowd like the good Lord himself, his long hair flowing,
and his expression like an angel. Tall as she was, she had pushed
her way through the crowd to get closer, eager to hear every
word and see at close hand his every gesture. And when she
reached the front, she had cast herself down on her knees and
become at one with all the other praying souls, feeling suddenly
calm and peaceful, spellbound in bliss. His words drew her into
his soul, as a father gathers his children to his bosom. Later she
could not recall much at all of his sermon, only the balm-like
sensation that had made them all breathe as one, as each breast
had combined in the same mighty heartbeat.

A week later she returned with Tom. Again, she sank to her knees
and surrendered to the preacher's sweet speech. In the rarely touched
depths of her being, she was reminded of her true father. He had
died long before her mother had married Joshua Saxton and she
commonly spoke of never having known him. Now memories arose
like dazzling, painful lights behind her eyes. There had been a room,
a game played on a man's lap, the warmth of strong muscular hands.
Tears flowed down her face, though whether of pain or joy she could
not say. I am home, she repeated without speaking. Baptist Gunn
had reached inside her and woken that neglected spark of love. And
now she believed she would die for him. She would follow him
wherever he led, from this world to the next.

That night Jennet found it easy to question the other camp
followers as Tabitha had directed her. The atmosphere was

feverish with talk of America, so she could directly ask about
payment for her passage. 'God will provide,' was the answer.
Then Baptist himself appeared and she knew instantly that he was
looking directly into her thoughts. He lifted his long white fingers
and pointed at her and Tom. 'You. The Lord tells me He
has chosen you both to populate the land of milk and honey.'

As Jennet and Tom left the camp together, she thought it the
sweetest day of her life. They drifted away from the others into
the late evening glitter of the groves. Baptist's presence still
echoed in Jennet's being, like the summoning of a heavenly bell.
At first she walked hand in hand with Tom until they spotted a
pale figure lingering ahead of them in the failing light. Tom
stopped, signalling they pull off the path until the woman had
gone. They found a pleasant bower and sank down to rest on a
bed of ferns. Jennet told herself that if they kissed it was no sin,
for Tom said often how he longed to marry her. They lay deep
in each other's arms, hearts thumping and bodies half-mad with
longing. And Tom whispered, 'If we go to America we will be
free to do anything we want.' Jennet solemnly nodded, feeling
the thrill of it, partly from holding a secret, and partly from
dreams of a wild and yet noble life as Tom's wife.

She did not allow herself to worry about leaving Netherlea. She
told herself she would soon be forgotten and that Joshua was not
her true father and had no notion she was now a grown woman.
And Tabitha had been harsh to her, letting Sukey take her place
as her companion, distracted by foolish tiffs with Nat, and making
ready for her new baby. No, Tabitha would not miss her either.
Tom alone filled her mind, heating her blood and intoxicating her
spirit. And the secret of their elopement gave the plan a thrilling
life of its own. Tom talked of the wonder of it and how they would
finally taste liberty. The words America and Pennsylvania, and
voyage excited her like charm words in a spell. In America they
would need no money. Baptist said that if everyone laboured for
only four hours a day the remainder of their time would be at
leisure to study the Bible and teach their children and sing psalms.
It was true that sometimes she felt suddenly startled at leaving
behind all she knew. Then she took comfort in the little book of
prophecies that proved, in God's name, that all would go well for
them, blessed as they were to be the chosen ones of God.

THIRTY-SIX

17 June 1753

A few days later Tom delivered a letter to Tabitha as she rested in the shade of the gazebo. It was addressed to 'Mrs De Valrey' in large and clumsy letters and had been posted in Chester. Distractedly, she tore it apart and perused its contents with some difficulty, for her eyes that day were weak and the spelling was fanciful:

> *'Mrs De Valrey*
>
> *I right these lines having give some thort to what you axed of me. Today I saw this paper & reckulect the name of the Jentleman our friend Maria took off with Namely Babtist Gun.*
>
> *I pray you do pursew Him without any delay & he be chokd by the hangman for the pityfull sake of our dear friend Maria.*
>
> *N. B.'*

Enclosed within was a page of Baptist Gunn's prophecies torn from the pamphlet. She re-read the letter with a stab of vindication at being right. To her consternation, Nat just then appeared, and she pushed the letter out of sight beneath a cushion.

'My dear. Might I speak to you for a moment. I have just called on Gunn.'

She nodded and he settled beside her.

'He has agreed to make a trial of his powers for me on Thursday evening. It is the summer solstice, a most auspicious time. I will ask him a question while he is in his sleeping state. It cannot be a simple yes or no. And then I shall study whatever prognostication he makes.'

'Where will this performance take place?'

'Here in the chapel. Some sort of holy place is best.'

Remembering Maria's blue-tinged body, Tabitha felt a quiver of apprehension. 'It is an odd choice.'

'It was once sanctified.'

She shook her head. 'I too have received news about your friend, Baptist Gunn.' She pulled out the letter as if it were a hand of winning cards and passed it to him. He read the few lines, suddenly catching his breath.

'How do you know this woman?' he asked.

She explained how she had waylaid Nancy Blair after the inquest. Nat cast his head down so she could not see his expression.

'It is proof that Gunn is involved,' she concluded.

'Proof only that she left with him some time ago.'

'He is lying when he says he never knew Maria.'

'It proves the connection. I agree.'

'And that he lies to us,' she urged.

'Yes. We must be ever vigilant.'

She waited for him to say that the test of prophecy would be put aside and forgotten. Nat was frowning, clearly calculating what to say next. 'Tabitha. I still want to go ahead. If there is any mischief behind his prophecies, is it not better to be fore-warned? I am trying to protect you.'

'Please, Nat.' She was begging him at last.

'I am sorry, I feel very close to an answer. But you need not be present, sweetheart. It is unfair of me to ask you. I will be alone.'

Perversely, she was suddenly overwhelmed with concern for her husband. She looked up into his face, the good bones and long-lashed eyes, and felt a welling up of tenderness. 'Nat, if you will not put an end to it I should be at your side. I shall speak up at once if I see any tricks.'

'Are you sure? Is it wise in your condition?'

'Well, I am not even leaving the house,' she said bravely. 'And I should so like to show the world what a cunning sharper he is.'

They began to walk back to the house and he took her arm. 'If you do expose him, I will be forever grateful. And Tabitha, our situation is not so bad. I have been considering matters. So, Bold Hall loses a tract of forest land. My father need never know.'

She halted, appalled at his relinquishing his pride like this. 'Nat, we cannot give Lord Langley the land.'

Her husband appeared stricken. 'Then what must I do?'

'Can the lawyer do nothing at all?'

'Their lawyer is in some cabal with the local judges. He does as he pleases.'

Tabitha pulled him closer to her body and felt a comforting pulse of warmth. They had reached the iron-studded front door to Bold Hall which stood open and welcoming on these summer days. 'Nat, you are far, far cleverer than the Langleys. We will think of a way to confound them very soon.'

THIRTY-SEVEN

21 June 1753
Summer Solstice

On the day of the solstice Tabitha learned from Jennet that Baptist Gunn scarcely had two pennies to rub together. 'The fault lies in his generous heart,' Jennet announced in her new ridiculously pious manner. 'Yesterday he visited the workhouse and laid his hands on a man with the King's Evil. Afterwards, the warden fetched a bowl of water so Baptist might wash his hands. He was so disgusted at such niceties he took the bowl and smashed it on the floor.'

Tabitha suspected such acts were a form of roguery. 'Smashing other people's bowls will not pay to send all those poor folk to America.'

'There is a rumour he has found a benefactor.'

'Do not tell me. His name is De Vallory.'

Jennet looked startled. 'I did not think of that.'

After Jennet had left, Tabitha retreated to the coolness of her chamber. It was the longest day of the year and the sky stretched hot and white and heavy. Gunn was to make a trial of his powers after the sun set at nine in the evening. Standing at the open casement she watched the tops of the shrubs moving in the breeze and noticed the birds' piping melodies were replaced by shorter staccato cries. Anna might be right; maybe humans could understand the birds' moods. Change was on its way – she could feel it in the crackling of the air.

The door swung open and Bess ran into her chamber. Tabitha scooped up her little sister and buried her face in the girl's hair, which was as soft as a dandelion clock.

'What's that?' Bess pointed outside to where the horizon was darkening and the sheep were retreating beneath the hedge. They both heard low rumbling, at first so distant it might have been a heavy cart or falling stones. Then a thunderclap rang out. Bess giggled, and looked over her shoulder towards her sister. Together they watched trickles of rain appear and then run races on the glass. Tabitha was comforted by the monotonous pattering. Bess started to sing out cheerfully, her eyes as blue as moonstones, alight with some inner vision.

'*She is dead, she is dead, says Robin to Bobbin,*
She is dead, she is dead, says everyone.'

'What is that you're singing?' Tabitha asked.

Bess thought hard for a moment. 'The ghost song I told you about. About my dream.'

'Shush, little one,' Tabitha murmured. 'There's nothing to be frightened of now.'

Yet it was not Bess who could bear no more of the sinister song, but Tabitha herself. Baptist Gunn had gained entry to their home by now, she was certain of it. And the shadow he cast over their lives was deepening every moment.

Nat and Tabitha walked together to the chapel just before nine that evening.

'Nat, remember I shall be an extra pair of eyes – and exercise my wits,' she whispered as they passed along stone-paved passages.

He nodded and she steeled herself for trickery. Reaching the chapel door, they paused and exchanged hopeful smiles of reassurance. Nat pushed the door open and Tabitha turned aside to rapidly make the sign of the cross upon her body. Then together they entered the dusky chamber of the chapel.

Gunn was waiting for them beside a burning flambeau, as soberly dressed as an undertaker in a black coat and breeches. At his side stood the scab-faced youth whom Gunn had requested should assist him. I shall be keeping an eye on that young fellow's movements, Tabitha told herself. Now that the sun was finally setting, the chapel's far edges and ceiling had disappeared in creeping darkness. Candles sparsely lit the faded splendour of the nave as Nat and Tabitha walked hand-in-hand towards a pair of carved chairs set out before the raised chancel. The rain had continued all afternoon, settling an icy chill on the evening, and Tabitha fretted that she should have brought her woollen shawl. Before Nat could turn back to fetch it, Gunn began to speak and she murmured acquiescence, resigned to shiver and take her place.

Gunn smiled benevolently down upon them both; Tabitha wondered what secret cogitations moved inside his brain. 'Welcome. And thank you.' He strode first to Nat and took his hands in his, shaking them gently, even gratefully. Who the devil did he think he was? This was their home. Then Gunn stood before her, his roughened hands enclosing her fingers. Dark eyes probed her face, her lips, her eyes that nervously blinked: he was searching, hunting, seeking entry to the chambers of her mind.

To Tabitha's relief, Gunn drew back on to the raised dais where a Christian altar had once stood. He stood against the inky-blue glass of the darkening window; with his pale palms outstretched he was a captivating sight.

'I feel this place of God welcomes us,' he began in his slow, sonorous voice. 'The walls, nay, the very stones here are alive with questing souls.' He raised his hand towards an elaborate memorial to an ancient scion of the De Vallory family. 'Those spirits who gather here know who you both are. They seek to help you. Do you not feel them crowding the air, listening?'

Certainly, a curious hush had fallen on the room. Tabitha reached for Nat's hand and gripped it tightly. He returned the pressure warmly.

'Now, in order to comply with your wish, I must surrender my own will to the Holy Spirit.' As before, Gunn slumped into a chair while the bony youth held the flaming torch aloft. The temperature in the room was dropping fast, and the brighter the torch burned, the darker the shadows appeared in relief. Tabitha was struck by an unwelcome memory: of Maria dead and waxy blue in this very place. What was left of Maria's unborn baby had been discovered here, too.

She pushed herself closer against Nat, trying to draw warmth from his body. When she next looked up, Gunn appeared to have fallen into his sleeping trance. At last he spoke, in the same eerie, rasping voice as before at the camp. 'Nat De Vallory. You have summoned me here. I am bound to answer your question. What is it you wish to know?'

Nat tensed and straightened. 'There is only one matter that concerns me,' he asked in a strong voice. Tabitha listened, expecting his question to concern the forest land or his father's health. Instead he entirely surprised her. 'Tell me how Tabitha will fare in her confinement.'

'No,' Tabitha hissed. She grasped his arm hard. 'Don't ask that.'

'Shh. Let me hear what he says.'

The slumbering figure stirred uneasily, tossing his head from side to side. A spasm of what looked like pain passed over the preacher's handsome features. If the vision hurts him even in repose, it must be a bad omen, Tabitha fretted. He began to speak again, in a whisper. 'He will be born on Midsummer's Day.'

She felt an inner jolt. Why, that was this very Sunday. She laid her hand on her stomach but felt no answering movement. The baby was asleep.

'A boy, then. Will mother and child be of good health?' Nat interjected.

The long silence was almost unbearable. Tabitha strained to hear Gunn's next words.

'I foresee danger.'

'No.' Tabitha wailed as her hand clasped her mouth.

'So is our child this saviour you speak of?' Nat demanded.

Though still unconscious, Gunn covered his eyes with his hands and writhed in his seat. 'It is hard to make it out. I foresee jealousy. The need to escape.'

'What do you mean?' Tabitha's voice was shrill.

'A secret plan.'

Tabitha sprang up from her seat and cried out, 'Who is it? Who is jealous? Who has a secret plan against us?'

Gunn's chin dropped to his chest and he appeared to sleep again. She turned on Nat. 'Was this wise?'

He looked back at her, his face grim. 'I needed to know you would be safe. Shall I stop him?' he asked.

Before Tabitha could answer, Gunn's head rose and he spoke again. 'There is another spirit here among us. One who has crossed into the valley of death. One who sorrows for you most piteously. She begs me to act as her vessel. To speak to Tabitha.'

Still standing, Tabitha froze. 'Is it our hidden enemy?'

'No,' Gunn's wheedling voice replied. 'She loves you. She urges me to let her speak to you. She begs to take the form of the living through my own animal vitality.'

Nat urged more loudly, 'Shall I stop him?'

Tabitha struggled to decide. All good sense told her they should stop Gunn's performance. She had underestimated him. This was not the harmless parlour game she had anticipated. Yet she had to be forewarned if the baby was in danger. There was only one dead soul who cared enough to return from the afterlife to help her. If there was the smallest chance that Gunn's powers were genuine, she had to gather her courage and let that spirit speak.

She felt unnervingly determined. 'Let her come,' she said.

Tabitha and Nat waited. Her senses ranged around the room in search of trickery. The youth continued to stand immobile, holding the fiery torch. Gunn slept on like a king of long ago, enchanted on his throne. Beyond the tall, blue-tinted window the sun must finally have set. There was a sudden darkening of the room; the candles bent and quivered. The ancient stones of the place exuded intense cold. She is coming, Tabitha told herself, taking Nat by his icy hand.

Gunn slept on, his features mask-like, save for the fluttering shadows cast by the agitated candlelight. Something was coming, Tabitha was sure of it. Seconds turned to minutes. Finally, she grasped the hope that Gunn's trick had failed. She gave Nat a quick smile and mouthed, 'Nothing.'

As if at a signal, Gunn's right arm began to move. She watched him raise it very slowly, his forefinger extended. He was pointing towards a small chantry chapel at the side of the altar, a side room with a heraldic altar built for the repose of some long-dead De Vallory ancestor. There was a curious window into the room behind which she noticed a grey light softly glowing.

'What's that?' The youth's voice piped fearfully. Torch in hand, Gunn's assistant darted over to join them where they stood, as if fearful of being alone. 'Can you hear it?' he whimpered.

Tabitha could. Someone was moving inside the chantry chapel with a slow unsteady gait.

She whirled upon Nat and said, 'It is some fairground trick. He has put a light behind that window and is trying to scare us.'

They watched together. Something was certainly moving behind the warped panes of old glass. Was this Gunn's doing, to send someone into the chantry and wave a lamp about? The need to unmask the hoaxer was so strong that she had to do it at once. With hurried steps she strode to the illuminated window, pressed her face against the glass and peered inside.

A figure was shambling towards her, barely three yards from where she stood. It was a woman; thin and bent, dressed in the pallid rags of the grave. Her face was overshadowed by a filthy shawl. As Tabitha watched, she took a tottering step closer, as if recognizing and hurrying towards her. Tabitha sprang back. 'God help me,' she murmured, clutching at the stone wall. 'What the devil is it?'

Nat joined her and pressed his face against the glass. She heard his sharp intake of breath and a whispered, 'No.' Then regaining himself, he muttered, 'She is moving. Is it possible? Tabitha, is she . . .?'

Tabitha looked through the warped glass of the window again. The wretched creature had reached a wooden chair and was slowly lowering her bony frame upon it in a macabre, jolting fashion. The sight made Tabitha think of loose, decaying bones held together only by worn-out strings of flesh. For a moment Tabitha remembered the waxwork exhibition she and Nat had visited and wondered if that was how the trick was done. Could it be one of those newfangled automata?

No, in the same slow and painful fashion, the ghastly woman raised her head. Tabitha saw the lower half of a chalk-white face, the chin bound up by a burial band to stop the jaw from dropping. Two long plaits hung past the shoulders. It was the thin grey hair that she remembered combing so well.

She struggled to gather her breath. Her eyes kept losing focus. 'Mother,' she uttered at last.

'But she is dead . . .' Nat insisted. It was true, her mother had been dead this last year and yet it seemed she sat here upon a solid wooden chair. Nat left her side and went to try the door into the chantry. 'It's locked,' he shouted. 'No key.'

Tabitha shrank back. If the door could be opened, did she have the courage for a reunion with her dead mother? Perhaps. Yes, for her mother had come to warn her of danger, she was sure of it.

'Is there another way in?' she asked. She looked back towards Gunn but he still sat silently sleeping. The boy was cringing by the chapel door, eager to escape, still grasping his fiery torch.

'The only other way inside is up some stairs from the crypt,' Nat said.

That was an even greater horror. She could not bear to think that her mother had climbed up slick black stairs from out of the cold earth. Yet still she was resolute. For her child's sake she must hear her mother's warning.

'Or we could break this window,' he suggested.

'Do it.' She leaned against the cold wall feeling queasy. Nat searched about and found a stout rod of iron. Then, ushering her out of the way, he swung it at the latticed glass and a score of small panes broke and fell tinkling to the ground.

'Wait!' Tabitha raised her arm to halt him and stumbled towards the broken window. At last she looked through the holes in the empty lead frame and saw the figure with her own eyes. Her mother appeared shrunken in size, wrapped in a ragged burial shroud that was stained yellow and filthy brown.

Tabitha spoke into the darkness of the chantry. 'Mother. Who is my enemy?'

She held her breath. There was no disputing that the true Widow Hart was dead. Yet still this figure spoke. In a high, reedy voice the skeletal figure uttered one word: 'Salvation.'

'Don't look,' Nat muttered. 'We should leave at once.'

Standing so much closer than Nat she could see every contour of the woman's rags and pitiful shape. And as clear as day she also saw the contour of the carved back of the chair. As if in a nightmare she could see both the woman's torso and the back of the chair on which she sat. Lord God in Heaven, she could see straight through the insubstantial substance of her mother's body. Her fingers clawed at the wall. What she was seeing was not a trick but supernatural – a transparent wraith or a phantom. Her eyes opened wide in disbelief. Her legs weakened; her vision grew dark. Though Nat tried to catch his wife as she fell, with a little cry Tabitha crumpled down on to the cold stone floor.

THIRTY-EIGHT

These signs will appear by the Prophet foretold,
Come Midsummer's Day in the world of old.

The New Prophet of the Forest

'No!' Nat sank to the floor beside the motionless body of his wife. Pressing clumsy fingers to her throat he found her pulse ran fast although her skin was cool and waxy. What had he been thinking? He ran to the door and jangled the old chapel bell, calling the alarm.

The next few hours he felt himself to be buffeted like a small bird on a storm. Higgott and Tom helped carry Tabitha upstairs to the solar. Doctor Caldwell was sent for but delayed by another case. When the doctor arrived after midnight Nat dismissed the servants and tried to explain how it was his wife lay senseless.

The doctor rounded upon him. 'What the devil was Mrs De Vallory doing in that unwholesome chapel of yours?'

'I was apprehensive of that preacher Gunn's prophecy. So I tried to draw him out—'

Caldwell left off his examination of Tabitha to glower in disapproval. 'And Gunn was doing what, exactly?'

'Demonstrating his powers of prophecy.'

'After all my sound advice, you allowed your pregnant wife to attend this . . . performance?'

Nat gave a mute nod.

'So, to be clear. What exactly precipitated your wife's collapse?'

'She had a shock,' Nat murmured. 'A spirit appeared.'

Caldwell's paunchy face grew rigid with contempt. 'I have heard of this preacher fellow. I suppose he played some charlatan's trick upon you?'

Nat was not entirely sure what had happened. 'The spirit was alive. Clearly moving, yet most apparently a corpse.'

Caldwell harrumphed indignantly. 'You do understand you

have gravely endangered your wife and child? Her heart is greatly overexerted. Has she complained of late, of any troubling symptoms?'

Nat was at first baffled. Then a series of tiny observations sprang to mind. 'She has been agitated. Yet that I fear is my fault. And breathless. I believe the baby is pressing up into her lungs. And tonight she complained of cold.'

'So, your wife has been cold, short of breath, her heart overworked? You did not think to call me?'

'I did not know . . .' Nat mumbled. 'My God, is she in danger?'

'I must bleed her. After that we can only hope and pray for the best.'

Nat stared at the floor while Caldwell unpacked a case of scarification tools. Tabitha tossed her head a few times but gave no sign of waking. Even above Caldwell's mutterings he could still hear Gunn's voice ringing out in his mind. 'The child will live. But there is danger.' No one could argue with those prophetic words now.

Nat had a bed moved beside Tabitha's four-poster and for the next twenty-four hours he would not leave her side. He fretted and dozed and wandered in his mind, while Sukey Adams kept vigil by the fireside. Dazedly, he observed the nursemaid: when not busy with her needle, she bathed Tabitha with scented waters, changed her shifts and bedclothes, and succeeded in feeding his wife spoonfuls of strengthening beef tea. She was a comforting figure in her neat blue gown and voluminous white apron. His decision not to dismiss her stood alone as one of the few sensible actions he had taken over recent weeks. He entirely forgave her indiscretion on his return from Langley Hall, for surely an abandoned wife could succumb to loneliness?

'Your wife is no worse,' the doctor announced at his next evening visit. 'I believe she suffers from a chloritic condition and her heart may be weakened. My apothecary is preparing a syrup of iron to give her strength. And thankfully, the child still lives.'

Tabitha only slowly regained her strength, occasionally opening her eyes and making little sighs and murmurs. The apothecary's potion arrived, a sweet syrup of wine in which iron filings had been steeped and then removed. Obediently, Tabitha sipped it and seemed to gain a little colour. Yet in reply to Nat's entreaties, Caldwell insisted there was still no sign of the child's arrival. 'And a good thing, too. The longer your wife can rest and recover her strength, the better chance she will have of a successful travail.'

Nat sat caressing her hand when Tabitha first opened her eyes and spoke.

'Nat,' she whispered, moving her hand awkwardly towards him.

'My love.' He dropped to his knees beside the bed and pressed her cool fingers to his mouth. 'I am so sorry.'

A smile fluttered on her lips. 'Is it over now?'

'All is well. Our baby is still safe.'

She sank back on to the bolster, looking weary. 'Good,' she said softly. 'Now I can sleep again. Kiss me, Nat.'

He leaned down and pressed his lips to hers. Then he thanked the Lord he had been saved from the consequences of his own folly.

Later that day, Tabitha sat up in bed and ate a little mutton jelly. With Mrs Adams watching over her, Nat left the solar for the first time and headed to the chapel. Lighting an oil lamp, he re-entered the high arched chamber, struck by its expectant air, as of a stage play suddenly interrupted. He inspected the area where Gunn had sat in apparent deep sleep. He could find no sign of mischief. Then, walking over to the chantry window, his boots crunched on the diamond twinkles of broken glass. Peering through the broken lead frame he could see nothing save for darkness. He tried the door and as before, it was securely locked. This time, he seized the iron rod he had abandoned on solstice night and attacked the ancient door with gusto. It felt good to hit an object so devilish hard, and he had soon splintered the ancient wood and struck away the lock. When the door creaked open, he ventured inside,

On first inspection the small chapel was as he remembered it. There stood the chair upon which Tabitha and he had watched the spirit sink down. He touched its cool surface; it was a solid chair. He sat upon it and it bore his weight easily. Next, he searched the small room inch by inch. He found two further matching chairs in the corner. Beside them was a heap of abandoned rubble: broken furniture, a funeral bier, a lectern, and what looked like a glasshouse window. He moved to the chantry altar where the alabaster figure of a long dead De Vallory knight reclined in full armour. Nat had no recollection of seeing the effigy before, nor of noticing the elaborate fan-vaulted ceiling. He touched the knight's cold gauntlet with his fingertips. The effigy had reclined there for centuries; it was securely plastered into an ornate funerary arch.

Nevertheless, his uncertain memory recalled only the ghostly figure hobbling across the room exuding its own sickly illumination. This was most curious. Could the visitation of a spirit overwhelm the human mind and alter human perception? Raising the lamp above the altar he noticed a short thread of black cloth snagged on a barbed excrescence of stone. Inspecting it under the lamp's glow he saw it was a thread of black wool about an inch long. This was clearly no relic of his mouldering ancestors but fresh and clean. Carefully, he tucked it inside his pocketbook.

As he had suspected, there was a second exit from the room by a low door which he supposed was the entrance to the crypt. When he tried the door it swung open, revealing a hole as uninviting as a dungeon. Slowly, he descended steep stone steps that dropped into the ground, ducking his head to avoid the arched roof which hung with dripping lichens. At last he reached an uneven paved floor. The air tasted sweetly putrid and was as cold as a cave. He was in a low stone chamber perhaps half the size of the chapel, paved with unwholesomely gleaming flagstones. He did not like to wonder what that fluid might be, for against the walls stood deep shelves that had once stored the dead. Nevertheless, in a few minutes he had inspected each dark corner and found no other exit, not even a trapdoor. Neither did any coffins remain, save for one imposing stone sarcophagus standing against the furthest wall. He began to inspect it, noting that the heavy lid had been pulled aside. He lowered the lamp to look into its interior. Something – or someone – was lying inside. Catching his breath, he waited, not certain if the bundled shape would move. When nothing stirred, he lowered the golden light of his lamp so it illuminated a mass of stained rags, much like those the spirit had worn when moving across the chapel. Not having the stomach to touch the bundle, he pulled a penknife from his coat and tentatively poked at the rags. Good. The death shroud no longer contained an entity. Cautiously, he cut a scrap of fabric and put it in his coat pocket.

Desperate to leave he took one last look about himself, into the impenetrable blackness beyond his lamp. He felt a momentary jolt to his senses, as if he had fallen into a bottomless pit or other great void. And it seemed to Nat that this physical loss of orientation entirely reflected the present state of his life. He wondered if Gunn had hoaxed him but could make no sense of it at all. And now, having lost his bearings, he felt entirely ill-equipped to take even the smallest step forwards.

On his return Nat assembled all the servants and questioned them about all the comings and goings on the day and night of the solstice. No, each and every servant assured him, only Mister Gunn and his boy had arrived and left their wagon in the stables, passing back and forth to the chapel by an outside path to a side door. Just as the master had instructed the pair had never ventured into the main part of the house. So far as anyone could remember, Mister Gunn and his lad had gone on their way shortly after Mrs De Vallory had been taken ill. No, Gunn had shown no signs of being in a trance and driven away as wakeful as a young cat. As for the chantry chapel, Higgott assured him that it was at least five years since anyone had taken the key and ventured inside it, or into the crypt below. Finally, Nat gave orders that if Gunn or any of his followers were seen nearby the constable must be sent for instantly.

THIRTY-NINE

24 June 1753
Midsummer's Day

Upon waking, Nat took a breath of air at the window, noting the luminous blue sky and sweet balmy air of Midsummer's Day. He spent the day in anxious expectation, questioning Tabitha. 'You are sure you do not feel any pains yet?'

She shook her head. 'No. It seems both Doctor Caldwell and . . . your preacher friend . . . were wrong about the date of my confinement.'

It was the first time she had mentioned Gunn and Nat was at once uneasy. 'He is hardly my friend. Let us hope he was wrong. About everything. I have set a watch against his ever returning here.'

She laid a finger on his lips to silence him. 'Thank you. Then let us be glad,' she said. 'The baby is well. Fate has been good to us.'

When Caldwell arrived he was unruffled about the matter. 'Your wife was never especially certain of the date,' the physician said smoothly. 'First pregnancies often run longer than subsequent births.'

At midnight, Nat heard the church bell tolling twelve times as he watched Tabitha sleep. There had been no fateful birth of a saviour, or at least not here at Bold Hall. Gunn's prophecy was proving false. Sukey Adams also looked up from her needlework and paced over to touch Tabitha's cheek and stare intently into her peaceful face. And so, to the disappointment of both master and servant, all three had an undisturbed night.

A few days later Tabitha woke to find not only Nat but Sukey absent from her side. It was Grisell who came tapping at the door to the solar with a tray of titbits and an oilskin packet posted to her from Chester. Inside was a message from Joshua explaining that the gimmel ring had been returned to him now the inquiry into Maria's death had been closed for lack of evidence against any credible suspect. As it had been found on De Vallory land and Tabitha had expressed an interest in it, he now enclosed it for her safekeeping. She opened a small cotton bag and inspected the half-ring. It was a pretty trinket and now she studied it again she was convinced it was one half of the ring worn by Phyllis Langley in the portrait.

Joshua also directed her to a dirty and tattered handbill folded inside the package. She read it rapidly:

20 POUNDS REWARD

~~~~~~~~~~~~~~~~~~~~~~~~~~~~~~~

Whereas a most cruel THEFT and DECEPTION was committed in the house of Mrs Elizabeth Green in Wardle in the County of Lancashire, whereby from the use of pretended Fortune-telling was defrauded Seven Guineas, a Silver Watch, several Bottles of Wine, and some other articles, by use of certain subtle craft to deceive and impose upon the said Mrs Green, by pretending to tell her future, and for telling her of certain things that concerned her husband.

Two suspicious characters are being sought, a man and woman working in league. The male is a tall Man of good genteel appearance and was last seen about the town as a travelling preacher known as Bradley Gun, also called Baptist or David; and the woman is supposed his Wife, a pretended sibyl, known as Sarah Bracewell, also called Sal or Salvation Gun.

If any person concerned in the above matter shall Cause one or more of these persons to be convicted, the utmost Means shall be used to obtain a Pardon for him, and he shall receive the above Reward.

October 1752

Tabitha felt all the keen pleasure of vindication at being right. There was no doubt that the man they knew as Baptist Gunn was a rogue and a thief. Yet to her frustration the handbill did not go far enough and condemn him as capable of murder. Tabitha twice read the description of Gunn's wife. This must be the barren first wife whom he had cast aside. Had it been this woman who play-acted her own dead mother? Or, she wondered with a sudden thrill, could this supposed wife be a false name used by Maria? Many street-walkers did have light-fingered habits, and even Tabitha herself had been known to lift a pocketwatch from a sleeping gentleman's waistcoat.

No, she decided. How could tangibly pregnant Maria have been discarded for not bearing children? Oh, she would give a heavy purse to question this Salvation woman about these goings-on. Dammit, though the handbill corroborated Gunn's criminal past it offered little help in discovering Maria's killer.

She rose to ring the bell and then stopped herself and pulled on a loose morning gown. It would be pleasant to spend more time alone and unobserved. The curtain at the window was half open and a breeze as clean as spring water was freshening the room. Two days had passed since Midsummer's Day and the baby might arrive at any time. From that moment her old life would vanish. What was it that Nat said? That she could not change him; that she had known well enough when they married that he needed to exercise his intellect. Well, so must she be true to her own self. And there was one thing she had vowed to achieve before she faced her ordeal.

She traced her way along the passage to her old chamber. Opening the large doors of the linen press, she saw that Sukey or Grisell had moved a good few of her garments to the solar so that the shelves stood half-empty. The two great wooden doors stood open as bare as empty canvases waiting for a painter to fill them. Opening her mother's box, Tabitha gathered up the items she had collected. There were the pressed flowers that had once decorated Maria's corpse. She pinned them to the open door. Next to it she hung the lace-bedecked poppet doll, and beside it Gunn's pamphlet of prophecies. Next she pinned up Nancy Blair's letter identifying Gunn as the man Maria had left Chester with. Finally, she added the handbill naming Gunn as a fraudster. She sat back and pondered.

Slipping the half-ring on to her middle finger she let her mind roam free, looking for a deeper pattern. Random notions floated in her mind: the oak tree's winter sleep and spring rebirth, Joshua's carving the poppet to hang upon the tree, the prophecy of the birth of the saviour, the mother's love expressed to her daughter etched on the gimmel ring's surface. Beyond the obvious connection with Baptist Gunn there lay one common thread that bound each item together. It was the birth of a baby. She recalled his sinister words that she and her child were in danger. Gunn was not to be trusted; whenever she came close to him she felt fear in her blood, in her bones. Perhaps it was not manly lust that made him watch her, but something quite different. The insane wish to take her to America, perhaps? Lord, it was almost ridiculous. Or even worse, to take the child alone across the ocean. Such was her anguish that she gave a little sob and laid her palms on her stomach as if her own two hands alone could protect her child from danger.

At her bureau Tabitha wrote a friendly message to Sophie Rix, relating that she was now recovering from a bout of sickness and inviting her call at Bold Hall as soon as she was able. She reminded her friend of the favour she had requested, to speak to Langley's daughter, Lady Maud, about the gimmel ring. Then, not certain she wanted to discuss her plan with even a servant, she carried the missive downstairs and slipped it into the post box in the entrance hall.

FORTY

28 June 1753

On Thursday morning Sukey announced that a Mister and Mrs Rix were waiting below, enquiring after Mrs De Vallory's health.

'I must dress and go down and greet them,' Tabitha insisted to her disapproving nursemaid. 'Sophie was my only friend at Langley Hall. To see her will do me more good than a hundred iron potions. Keep my stays very loose, mind, as the doctor advised.'

Down in the parlour, Tabitha and Sophie shook hands and found they could scarcely let each other go for the sheer pleasure of meeting again. In answer to Sophie's enquiries, Tabitha made light of her illness. 'They kept me in bed as a caution because the baby is expected so soon. But truly, I feel quite recovered.'

'You certainly look well,' Sophie agreed. When the gentlemen went away to Nat's study, Sophie announced her news. 'You asked if I might call upon Lady Maud. I did so yesterday and she is eager to see you – today. Here is her card. She will call here at eleven o'clock and speak to you if you are taking callers.'

Tabitha instantly revived at the prospect of renewing the chase. 'That is perfect. What could be better?'

While they waited Tabitha drew out the circumstances of Lady Maud's life from her new friend. 'She married Lord Randall-Scott in order to unite their two fortunes. A horrible man, with something of the angry bulldog to his manner. Swinging jowls and bloodshot eyes, you know the sort? Fortunately, he generally stays at his own estates on the Scottish Borders. Well, matters went fairly well at first. Lady Maud had a difficult confinement but successfully produced a son and heir for the Langley family.'

'So the line runs through Lady Maud? There is no male heir?'

'No, the Langleys have no other surviving children. Hence the jubilation at Maud producing a son. Or so it seemed, for little Eddie was said to be somewhat wanting in brains, though he was amiable enough and adored by his mother. She had been told she would never bear another child so had little else upon which to throw her affections. The family were rarely seen in society and little Eddie, never at all. Then, it must have been a few years ago now, in 1750 I believe, we all heard that Eddie had drowned in their lake. He had escaped from his nursemaid and set a toy boat on the water and, utterly careless of the danger, had waded in. Oh, it is too tragic to speak of. He was only eight years old. Lady Maud has remained in deepest mourning ever since.'

As Tabitha listened, she felt the heavy burden of her self-appointed task. Hearing the rumble of wheels, she glanced out of the window where a very grand black carriage was winding its way up the drive. Who was she to meddle in the business of these grand people? Momentarily, she felt a wave of giddiness return. If Lady Maud had not been expecting to meet her, she would have been tempted to return to bed at once.

Lady Maud had expressly asked that Mrs De Vallory should speak with her alone, and so Sophie reluctantly went outside to admire the garden. Tom ushered in a woman of forty or there-abouts, scarecrow thin and dressed in severe mourning. Tabitha rose and curtsied awkwardly, and then raised her eyes to a countenance more ravaged by unhappiness than any she had ever before encountered.

'Welcome, Your Ladyship. Please make yourself easy and I'll send for some refreshments.'

Lady Maud's moist grey eyes flickered over the swelling beneath Tabitha's silk bodice. 'I need nothing, pray be seated. I believe you are Sir John's daughter-in-law. I am intrigued why you should wish to speak with me.'

Tabitha sank back into her comfortable chair and forced her breath to grow calm. 'I am most obliged to you, my lady. I shall endeavour not to waste your time. I have been searching for the other half to a gimmel ring. When staying at Langley Hall I happened to notice the same ring in a portrait of your late aunt Phyllis. Upon making enquiries I understand it may have been bequeathed to you upon your aunt's death.'

Tabitha reached into her pocket and drew out the half-ring found in Maria's cold hand.

'Oh.' Lady Maud came forward, hesitating before touching it, as if it might scratch her. Then she stared at Tabitha, blinking like a stricken rabbit. 'How did this come into your possession?'

'It was found on my husband's land in Mondrem Forest.' When the silence lengthened, she continued. 'Prepare yourself for bad news, Your Ladyship. This ring was found on the hand of a young woman who was tragically deceased when we discovered her.'

Lady Maud sat down, as stiff as pewter. 'Who was this young person?'

'She was known as Maria St John. However, I understand St John to be a foundling name as she was raised under the auspices of the Blue Coat Hospital.'

Lady Maud produced a black-edged handkerchief and wiped tears from the deep furrows around her eyes. Then pulling on a black ribbon at her throat she retrieved a second ring. At last, Tabitha thought, with bitterly mixed emotions. It was the matching half of Maria's ring, a mirror image of the first gold band, bearing a second outstretched hand worked in enamel. Leaning forward, Tabitha could see that it bore the completion of the ring's motto. '"As these hands part",' her visitor recited in a cracked voice, '"so breaks my heart." How prophetic those words have proved.'

Now Lady Maud unloosed her own ring from the ribbon and slotted both parts together with a gentle click. She studied the result on her outstretched hand. 'At last our two hands are reunited. I had to break the tiny gold pin to separate them,' she murmured. 'Seventeen long years ago.' Then raising eyes full of tears, she asked Tabitha, 'She was my daughter. How did she die?'

Tabitha said gently, 'She was killed by another's hand. I have been attempting to unmask Maria's murderer. So far, in vain.'

Maria's mother made an attempt to restrain her tears, but her voice was choked with sorrow. 'I understood she had left that institution. I had not seen Maria since observing her secretly in the chapel some years ago.'

'How dreadfully hard for you,' Tabitha said quietly. When Lady Maud lifted her face, it was entirely raw with grief. 'Tell me. Do you know where Maria now lies?'

Tabitha explained that the coroner had intended to place her in a pauper's grave when no family came forward to claim her. 'I arranged that she be buried in a modest grave in Netherlea churchyard. There is no headstone yet, for I was not certain of Maria's full name.'

Lady Maud shook her head. 'I had no choice but to give her up. Maria was conceived as the result of an alliance with a servant; yet I console myself, she was at least conceived in love. When my father discovered the facts, he ensured my sweetheart vanished from my life along with my beloved baby. My husband also forbade my ever meeting with Maria.

'I could bear it while little Eddie was with us. Though my heart never mended at the loss of my daughter, my son was some consolation. But to lose both – to lose all my children and to be told I could bear no others . . . what kind of cruel God would do that to a woman?' Rising, Maria's mother crossed to a table with a decanter and asked, 'May I?'

At Tabitha's acquiescence she poured two glasses of brandy. Setting one to stand untouched at Tabitha's side, she took a long draught and asked, 'Did you know her?'

'Only briefly. I believe she tried to improve her situation.'

'Yes. She tried. Yet she had little hope of a happy life. Beaufort ruined my daughter.'

'Beaufort Langley? Surely they are kin?'

'Yes, they are cousins. Beaufort came upon her by chance on the streets of Chester. He set her up in a rented house as his kept – well, his *demimondaine*.'

'And did he abandon her?'

Lady Maud unsteadily returned to sit at Tabitha's side. She stared forlornly at the ring. 'No, I understand it was Maria who wanted to end it. Beaufort is not a gentleman. I wanted to give her shelter but the men in my family have various means of preventing their wives any liberty. I know she became a common prostitute. And then she disappeared. I have long expected the worst news.'

Tabitha gathered her courage to ask some keener questions. 'Is it possible Mister Beaufort Langley could have harmed Maria?'

'No.' Lady Maud was entirely firm. 'Beaufort, for all his many sins, was besotted by Maria. However, it was not a mutual affection. He has confided that she was his life's love despite Maria's dislike of him.'

Tabitha thought quickly; she still did not entirely trust Nancy Blair. 'Maria told a friend she was leaving her old life on the streets to join some sort of family. Could it possibly have been Beaufort?'

'No. Certainly not Beaufort.'

'Some say she left with a preacher named Baptist Gunn. Do you know him?'

'I do not. Is he a good man?'

'I am afraid he is a cruel hoaxer.' Then after a long silence, she added, 'In confidence, Your Ladyship, I fear my husband has been cheated by Mister Beaufort Langley.'

Lady Maud appeared to wake a little from her grief. 'I am sorry to hear of your husband's troubles. I have heard Mister De Vallory's name much of late. I believe my father covets a tract of your land.'

Tabitha had no alternative but to be honest. 'It is true that Sir John owns the land. Lord Langley . . . he disputes the claim, shall we say.'

An expression of disgust pinched Her Ladyship's thin features. 'My father is trying to steal it, is he not?'

Tabitha bit her lip. 'I cannot disagree.'

'I have a notion, Mrs De Vallory, of how I might stop this nonsense of stealing a neighbour's land.' She took Tabitha's hand and though her touch was as cold as an iron key, the pressure was gentle. 'After Maria left the charity school, I wanted to reclaim her as my own child. You do know that, after Eddie died, Maria would have inherited the Langley Estates after me? And now we have Beaufort Langley picking our pockets. My father calls Beaufort the family saviour. I call him our curse. Poor Maria. A mother's sorrow for a lost child is the cruellest of all fates. Yet I do believe that over time grief may be distilled into a most useful weapon.' Her voice breaking with emotion, she stood and signalled that she would leave. 'You have been most kind. I shall do my utmost to assist you.'

When her friend returned Tabitha gave a somewhat censored version of Lady Maud's revelations. 'Such a woman does not

deserve to be the entertainment of her neighbours,' she said
soberly. 'I have returned the lost half of the ring to her. I should
be grateful if you do not speak of today's visit.'

After Sophie gave her word, Tabitha said, 'Enough of me. Tell
me, how are you?'

Sophie sighed and stared at the carpet. 'I have no news. Though
I have attempted a number of charms in the hope of becoming
a mother. Unfortunately, mandrake tea was not to my taste. And
I have carried the heart of a female quail in a little bag at my
waist since Eastertide. And . . .'

'My dear,' Tabitha interrupted gently. 'Do not waste your time
on such follies. These are rational times, my friend. Here, let me
show you.'

Pulling a little almanack from her pocket, she opened it at
the next month's calendar and soon set out a plan of campaign.

'So you are saying I will only make a child within this middle
time of the month?'

'Yes. Turn your husband away if he comes to your bed outside
those prescribed days. This is especially important if he is weak
due to age or sickness.'

'Heavens, to have such knowledge. Do you know these matters
because of your former profession?' Sophie awaited the answer
like a mischievous child.

'What is it you wish to ask?' Tabitha could not keep a smile
from her lips.

'Well, I have secretly read . . . that particular book everyone
whispers of. The extraordinary adventures of a certain Miss Hill.
My dear Tabitha, all the ladies of the neighbourhood are agog
about your former profession. What a life you must have led.'
Her brown eyes grew round with curiosity.

Fiddlesticks, her new friend was waiting for a saucy
anecdote.

'I assure you,' she said gravely, 'my London life was never
so full of incident as any masculine author would write it. How
my friends and I laughed at young Fanny's relentless contortions.
The poor girl would have been worn to the bone by her sixteenth
birthday. No, Sophie, many men desire only the swiftest of
connections. And others, tedious as it may sound, merely want
an amiable companion to wear upon their arm.'

'Truly?' Sophie looked disappointed.

Tabitha nodded sagely, intent upon destroying her reputation with such dull stories. Heavens, if only Sophie knew of her London romps Tabitha doubted very much their friendship would survive.

Nat was dutifully entertaining Mister Rix in his basement study in the dower house. The man was unimpressive in appearance, seeming more than his fifty years of age, grey-haired, spindly, with a wrinkled countenance that did, thankfully, combine with a most engaging mind. He leaned upon his cane, admiring the room's classical frescoes and spontaneously described the history of Chronos. Nat found himself looking again with interest at the Roman fresco discovered by his late uncle, depicting the forefather of Time replete with a sharp sword and grey beard.

'This room of yours is perhaps the most exquisite survival of the classical past in the county,' Mister Rix said in admiration. 'I am merely an antiquarian, De Vallory,' he confided as he turned to Nat's precious library. 'My collection is mostly books and stones and bones, I'm afraid. You must have many fine relics hereabouts, judging from the number of tumuli and what the common folk call giants' stones.'

Nat warmed to the man. He hesitated, then decided to confide in the scholarly fellow. 'In truth, I am in something of a predicament, sir.' He told Rix of his commitment to present a paper to the Cestrian Society. Then, rather sheepishly, he described his experiment on the veracity of prophecy – and its disastrous consequences. His new acquaintance questioned him closely, occasionally refining Nat's account when he allowed emotion to colour his description. 'The facts alone please, sir. Tell me only what your senses recorded.'

When all was told, Mister Rix sat back and considered for a while, tapping his bent fingers on the silver top of his cane. 'What a fascinating experiment you made, sir. However, I predict your hypothesis will be explained by human motivation rather than the occult. The essential question is, what does this fellow want from you?'

'That is a question that puzzles me mightily. Firstly, there is the prediction Gunn made of imminent danger to my wife and child. I admit I wanted to draw him out, but God forgive me, I was badly startled. Presumably, he wants to frighten us. And there is the fee of fifty pounds, I suppose. Though I have not yet paid him.' Nat was finding it a prodigious relief to speak and, once he started, he found it hard to stop. 'Yet still, the artifice of the whole affair: his choice of location, the dim candlelit chapel and the creation of a sinister atmosphere. Most prophets I've studied are meticulous in managing the staging of their act, baffling their watchers with esoteric chanting, darkness, surprises, and so forth. It is the apparition that baffles me.'

Mister Rix nodded the grey thatch of his head, but his shrewd eyes shone. 'Why so?'

'Because to our astonishment it was not solid. It was made of air.'

The gentleman raised his grizzled brows and gazed into space, considering deeply.

'Curiously,' Nat added thoughtfully, 'I do have a clue, a thread to follow in this labyrinth. I found it attached to the wall above the altar.' He pulled the black fibre of wool from his pocketbook.

'Fascinating. We have a conundrum worthy of Theseus himself.'

'Indeed. As it was so well expressed by Chaucer: *By a clue of twine as he hath gone, The same way he may return anon.*'

Nat had walked outside to bid farewell to Mister and Mrs Rix while Tabitha retired to rest.

'Please do visit us,' Mrs Rix begged. 'You can test my husband's prodigious memory. Name any book on earth and he can at once tell if it is one of the three thousand volumes in his library.'

Nat considered. What the devil was that book he had been meaning to search out? Yes, the unlikely volume he had seen in Gunn's possession at the camp. 'Do you know an author named Della Porta?'

Rix nodded vigorously. 'A Neapolitan. Natural philosopher of the last century. A playwright, and inventor, I believe. I have an edition of his work. Call on me and you may borrow it.'

FORTY-ONE

30 June 1753

On Saturday morning Nat rose early, eager for a long ride. The year had reached its sunlit zenith and his bones, stiff from sleeping on a thin and narrow bed beside Tabitha, warmed pleasantly in this golden season. He rode out to the forest and noticed for the first time the subtle darkening and drying of the bright springtime leaves. The air was very still and scented with old sap. Along the familiar bridle path Nat felt the sweet melancholy of summer's peak that was slowly passing. He was humming a song that revolved in his brain: the one where a fellow's mother-in-law bewitches his pregnant wife who is cursed never to give birth to her child:

> *'Of her young bairn she'll never be lighter,*
> *Nor in her Bower to shine the brighter.'*

His mind ran over the ugly verse: a nightmare of death in life for both mother and child. What tosh. Caldwell had to know best and any day now their child must be born. With luck, the whole worrying event might even be ended by the time he arrived home. He was mightily looking forward to presenting young John or Hannah to his own father. He and Tabitha had agreed the baby's names to follow De Vallory family traditions. 'For if little John has your jackanapes manner we can always call him Jack,' Tabitha had teased. Jack or Hannah. He liked the names well. It would be his one achievement, for he considered himself a disappointing son. In some inexplicable way he believed he had brought ill luck to Bold Hall. Well, it was time for a new start. Today he would speak firmly but civilly to Gunn and demand an explanation for that mountebank show in the chapel. As for the fifty pounds, he had no intention of paying the man for such a gruesome spectacle.

As Nat emerged from the tunnel of thorns into the camp's circular clearing, he drew Jupiter to a halt. The place was eerily empty. Gone were the barking dogs, tatterdemalion tents, and collection of ragged but hopeful believers. All that remained was the forlorn shell of the treehouse and a scattering of grubby detritus. Nat ruffled Jupiter's mane and uttered a silent prayer of thanks that Gunn had vanished. He could scarcely wait to tell Tabitha. Next, he would send over some labourers to clear the place, for filth and rubbish lay strewn about and a stink of privies and rotten food spoiled the air. Soon Nature would creep back over the pockmarked grass. Suddenly Nat was convinced that – with Gunn on his way to America – he could overcome Langley's claim to this precious land and soon all would be well.

An hour later Nat's entire world spun around him. He was inside the strongroom at Bold Hall. He groped inside the empty money chest, stupidly hoping that his eyes were deceiving him. Higgott had met him at the gate and led him to the windowless repository with scarcely a word.

'You are sure it is all gone?'

Higgott nodded, his expression dazed. 'I have searched everywhere.'

'Yet the door was locked.'

The man swallowed and nodded again.

'Who had the key?' Nat could scarcely believe his voice was so steady. According to the ledger, there had been six hundred and forty-eight pounds in the strongbox, representing the Bold Hall estate's entire stock of coin.

'I keep the key upon me.' The steward pulled out an iron chain attached to a ring on his belt. 'I never remove it, sir.'

'And at night?' Nat asked.

'It is hung on my bedpost as I sleep.'

'And your door is locked?'

'Well, sir. Not generally.'

'And no doubt you sleep soundly,' Nat said irritably. 'Go and assemble the servants. We must untangle this matter at once.' Standing alone, a mist of despondency fell upon him as he stared stupidly around the room. What was it Gunn had warned him of? Danger. Jealousy. Escape. What variety of malice had he invited into his home when he invited Baptist Gunn through his door?

All the household assembled in the servants' hall, muttering at this second unorthodox summons within so few days. When the news was given out, no one could offer a single sensible notion of how the money had vanished. Nat was gathering his thoughts when a cook-maid spoke up. 'Where is Grisell? I never seen her since she went to the village last evening.'

Mouths fell open as the household stared at one another. Someone was sent to search Grisell's chamber and it was established that she had vanished and taken her travelling box besides. Nat quieted the chatter. 'Silence! Grisell made it no secret she was a follower of Baptist Gunn's creed. What do any of you know of her connection to him?'

'She gabbled on of little else,' the cook grumbled. 'I have no doubt she will be camped out amongst his followers in that there wood.'

'No,' Nat corrected. 'They have gone. The camp is empty.'

A collective groan filled the room, smattered with curses. Cook began to wail, 'Oh, Grisell, did she steal that money to get to America? She will be drowned at sea, the foolish article.'

In search of a more rational witness, Nat turned to Tom. 'You have visited those gatherings, lad. When did you last see Grisell at Gunn's camp?'

Tom looked more than flustered; he might have been about to flee away himself. 'I can't think right, sir. I cannot say. They've all gone? What, all of them?'

Nat repeated that they had. A knock at the door announced Joshua's arrival direct from the sheriff's business in Chester. With some relief Nat dismissed all save the constable and called for bread and ale while the two men conferred.

Nat considered. 'I need you to stop them on the road. They will be heading to Liverpool, the only port hereabouts giving passage to America. Take a few stout men. And help yourself to any fast horses you need from my stable. But listen, Joshua. If you do find them alert the local law officers at once and arrest them with the greatest care. I don't want that devil Gunn slipping down an alley and on to a waiting ship.'

'May I go with the constable?' Looking up, they saw that Tom was still hanging halfway through the door.

'No, you may not, Tom. I want strong men in this house tonight. I shall be off to Chester and speak to the sheriff myself. Tom, your duty is to check all the doors are locked and keep watch through the night.'

FORTY-TWO

1 July 1753

I t was not until the following day that Nat returned from Chester, having been forced to lodge at an inn for the night and then wait in a fury of irritation before he could persuade the sheriff to take action. On his return he found Tabitha alone and waiting for him in her old chamber. She grasped him tightly in her arms.

'No news,' he murmured softly. 'And according to Joshua, no sign of Gunn on any road. Today he is searching all the inns and seagoing vessels of Liverpool.'

'And there is no news of Grisell, either,' she added. 'The silly fool of a woman.'

He looked seriously into her face. 'Grisell wished her fate upon herself. It is your safety that is everything to me. Promise me, you shall not leave these walls.'

She smiled grimly. 'Do not fear. I am glad to be safe at home. I have heard these voyages are a form of hell on earth.'

'Well, my love, I hope Gunn suffers every torment. That is a great deal of my father's money he has spirited away.' He sighed, pressing his long fingers to his brow. 'You should never have married me, Tabitha. We may have to borrow against Father's land.'

A light-hearted chuckle escaped her lips. 'Heavens, Nat. I longed to marry you when you were a penniless poet. What is coin if we have love?'

He didn't speak again as he worked to remove his boots. He was dog-tired and vastly downhearted. Stupidly, he felt his eyes prick at her kind words. She was so trusting, so much more than he deserved. This was what he would lose when she learned about Maria. He was severely tempted to tell her and have it over with. Her anger could scarcely make him feel any worse than her sweetness.

'Nat?' Awkwardly, she lowered herself to kneel in front of him. 'You do know that I love you. You – and not this carapace of a gentleman. Sometimes, I wonder if we should have run off to London to live by our wits as two out-of-pocket rogues.' She smiled broadly at the fancy of it. 'Instead, my darling, you have had to take on the burden of all these calamities.'

He nodded, then reached for her face and lifted a stray hair with his forefinger. 'Since Gunn came everything has gone so ill.'

Her clear eyes examined his face. 'Do you believe Baptist Gunn could be Maria's murderer?' She gave the handbill to him and he rapidly scanned it. Death and fire, it was all as clear as day now. He had been duped by a known fraudster. 'How did you get this?'

Tabitha was admirably serene. 'I asked Joshua to find out Gunn's history.'

'A fine upholder of the law I have proved. I should have listened to you from the start.' He leaned down and kissed her, drawing her hair up from her neck so that she shivered beautifully.

But instead of succumbing she pulled back and asked, 'So you no longer forbid me an opinion on these matters?'

He shook his head. 'You never liked Gunn. You warned me he wanted my money. I have been a numbskull.'

'You are lucky to be such an attractive specimen of numbskull.' She rose to her feet and said, 'I must show you something. Now do not mock me.'

'Very well. Only send for some meat and drink first.'

She rang the bell and when the maid had left Tabitha shyly walked to her linen press and swung open the two tall doors. On the left-hand side were pinned a number of peculiar objects. She began to expound her ideas on the pressed flowers, the poppet, Nancy's letter, and Baptist Gunn's prophecy. His curiosity was reluctantly kindled. He ate and drank eagerly but fixed upon her, considering her argument. Finally, she concluded with the drawing of the gimmel ring that had been returned to Lady Maud. 'Do you agree that it is birth that is the common factor here?'

He took a long draught of ale and wiped his lips. 'Hearing your account, I would agree. Yet there is more to it than this.

I have also collected a few scraps. But be warned, Tabitha. I must speak of that apparition in the chapel.'

'Naturally.'

He stood and opened the bare wooden right-hand door of the press. 'To begin, there is this issue of my father's land.' He pulled the letter sent by Lord Langley's lawyer from his pocket and pinned it roughly into the wood. 'Does that relate to birth? Is it my sudden appearance as Sir John's heir that has prompted this theft of Netherlea land? No, I think the Langleys intended to take it from my father any way they could. My involvement is simply an inconvenient obstacle to them. Just as Hector's being taken was probably no more than petty spite by their gamekeeper, Mullock.'

'Very well,' Tabitha agreed amiably.

'And here is the written account of what was locked in the strongbox. The thief kindly left Higgott's record of the sum to console us in our misery.' He pinned a paper neatly scribed giving the total of more than six hundred pounds.

'Now this will interest you. When Cook cleared out Grisell's room she found these.' He attached a bundle of handwritten verses to the door. 'She must have kept a tally of every prophecy she heard at the meetings.'

Tabitha rose to read them. In style they were much like those printed in the prophecy pamphlet, only there were a great many more of them.

Nat opened his pocketbook and showed her a tiny thread of black wool. 'And a further intriguing piece of evidence is this. I found it snagged on the chantry chapel's altarpiece after we saw that apparition. I am certain it was newly placed there. Then I found this by going down the steps into the crypt.' What he unfolded this time was larger – a stained rag of linen. 'It is part of a much larger shroud I found inside an open sepulchre. The apparition was draped in this cloth. Surely this proves that a mortal trickster tried to frighten – or distract – us?'

Tabitha stepped forward to inspect it. Her eyes shone as she placed it back in his hand. 'This may be a shroud but it is not the one my mother wore in her grave. Hers was white wool, not linen. It was a poor thing but it was not this.'

He nodded. 'That is useful. It proves further that we were

misled by appearances.' Nat pinned the piece of cloth and the black thread beside the other clues. 'The servants insist we had no other visitors that day save for Gunn and his helper. So who paraded in these rags?'

For a while they both studied the objects until Tabitha shook her head. 'I do not know the answer, Nat. But if anyone can solve this conundrum it is you and me. For at last we are true and honest with each other.'

The room fell silent. Nat fixed upon her, brooding. Her childlike trust in him was too, too much. His conscience would no longer be bound. 'My love. Sit down. I want you to remain as placid as you can. There is a matter that has troubled me a long while.'

Awkwardly, she sat in her chair, rather pale and anxious.

'Now you are up and about again, I must speak. I have not been quite honest with you.'

She eyed him warily. 'What is this? You frighten me. Tell me quickly.'

He wiped his mouth. 'Well. I once knew Maria. I recognized her the moment I saw her lying beneath the tree. I didn't like to tell you. And I confess I had no wish to be questioned by the authorities.'

She blinked and frowned but remained composed. He knew it was a trick of hers to mask her true reaction when wrong-footed.

'Now I see that was folly and—'

Her placid demeanour suddenly cracked. 'How do you mean it? That you knew her.' She was watching him keenly.

'She worked at the Kaleyards, as you said.'

She stiffened and instinctively cupped her stomach. 'Oh, Nat.' Dismay tightened her features. 'How could you? It was not . . . your child?'

'What the devil do you take me for?'

'A man,' she said in a small voice.

Unable to look at her, he mumbled, 'No. I last saw her in . . . in the middle of August of last year.'

'Saw her? Speak clearly. You mean you enjoyed her?'

He nodded like a guilty child. 'Yes. There were transactions.'

'Oh, God. Often?'

'Lord, Tabitha. No more than four or five times. My darling, it ceased soon after we two met.'

'Soon? When is soon? When did you last visit her?'

He dropped his head into his hands. 'I believe the last time was the night of the fourteenth of August. Remember, you and Joshua found me the next day still slumbering at noon. But scarcely a week later we rode to Chester together where you had arranged to see your paramour, Robert. I also had an assignation. I was to meet Maria. Yet as we both talked and travelled we found each other so agreeable we turned around and never reached the city. Remember?'

'Did you visit her after that?'

'I swear I never had business with her again. Though I did try to find out how she fared. Don't look at me like that. We had been friendly before I knew you. I was passing the Kaleyards the night before we found her dead. Another of the street girls, Nancy Blair, told me she had gone away. I swear I wanted only information, not the usual business.'

'Ha! That night you went to the Cestrian Club? I cannot believe those hussies turned you away.'

'I didn't say my company wasn't wanted.'

When she looked up at him, he was shocked to find her face stricken with anguish. 'Tell me you are jesting. That it isn't true.'

He reached out to console her. At his touch she snatched herself away. 'I didn't speak because I wanted to protect you from any pain,' he insisted.

'No. You are not who I thought you were.' Her voice was shaking. 'I cannot look on you. Please go away.'

FORTY-THREE

2 July 1753

At five the next morning Nat was still lying sleepless, regretting his confession, when he heard raised voices outside his window. Throwing on his riding coat he dashed downstairs and found Joshua remonstrating with Mister Higgott.

'Tell me where he is!' Joshua's brawny fist lunged at the older man's head. The steward cringed back in fear.

Nat pushed his way between the pair. 'Hold off. What troubles you, man?'

Joshua squared up to him, red-faced. 'Jennet has disappeared. I came home to a cold hearth and both herself and her best gowns all gone. No one has seen her. I reckon – God help me if I'm right – she may have run away with Baptist Gunn and his lot.'

Nat shook his head, incredulous. Beside Jennet's disappearance his own loss of money was a paltry matter.

'Where is Tom Seagoes?' Joshua growled. 'That dolt of a footman will know where she is if anyone does.'

Tom appeared in Higgott's office, quaking like an aspen leaf. His frogged coat was unbuttoned and his white stockings at half-mast. Nat bore down upon him. 'Where is Jennet Saxton?'

The lad's lips worked noiselessly before mumbling, 'I cannot say, sir.'

Nat slapped the desk with his hand and Tom jumped like a rabbit. 'Tell me what has been going on here. Spit it out now, or I shall see you thrown into the dungeon at Chester Castle.'

Tom's face appeared on the brink of unmanly tears. 'I know not where she is, sir. I wish I did.'

'Then tell us what you do know.'

The lad swallowed hard. 'I was to meet her. On Friday night, it were. We was decided on going to America with Mister Gunn. Jennet were fair sick of life here in Netherlea. I loved her so,

we could not bear to be apart no longer. I never known a girl
so—'

Nat interrupted. 'Tell us where and when you arranged to
meet.'

'At the Mondrem Oak. At ten o'clock. I had all my goods
hidden beneath a wall in the garden and needed only walk through
the woods to meet her. Then I got it into my head how I'd left
me tankard at the inn. And how if I fetched it I could raise a last
toast with the lads.'

At this, Joshua shouted, 'So you chose a pot of ale over my
daughter!'

'Stay back, Constable,' Nat ordered, raising his palm. 'Carry
on, Tom.'

'I'd collected my year's wages from Mister Higgott by telling
him my ma was sick and in need of physic. So I shelled out for
a round of ale as a farewell to my old pals. And then some other
fellow paid for more. And we sang songs and raised toasts and
each bought a round and I don't recollect any more than that.'

Mister Higgott interjected. 'Aye, next morning I had to collect
him dead drunk from the lock-up on the High Street.'

Nat shook his head in despair. 'Tom, tell me all you know of
Gunn's plans.'

'We knew they was leaving. That's about it. Mister Gunn was
going to pay our passage to America.'

'What road, what port? Tell me!'

Tom shook his head like a woolly sheep. 'I never took no
notice. Then the next day I were that bog-eyed I couldn't think
right, though I turned up for my duties. When I did get an hour
off I went searching for her up at The Grange. It were all locked
up. I couldn't scarce believe she'd gone and left me. I were
heart-broke.'

Nat watched him coldly. 'Yet you were not heartbroken enough
to tell her father. And you never thought to raise the alarm? She
has run off with a band of thieving rogues while you lay as drunk
as a hog in gaol.'

'Oh no, sir,' said the boy. 'They are good Christians. Jennet
at least will be free and happy on her way to the new world.'

In an instant Joshua had darted around the table and the foppish
lace at Tom's throat was yanked tight in the constable's fist. 'You

toss spot.' He snarled into Tom's terrified countenance. 'You have betrayed the trust of an innocent girl.' He hurled the lad against the wall where Tom slumped and slid down on to his haunches.

Nat watched the confrontation coolly. 'Mister Higgott. Return this milksop to the lock-up and keep the key safe. And that, lad, is a great kindness, for otherwise Mister Saxton would no doubt skin you alive with his own hunting knife and leave you for the flies to eat.'

FORTY-FOUR

4 July 1753
Old Midsummer's Eve

On Friday night Jennet Saxton had waited for one long harrowing hour at the Mondrem Oak until she heard distant church bells ring out eleven o'clock. She looked about herself, praying that she would hear Tom's cheery whistle or see his shape approach along the track. Over the last hour her spirits had plummeted from giddy anticipation to fearful disappointment. She did not know what to do. In the end she persuaded herself that Tom must have misremembered their place of assignation and was waiting for her at the camp. It was not much further on into the forest and she held her lantern high as she ventured past the whispering, rustling trees. Beyond the track she could hear the shrieks of small creatures, the hunters and the hunted, and strange rustling sounds as if invisible watchers were following right behind her.

When she reached the clearing, she hung back in the shade of the thorns. Baptist Gunn's followers were making ready to leave, hurriedly loading carts and hauling bundles. There was no moon to see by and in the murk Jennet could scarcely make out any faces. Why was Tom not looking out for her? In a fit of nerves, she was tempted to turn back straight for home. Joshua was out on the sheriff's business and with luck would never even guess she'd been away. And if Tom then had to come and search her out at The Grange? Well, that would teach him not to fool with her affections.

'You are Jennet, are you not?' Out of the dark undergrowth a man emerged. Not Tom. It was Baptist himself.

'Have you seen Tom?' she asked.

The preacher's teeth shone white in the dark as he smiled. 'I believe I have. Come and load your bundle. Let's go and find him.'

It was the woman Repentance, who Jennet disliked, who took charge of her. First, she was made to wait beside a wagon with the other new recruits. It was a long time until Repentance returned with news that Tom had been delayed on an errand and would join them on the road. Jennet gratefully thanked the woman and soon afterwards the whole company set off with no more sound than the rattle of harness and creak of axles. She had no notion of how much time had passed when she was jogged from sleep and hurled forward on to her bundle. The wagon had come to a sharp standstill. Through the darkness she heard a faint whisper. 'The road is blocked.' Struggling to hear, she gathered more fragments of news. The Langley Hall gamekeepers were hunting a band of poachers and had cut off the principal byways that led out of the forest. How could Tom find her? She looked at the black massy shapes of the trees against the luminous night sky. She pondered jumping down from the wagon and making her own way back to her bed. If Tom was going to play catch-as-catch-can in the dark, he must chase her all the way home. Besides, she was less sure of wanting to travel so far as America with the likes of Repentance giving the orders. She wriggled to the edge of the wagon and contemplated dropping into the dark vegetation below.

'Keep still. No one must leave the cart,' hissed Repentance, turning to address them from the seat beside the driver. 'Langley's keepers will shoot aught that moves tonight, whether a poacher or innocent child.' Jennet froze, wondering if Repentance had the same powers as Baptist to read her secret thoughts. It was not a comfortable notion. Warily, she slid back on to her hard seat and when the horses jogged on again she tumbled back into a fractured sleep. She dreamed of finding and then losing Tom, and of being hastily woken and made to shuffle forward into an icy place deep beneath the ground.

When she at last came to her senses, Jennet discovered her nightmare was chillingly real. She was in an underground place and as cold as the north wind's teeth, huddled over her bundle on painful rock-strewn ground. A few crude torches and tallow candles flickered around her, giving off more smoke than light. She could see enough, however, to be sure she had no notion on earth of where she was. Hiding her face in her bundle she let the tears flow, hot but quickly cooling. She knew, as sure as the cloak lay on her back, that Tom was not here. He had abandoned her. She had become that common object of sport – a maiden made a sorry fool for love. Love. What a strong potion it had been. Now, weeping in the dark, love gave no comfort, only the worst of pains – the unclouded brilliance of clear sight.

FORTY-FIVE

All day Tabitha fretted for news of Jennet. Her anger towards Nat had dwindled to a gentle simmer, kept alive as much by fear as sorrow. Was it any surprise she was fearful? She had spent most of her life in the company of men who betrayed their wives. Alas, the shoe was now on the other foot and it was a mighty pinching fit. She knew only one way to keep a man in thrall and even that had been denied her by Caldwell. And the worst of it was, the less secure she was of Nat, the more she felt love's bittersweet torment.

She had seen him scarcely at all since Jennet went missing, and then only when he had told her he was bound to be late back. He had kissed her cheek, quickly but affectionately, and gone. Since then the hours had dripped past as slowly as unctuous jelly easing through muslin. Sukey Adams fussed over her, insisting she try some gentle purges, bringing her mistress cups of tansy tea and pepper cake. Tabitha tried to drink and eat but the heavy air inside the chamber exhausted her. The heat of the dog days would soon fall upon them; it would be better if the child was born before Sirius released its sickly influence. For a few hours now she had experienced a sensation that was not a pain or spasm but a new understanding of her body. The baby kicked and turned so powerfully that when she stripped to her shift she could see the telltale impressions of its thumpings rippling across her drum-hard stomach. She wondered if the baby was demanding release into the world.

In the hope that motion might start up her labour, she sent Sukey on an errand to the village and ventured outside into the garden. At once she felt relief from a delicious fresh breeze. She quickened her speed, willing her body to relinquish its burden. Reaching the gate that led to open pasture, she gratefully rested on a bench, inhaling the sweet air. The manor house rose beside her, its intricate magpie patterns in black and white rising comfortably above the flower gardens. The pointed oak gables and tall chimneys stood as strong as any tree. She tried to engrave in her memory this waiting at the threshold of motherhood. If only Jennet could be safely returned, she would be free to celebrate her home, her husband, and the coming into this world of their child.

'Tabitha?' A wavering voice interrupted her musings.

'Let no one inside,' Nat had said. But it was only Anna Hollingsworth calling to her from the gate.

Tabitha stood awkwardly and unfastened the latch. Offering her arm to the old woman, she led her to the bench. 'The man at the door would not let me through. I need to know how you and the little one are faring.'

'My husband has set a guard upon the house since we were robbed. As for the child, I feel it will come very soon,' Tabitha reassured her. 'I wear your eagle-stone constantly near my heart. Since my friend Jennet disappeared, we all feel in need of protection.'

Anna nodded her head. 'I wish I could tell the constable I had seen his daughter, but I have not. I heard the commotion in the forest on Friday. Jacob was captured by Langley's men but when they found he had no net or snare, he was released.' Suddenly Anna grasped her wrist with a hand as bony as a turkey's claw. 'Tabitha, I came because I dream of many omens. I had such a strong notion you are sick or hurt.'

She smiled in reassurance. 'No, I am only hot and weary.'

'It was such a strange feeling. Here, in my—' She pointed at her shrunken breast. 'It is the time of *Litha*, the Midsummer moon. The earth is older and wiser than us mortals. Every rebirth demands a sacrifice. Even your own birthing, Tabitha, demands Eve's sacrifice of pain and suffering.'

Tabitha nodded, mildly alarmed that Anna appeared confused, and perhaps even a little mad. Her glittering eyes seemed not to see the garden but some other distant place.

'Does your son still see ghosts?'

Anna's hanging lower lip quivered as she nodded. 'The pale woman walks in the moonlight.'

'Anna, Baptist Gunn came here and pretended to raise a ghost. It looked like my mother risen from the grave. I was frightened and fell ill. What was it?'

The old woman shook her head unsteadily. 'He has the power to lodge a splinter of himself in another mortal's mind and they cannot dig it out. He can make them see what is not there. Did it speak?'

'Not like my mother, no. It whispered, more like the voice Gunn uses for his prophecies. It spoke the word, "Salvation".'

'And what do you believe?' Anna was watching her intently.

'I think it was a clever trick. Besides, Gunn used the diversion to rob our strongroom.'

'The pale woman that Jacob sees is not of that sort. He is bewitched. It was a hard task to even make him drive me here today.'

'He is here? May I speak to him?'

Anna nodded and Tabitha passed through the gate and found Jacob Hollingsworth on the seat of a donkey cart. When he saw her his angry gaze slid away into the distance.

'Jacob, I need your help.'

He gave a surly nod of his grizzled head.

'You know I found Maria beneath the tree. I knew her when she lived. I long for her to rest in peace. So if you have seen her spirit, can you give me an account of her looks and manner?'

Jacob jumped down from his perch and began stroking the coarse grey of the donkey's cheek. He assumed a sheepish expression. 'The woman I seen be a fair woman. A bonny woman.'

'Aged seventeen years or so?'

As he had done before when questioned, Jacob grew fretful and looked the other way, turning the ring of the donkey's harness round and round through his fingers. 'Not so young as that. Yet such fair white skin as a young maid.'

'As tall as me?'

'Not quite so tall.'

'And did you see her hair?'

''Twas down her back. A glory of it.'

'Was it brown or red or black?'

'In the moonlight it were not black. More shiny like an angel's.'

'So she unloosed her hair for you? She is an exceedingly bold phantom.'

Tabitha could see the man was torn between his customary silence and a fierce urge to speak of the object of his love. 'She

took my hand and led me down in the shade beside her. And . . .
she has right hot blood. Just as they spoke of that dead girl.'

'Was her belly big with a child?'

'No, mistress. I could near span her waist with my two big
hands.' So it could not have been pregnant Maria, Tabitha was
sure of that. Jacob was looking up and down the lane, eager to be
off.

'She has solid flesh? Not a vapour or moving light?'

He stretched out his coarse knuckled fingers. 'She be as solid
as my own hand.'

'And does she speak?'

The hot blood rushed to the soldier's face. 'Aye. Calling me
to her through the whispering leaves. Bewitching me in the
moonlight.' He looked sorrowfully into the donkey's gentle eyes
and then came quickly to himself. 'I must be getting my mother
back home, mistress.'

'Very well. But tell me of any sighting of Jennet Saxton, won't
you?'

'Aye. When I've took my mother home I'll go join the men
who are searching. If it's true she's been taken by that Devil-bater
Gunn, I shall do my best to see him hang from the gallows tree.'

FORTY-SIX

By dusk Tabitha knew that it was written in her flesh and blood that the child was ready. Like the ticking of an overwound clock, a tension was building that could only end in the explosive clamour of birth. She was waiting, waiting – for the child to finally free itself, and at the same time waiting to hear the worst of news. God forbid that Nat, or Jennet, had been hurt. She paced back and forth in the entrance hall, and then ventured outside beneath the night sky. A vast half-moon turned evasively from the earth, its silver face pitted with pockmarks and shadows. She surrendered herself to the glittering strangeness of the stars. The infinity of the universe was so vast and she was so small. And the child was smaller yet, a tiny cog about to be set free into the machine of the ever-spinning world.

All in a moment she understood something new about herself. She knew her weakness well enough, a vanity bred from years of shallow admiration. Back in London she had gained proof that she was good at her profession in the solid form of gold sovereigns. Yet with that sense of her desirability had come a craving for attention, and most especially every grain of Nat's devotion. Please come home tonight, she repeated silently. If so, he might go to the Kaleyard every week for the entire coming year. All that mattered was that he was alive. And like a revelation she understood that married love could not be a continual contest of flirtation and proofs of affection. Such were the drolleries of rakes and their molls. What she felt for Nat was a raw terror of his extinction. She must have him as a stem has its leaf, as a bird has its wings. And it was her duty not to fuss around him but to help him become the man he deserved to be – as he must help her to one day become a worthy woman.

A noise sounded from the entrance gates. Snatching up the lantern, she hurried to the drive and peered into the black mass of shrubbery. She heard the sound of steady hooves and saw the black silhouette of a horse and rider.

Nat rode silently towards her. 'No news of Jennet,' he called, then dismounted at the block. 'And no sign of Gunn on the roads. I have a notion they are hiding nearer home.'

She threw her arms around his neck. 'I was so frightened you had to fight.'

He kissed her and relief flooded into her like a draught of strong wine. 'If only there had been a skirmish,' he said. 'We've played it too safe. Tomorrow I'm going out with Cam and his poacher friends. If anyone can hunt Jennet down it will be those hounds of theirs.'

'It is my fault,' Tabitha confessed. 'I sent Jennet to spy upon Gunn. I wanted to know what he was planning. God forgive me, I even encouraged her and Tom to go to the camp together.'

'You cannot blame yourself for those two running off together. As Joshua often says, forbid a fool a thing and he will always do it.'

She put her arm through his. 'Come up on the roof with me. I want to say something.'

'Gladly.' Nat whistled for the stableboy, then followed her through the stable arch and into the inner courtyard. A flight of narrow stairs took them up to the old lead lights above the roof. It was cooler up there, though when Tabitha seated herself on the sloping surface the lead itself was sun-warm to the touch. For a while they talked only of the twinkling spectacle above them, of a million silver spangles in the black velvet sky. A languor settled upon her as Nat pulled her close into the crook of his body.

'There is your planet, Venus, sweetheart. We must find another star for our child.'

A week earlier, she might have hushed him and told him not to tempt fate, just like Sukey who would still not allow the cradle into the birthing chamber. Tonight, why might they not choose a star? Inside her the infant stirred, no doubt exercising his limbs in readiness for his great entry into the world.

'What of Jupiter? Do you see it there, almost orange and shining so brightly?'

She smiled in the darkness. 'Yes. The little one is kicking in agreement.'

She leaned her head upon his shoulder. 'Tabitha, I want you to know . . . I have been so selfish.'

'Listen, I am more wounded by any untruths you told me than . . . than if you took a thousand girls in a dark Chester alley.'

'Well, there were perhaps not that many . . .' They both released a tight burst of laughter. Nat gently took both her hands in his. 'Untruths, my love, have many guises. I knew you watched the examination of Maria's body in the chapel.'

She shrank back, startled, as he talked freely. 'I have come to understand we are still learning about each other, Tabitha. Your boldness has rattled me. I have feared for our child – for it is our child, and not only yours. And I have feared for you. I know your inquiries into Maria's life were prompted by justice but at each discovery I felt ever more trapped. I feared I would at any instant be put on trial myself. Think of how our neighbours would glory in the scandal of it. That I, with all my recent good fortune, might be entangled with a murdered ward of the Blue Coat School. That I searched for her one night, and the very next day, she was discovered by me, of all men, on my father's land. And that while I, newly married am expecting an heir, this unfortunate harlot was despatched along with her own ill-gotten child. And what of you? Your reputation would have been thrown in the mud, for it cannot have escaped you how your former profession is well-known hereabout. Yes, I could swear on the Bible that all was a coincidence, a cruel trick of fate, but a hundred gossips – and maybe even twelve jurors – might have judged it otherwise.'

Tabitha considered for a long spell before breaking the silence. 'Nat. I am sorry I was heedless of your concerns. I have been too used to following my own careless ways.'

He watched her gravely. 'I love your spirit, darling. Let me never confine it. But I suppose the consequence of true love is responsibility to one's beloved. It is a new, unsettling sensation for me, too. To protect you and our child. I apologize if I was slow learning my lesson.'

Tabitha's smile was resigned, and sadly self-knowing. 'Thank you. It has also been a hard lesson for me but I'm better for it. We are no longer two carefree lovers but bound by this . . .' She took his hand and placed it where the baby nestled. 'I shall strive to be your loyal wife. And now my heart is easy.'

He did not speak. The silvery starlight lit his dark eyes with emotion. 'Tabitha,' he said at last, very slowly and with a voice cracked with emotion. 'I knew when I first saw you that I loved you. But I swear I did not know what the word signified. You are the twin soul I have always searched for.'

'Yes,' she whispered. She lifted her face to his and they kissed, long and deeply.

'Listen,' she said after drawing back, her senses reeling a little, 'I have a notion how to seal our love.' The dim light must have revealed her smile for she saw the gleam of his teeth too. 'The baby is ready to come. I know it and the waiting is unendurable. I have been thinking, there is a long-held method to give him a . . . nudge into the world.'

Nat's answer was to run his hands freely over her hot skin. 'I am so tired of Doctor Caldwell's rules,' she breathed into his ear. 'I know what medicine is needed, husband. Will you administer a sharp dose?'

'God's blood, I will.'

Together they spread his riding coat upon the warm lead. On fire with anticipation she lowered herself upon hands and knees and felt his hands dive beneath her petticoat.

'Should I not be gentle?' he asked, his fingers halting on their exquisite journey.

Feeling more alive than she had in months, Tabitha twisted her neck to face his dark silhouette. 'No,' she murmured. 'I don't want to be safe anymore. Be as deep and hard as you can. You are the father. Now do your own deep magic to bring our child into this world.'

In their urgency ribbons and laces were abandoned. Nat bundled up her skirts and found the hot flesh above her garters. 'I need not be tender?' he asked again, though she could feel him unfastening his breeches.

'No, I have wanted you for so long,' she begged. Then she cried out like a creature of the night as he quested between her thighs, as ungentle as a young bull. Here was the moment she had waited for, undamming sensations that clamoured like an unstoppable flood. Nat licked the top of her spine and she savoured the roughness of his cheek and gasped at the hardness of him as he entered her. For a long moment Tabitha looked up into the star-strewn sky and wondered at what moment the soul would ignite inside their child. Then her eyelids squeezed closed as she cried out, lost in crimson caverns of pleasure.

FORTY-SEVEN

5 July 1753
Old Midsummer's Day

The next morning, when Tabitha woke in her bedchamber, she moved into the warm shelter of Nat's body, listening to his heart that beat as one with hers. He was dozing, his head a tangle of unruly dark hair, the shadow of dark stubble on his chin. She closed her eyes again, seeing a galaxy of stars as she relived the pleasures of the night before. Her body was sticky and languorous. She wished never to move again.

Discomfort prompted her to roll over. A needling pain darted into her spine. She twisted again but it would not go away. So that was what had woken her.

'Come here,' Nat croaked. His strong arms slid around her and she let herself be pulled back towards the musk of him. His voice was hot in her ear. 'What do you say to another dose of medicine, madam?'

She giggled and pushed hopelessly against his grasp. When he would not let her go, she told him: 'The first dose was quite sufficient, sir. I believe a little stranger may arrive very soon.'

He lifted the bedclothes and kissed her stomach. 'Shall I stay here today?'

Her spirits leapt at the thought of Nat waiting with her until the moment she could present him with the child. But before she could reply the sound of horses' hooves and yelping dogs reached them through the window.

'It's Cam and the dogs,' Nat said between yawns. 'I'll go down and tell him he must take orders from Joshua today, whether he likes it or not.'

She caught his hand as he made to rise. 'No. This is your day to show the villagers your mettle. It's time they realized you are your father's son and show respect to you.'

'I should rather stay with you.'

'No, my love. Go and search for Jennet. It may still take days for the baby to come. You will be wasting time here.'

'I suppose I should rather put Gunn in chains than wear out boot leather pacing the corridor,' he said good-naturedly. 'I shall set a watch over the gates. Let no one inside. I may be late back. And you have Mrs Adams, so I need not worry.'

As soon as Nat had left with a small crowd of servants, Tabitha called Sukey to her bedchamber to tell her the news.

'How could you not have rung the bell sooner?' she exclaimed in rapturous excitement. 'We must go to the solar at once, madam.' With her arm around the nursemaid's shoulder Tabitha shuffled along dim passages until they reached the birthing room. For the first time Tabitha welcomed the sight of the big, bolstered bed and gratefully lowered herself on to it. Sukey fussed around her, complaining that the stuffy room was too cold. And so, while her mistress huddled inside her four-poster, the nursemaid began sealing up the windows and then lit a high bright fire.

'I must see how far on you are.' Tabitha opened her eyes to see Sukey watching her eagerly. She allowed the woman to raise her shift and grope in what the nursemaid modestly called her privities.

'I have only an ache,' Tabitha explained. 'Perhaps the child is not ready yet.' The next moment she cramped as a sharp sensation made her cry out. A few moments later a warm flood of water gushed on to her legs.

'Well, well,' Sukey said, her pale eyes alight. 'He is on his way now.'

When the bedlinen had been changed the nurse prepared ragmoss tea. 'It will make the spasms run faster. The baby will be stronger if the birth is quick.' The drink had a taint of mouldering fruit that made Tabitha want to retch. While her mistress forced the drink down, Sukey set more water to boil on the fire. Freed from her attentions, Tabitha slid her hand inside her shift to find the precious eagle-stone and called on Mary, the Blessed Mother, to save her from the snares of death. By long tradition she had become unclean as soon as her travail began. If she should die, she would no longer be in a state of grace, as indeed the child would not be until baptized. Lord, she had not even left instructions for where Nat should bury her if the parson refused her the De Vallory tomb. Another spasm erased such worries.

By the time Sukey returned to her bedside the room was as hot and stifling as a bread oven. Sukey glowed crimson from the fire, standing above her mistress, as merry as a lark. With a great effort Tabitha smiled back up at her. Together they had shared long hours of preparation and spoken of this moment often. She considered how fortunate she was to pass all responsibility to Sukey for her delivery. She pictured a hopeful tableau in which she looked prettily flushed as she presented the baby to Nat on his return. No, it was not at all likely a first child would come so easily. She suffered another qualm of apprehension.

'Sukey, would you comb my hair?' The maid unloosed and tended her hair and then untied the ribbons of her shift. 'All laces and knots must be undone. I'll have no obstacles to the baby coming.'

Tabitha felt a tug on the silver chain round her neck. 'Who gave you this?' Sukey pulled the eagle-stone out from her shift.

'It was lent to me to ease the birth. By Anna Hollingsworth.'

Sukey handled the stone critically before releasing it back on her mistress's breast. It was then that Sukey's manner suddenly altered. 'That crack-headed witch,' she scoffed. 'You keep strange company for a lady. I hear all the men are out searching for that flibbertigibbet friend of yours today. Fancy her trying to run away with that straw-for-brains Tom Seagoes. And him so full of drink he forgot to even meet the girl. At least we shall be free of Jennet Saxton's whining today. And I told the kitchen maids not to bother us. So, I may as well make myself comfortable while we wait.'

Tabitha watched in baffled horror as her heavily pregnant nursemaid lifted her skirts and removed a horsehair cushion that had been tied around her middle.

Tabitha struggled to speak. 'You are not with child?'

'Ha, well done at last, Madam Clever-Clogs.' Sukey Adams' pink lips twisted in self-satisfaction. Tabitha stared at the abandoned cushion. Just then, another spasm of pain tore at her, like a dog snapping its jaws inside her. When the contractions passed Tabitha succeeded in pulling herself to a half-sitting position.

Sukey was laying out the very best baby linen for the child

to wear. Tabitha checked again how the maid's skirts fell flat against her stomach. If Sukey was not bearing a child . . . the consequences were too overwhelming to consider. 'Why did you pretend?' she asked hoarsely.

Sukey's face glowed with triumph. 'How else could I get close to the baby? I needed to be right at your side. Now who's lost for words? Haven't you worked it out yet, with all your famous wits? Your baby is the chosen one. I'm taking him to Baptist. My husband. And when I return to him as the mother of the second saviour, Baptist will open his loving arms to me and give prayers of thanksgiving to the gates of heaven itself.'

Though the room was overheated, Tabitha shivered as she groped to understand. 'No,' she pleaded. 'Sukey. You cannot do this.'

'It has been foretold,' Sukey continued with the brisk certainty of a zealot. An ugly smile broke out upon her face. 'It was Maria who led us straight to you, d'you know that? Back in April we arrived in Chester and we saw you. You never saw me for I was hidden in the midst of Baptist's folk, all dusty and draggled. But I heard that she-bitch Maria say, "Look over there. That's her who was a harlot in London and has got her sharp claws into the richest man in Cheshire. She has it all and not a farthing thrown in my direction."'

Sukey's voice grew dreamy at the memory. 'You were stepping out of a jewel shop, wearing silks and gemstones that shone like the sun. There was a glamour coming off you that drew all eyes to watch. And your husband touched your belly so gently and I saw you were with child.'

Recalling herself, Sukey swallowed and the spite returned. 'Baptist asked who you were. And that bitch told him both your names and he said, "Rich, you say? They look ripe for the plucking." And he found out where it was you lived and how in past times travellers camped on your land near the Mondrem Oak. And the night we set up camp the prophecy was made and I knew at once that God willed your child to be mine.'

'No,' Tabitha pleaded. 'You cannot take my baby. You have little Davey. Who will care for him if you are gaoled?'

To Tabitha's dismay the nursemaid left off folding baby linen and swaggered towards her, her gait unhindered by the false pregnancy. 'Pipe down. Why would I want your child if I'd already given Baptist the son he always longed for? There is no Davey. I spun a tale about a false child so I could come and go as I pleased.'

'Go where? To visit Baptist Gunn?'

Her smile was brim-full of malice. 'Naturally. He's recovered his senses now. The fever of fornication is over and he needs me again.'

Tabitha was piecing parts of the puzzle together. Lord help her, this woman was a known fraudster and maybe worse. 'What happened to Maria?' she asked, her breath very faint.

'Maria? Even that blessed name wasn't good enough for her. Called herself Trinity. As if the three of them was one. You know what? It wasn't even Baptist's child. That trollop was already breeding when she first came to us. I couldn't let that penny whore defeat the righteous.

'It was Maria who made him cast me off. Me – his true wedded wife. That she-dog thought she'd won the game when my own husband ordered me out of the camp. She told him she carried the true saviour. But I stayed close and watched and waited.'

Fearing the end of the tale, Tabitha tried to grasp the woman's hand. 'Stop, please. Recollect yourself. How could these dreadful things be God's will?'

'What do you know of God?' the nursemaid mocked. 'It was God who told me to send a message from my husband to lure that whore to the Mondrem Oak. When she got there, I heard her call his name, as sweet as a honey-bird. I crept out of the hollow trunk and killed her with my chopping knife. Chop, chop, chop, ridding the world of Satan's seed. I had to kill the false saviour before it was born. And after I'd chopped it up, she looked that untidy with all the blood and guts spilling out of her.' She shook her head like a fussy matron. 'I cannot bear untidiness. I covered the slut with forest leaves and flowers.

'I ran to Baptist with the wonderful news, but God had commanded him it was too soon to take me back. I needed to lie low until he gave me a sign to join him. He needs me, for sure. Now I serve him in my own way. I called on that pompous doctor and came here. Why, you were taken in from the very first tears that poor nursemaid shed.'

Tabitha buried her face in her bolster, wanting to hear no more. But the nursemaid's rant continued. 'I often thought how you were like her. It's been quite a jest these last weeks. You chasing about after Maria's killer when the strumpet hated your very guts. Whenever I met Baptist, he said your husband was a born gull but we must watch out for your harlot's guile. He needn't have worried. Couldn't see beyond your nose, could you? And you're not so rich now, eh? That pretty husband of yours cannot even be trusted with keeping the key to his strongroom safe. T'were but a moment's work to help myself and lead Baptist to the strongbox.'

Sweat beaded Tabitha's face. She closed her eyes and endured another fearsome bout of pain. Recovering, she racked her brain for a means to escape. Christ above, she had let herself be guided by this madwoman. And there were scarcely any other servants on duty now that Jennet was being searched for. I have brought this upon myself, she cursed silently, by pushing Caldwell away and insisting that only a woman attend me. And sweet Jesus, she had wished Nat away this morning. Stupid, stupid woman. When her attention finally returned to the birthing chamber Sukey was stoking up the fire so that red firelight danced across the walls.

'Stop that wailing,' demanded the nursemaid, with a new sharpness. ''Tis almost noon. 'T'will be best if he's born at the chime hour of twelve. The true Midsummer's Day, twelve chimes. He'll be born with all the gifts to see everything – spirits and ghosts and all the future will bring.'

While Sukey turned her back Tabitha frantically looked about herself. The birthing tools were set out on a low table: fresh linen clouts, scissors, a basin, a large knife. She pictured Nat's tender pride when he spoke of their child. For his sake, could she reach the knife and take this woman by surprise?

With a dizzy effort she pulled herself to the edge of the vast bed. 'I am in such pain. I need to walk.' The knife was only three steps away. Dammit, Sukey Adams was watching her with those unblinking eyes. Though her will urged her to act, terror left her legs trembling and unable to move a step. She could not get her breath. She fell back on to the bedclothes as her legs buckled beneath her.

'Do you want to push?' Tabitha's senses returned to the hellish room. Sukey's face loomed above her, close enough to see the blotchy veins across her cheeks. 'That's my special tea at work, quickening the spasms. I haven't got all day. Raise yourself, get on to the birthing chair.' Tabitha let herself be hauled to the chair; its horseshoe seat was set directly in front of the fire that pressed heat like molten irons against her. There she slumped, no longer knowing the limits of her body; only the vast acres of pain across which she roamed. Sukey's face appeared, as wet as a bather's, and the woman held her through the next rack of pain.

Tabitha's head fell forward, but Sukey lifted it by the hair and uttered broken phrases into her face. The nursemaid's face had changed again; now it was as cold and empty as a mannequin's. Sukey tied a sacred girdle, such as wise women use, tight around Tabitha's thigh and recited words she could not understand. These are the words of a murderess, ancient and devilish, Tabitha thought. She clutched ever harder at Anna's eagle-stone and prayed for mercy. Though the chamber wheeled and spun around her like the surface of a spinning wheel, she soon felt a fearsome force gathering within her. The child was being cast out of its darkness. With a groan, she gave a mighty push. The urge returned and she pushed again with all her strength.

'The head is coming!' cried Sukey. 'Gather yourself. At the next heave he will come.'

And so he did, as slippery as a fish, falling into Sukey's arms, wailing and spluttering. Exhausted, Tabitha sagged in her bloodsoaked gown, mutely watching the nursemaid take charge.

'As I foresaw, he is a boy,' the nursemaid crowed triumphantly. After the navel-string was cut she picked up the end of it and squeezed a good spoonful of scarlet blood into her palm. With great care she dipped her forefinger in the blood and dripped it into the infant's twisting mouth. 'That's to be sure he grows as lusty as a young ox.'

She cooed as she washed and anointed the child, muttering phrases: 'I, Salvation Gunn, received by God's grace the Second Saviour . . . and dressed Him in lordly raiment bearing all the signs of His Coming.' The neat pile of baby linen was laid out ready: fine muslin robes, caps and bands, all stitched by Sukey's neat needle. Pricked into the fabric were the holy symbols of a great oak tree, a Holy Crown, and the Lily of the Annunciation.

In a flash of understanding, Tabitha comprehended how naive she had been to think Sukey would devote such hours of labour to another woman's child. She had all this time been preparing to minister to her coming saviour.

Sukey scarcely looked at her now, only passed out orders. 'Hold that touchstone to your womb now. The magnetic force will draw out the after-burthen.' Tabitha did as she was told while fighting to clear her wits. The knife that had been used to cut the navel string lay abandoned by the basin. Yet still she was too weak to stand.

'My little lord, I forgot your milk,' Sukey muttered to the child as she bundled him in cloths and blankets on the bed. Tabitha urged herself to pay attention. It was becoming apparent that Sukey intended to take her son away. Stone-faced, Sukey checked the bloody basin set on the floor beneath Tabitha's legs. 'Stay there,' she ordered. Then she hurriedly tied the horsehair cushion beneath her skirts and left the room.

As soon as the door closed Tabitha dragged herself across the room to the bed. For a brief spell she was alone with her little one. He was asleep, his mouth pursed like a rosebud, his eyelids fringed with dark lashes still wet with tears. With bloodstained fingers she brushed his warm pink cheek. Never before had she touched such a wonderful creature; barely a few minutes old, he shone like a new sun in a dead universe. Her touch woke him and he blinked his eyes; grey like the water-stained marble of the De Vallory monument in Netherlea church.

'Jack?' Her throat choked with sorrow. No, now was not the time to weep. Could the pair of them hide? There were abundant empty rooms in this wing of the hall. She picked up the bloodstained knife and slid it inside the pocket of her shift. Then, a fit of the gripes attacked her, and she had to return to the chair again. The afterburthen was not yet free.

She sat, growing lost in confusion. In the midst of her stupor a sound roused her. Looking up, she heard three soft knocks tapping at the door.

FORTY-EIGHT

'Come in,' she called, gripping the chair's solid arms, praying it might be Nat returning, or even Cook visiting from the kitchen. The door opened a few inches and Bess cautiously stepped inside. 'Is the baby come?'

Tabitha struggled to speak. 'Yes, yes. He's over there.' The little girl appeared not to notice Tabitha's distress. Skipping over to the bed she crooned, 'Can I touch him?'

'Not now, sweetheart. Listen, Bess. You must go downstairs and find a servant. Any servant. Tell them the baby is here and I need help. Will you do that?'

Bess reluctantly looked up from the baby. 'Mrs Adams says I mayn't go downstairs.'

'She is a servant, Bess. I am her mistress. You must go. Now repeat what I said.'

As Bess attempted to repeat her sister's words Tabitha suddenly hushed her. 'Listen. Someone is coming.' It was the tip-tapping of Sukey Adams's heeled shoes growing ever louder on the wooden passage floor.

'Hide! Quickly. Behind the bed curtain.' Bess began to laugh at the prospect of a game. 'Hush. Not a sound. Mrs Adams must not know you are here.' Then, desperate to hurry her, 'She will beat you if she sees you. Not a sound till I call you.' Alarmed, the little girl slipped behind the heavy fringed bed curtains.

As the door opened Tabitha dropped her head forward and pretended to doze. She felt feverish but the nursemaid paid her scant attention. Instead she set some milk to warm on a trivet and walked over to the bed and stared fixedly at the child. If only she would disappear again. Or could she make her go away? At last, Tabitha formed an idea. She tried to calm herself, and then said in a shaking voice, 'You made a loop to tie the De Vallory rattle on his gown.'

'What of it?' The nursemaid glanced over at the milk warming on the fire.

'The rattle isn't here. You should take it with all the rest of his finery. It is his birthright.'

The woman tutted, distracted but annoyed. 'Where have you put it?'

'It is in my old bedchamber. In the bureau.'

Sukey stared dreamily at the baby again. 'He must be dressed mighty fine, as befits his lordly rank in the world.' After casting a resentful glance towards Tabitha, she took the milk off the fire and poured it into a stoppered jar. Then making her way to the door, she called, 'Don't you move an inch while I'm gone.'

When Sukey's steps grew faint Tabitha called to Bess. The little girl peeped out from behind the curtain and came to her. 'Now go carefully. If you see Mrs Adams you must run, understand? Find any servant, Cook in the kitchen or the boys in the stables. Tell them to come up here and see the baby at once. Now go.'

The blue leather pumps on Bess's small feet made no sound as she crossed the floor and slipped away. Tentatively, Tabitha hauled herself up. A clotted mess lay in the basin beneath the birthing chair. She accomplished a few awkward steps towards the bed where her child was now sleeping.

'My miracle,' she murmured, and caressed the damp fuzz of his dark hair. His fingers stretched and relaxed in small stars of pleasure, his fingernails the tiniest shreds of seashell. Tabitha found the handle of the knife inside her pocket. So this was a mother's true instinct, she realized. If Sukey Adams came back and tried to steal the baby, Tabitha would gladly protect him with that sharp blade.

Bess loved to play hide-and-seek. A smile lifted the corners of her mouth as she reached the wide oak staircase. She peeped through the gaps in the carved balustrade. No one was about. The hall boy was missing from his usual place and everywhere was very quiet. Tabitha's baby was born. Bess was bright with excitement, joyful to have a little nephew at last, a playmate she could share her games and toys with. True, he was still very small and sleepy, but she was hopeful he would grow very fast. And Tabitha had given her the news to tell!

She tiptoed down the stairs and ran into the kitchen. 'Cook,

the baby's come.' Cook was sitting by the open back door, fanning
herself with a pan lid.

'You playing your tricks on me, young miss?' the cook said
sourly. 'Not ten minutes ago Mrs Adams said the mistress were
still showing no signs. Be off with you. I'm running upstairs
after no one today.'

Bess jumped up and down on the spot. 'Tabitha says you have
to come,' she tried again, tugging on the cook's apron. 'It has a
little red face.'

'Oh aye. One of your dollies, is it? Get away with you.'

Tabitha stood unsteadily behind the door, wiping sweat-slick
hands across her stained shift. Her mind was reeling save for
one thought – that she would destroy the nursemaid if she tried
to take the baby. A trickle of liquid was moving down her thigh.
It was only blood. She felt herself newly baptized by it: the
common element to birth and death; the entrances and exits of
existence. She grasped dimly that Sukey Adams wanted to cheat
nature, to claim motherhood without the suffering. Well, she had
not reckoned on the power of birth to bind and to bond. In the
instant she had first seen little Jack, she had marvelled at his
being created as a new living entity. Between them, she and Nat
had set in motion a soul's destiny and she would not allow his
small spark to disappear.

A noise sounded from the passage. Tabitha grasped the handle
of the knife as tightly as she could, though her arm shook so badly
she feared she might drop it. The door opened and Sukey Adams
did not see her where she hid behind it. Instead she hurried past,
heading straight to the baby on the bed. Tabitha fixed her gaze on
the nursemaid's pink neck, where it showed between her white
kerchief and her lace-trimmed cap. Like a lioness, Tabitha leapt
upon her, driving the knife towards the band of livid flesh. The
nursemaid must have heard her for she twisted nimbly away.
Staggering, Tabitha felt a sharp blow spike into her head. Losing
her balance, she bumped against the wall and slipped to the floor.
She was winded and breathing hard, unable to move. Towering
above her, Sukey Adams glanced down, the coral rattle red with
blood, and then dismissed her. When next Tabitha lifted her eyes,
the nursemaid was rummaging through Tabitha's goods, packing

items inside the bundle. Then, with a blissful smile, the nursemaid lifted the sleeping baby into her arms and carried him past Tabitha, to the door and away.

Shooed out of the kitchen, Bess wondered if she should go back upstairs. No, Mrs Adams might catch her. And Tabitha – well, Tabitha had asked her to fetch someone. Out in the yard all was quiet. Bess tapped on Mister Higgott's office door, fearful of his shouting at her. No one answered. She looked in the laundry and that was empty, too. Finally, she heard movement in the stables. Running inside, she grasped Tom's coattails. 'Tom. The baby's come. Tabitha says come now. Come on.'

She knew Tom was in some sort of trouble and wasn't serving at table any more. Now she wondered if that was why he didn't move at once.

'Please,' she begged. 'Tabitha says fetch you. The baby's got a red face. Tabitha wants you. Come on.'

'Oh, very well,' Tom grumbled. 'I in't supposed to go indoors, little maid. Though I reckon no one will see me this once.'

So Tom and Bess set off upstairs; one tiny white hand clasped in another great red fist.

Tabitha was sitting on the floor beside a bloodstained knife. Seeing Tom and Bess, she lifted eyes near-blind with tears. 'She has taken him.'

Tom, the great lump, stared dazedly at the bloodied clouts, the basin of liverish afterbirth, and the hellish red light from the fire.

'Tom,' she croaked again. 'Sukey Adams has stolen the baby. Go and find your master or the constable. Stop her.'

Bess had started to weep for she could not find the baby anywhere in the room.

'Why would she do that?' Tom asked gormlessly.

'She is Baptist Gunn's wife. They reckon our child is their so-called saviour. Hurry, Tom. Take the fastest horse from the stable and find someone to stop her.'

FORTY-NINE

And when the rich thieves upturn the common land in war,
The child shall find sanctuary behind earth's secret door.

The New Prophet of the Forest

At first light Nat's spirits had been high but it had proved a fruitless morning. Cam had agreed to close his forge for the day and call up a good number of the night-hunting fraternity. His best scent hound, the lurcher named Nipper, had buried her muzzle in Jennet's old apron and sniffed and trotted her way to the Mondrem Oak. After that they had wasted time on a series of false trails. Nat's theory that Gunn and his followers were still in the forest was as yet unproven. As the sun rose to noontide, Nat, Joshua, and the servants from Bold Hall gathered at the bush tavern alongside a group of poachers led by Cam. The soldier, Jacob Hollingsworth, had appeared as well, though he hung back at the edge of the gathering.

'Any luck?' Nat called out as a few last stragglers joined them. They wearily shook their heads. Nat had paid the landlord to serve a good board of bread, cheese, cold meats and beer to the hungry men. Helping himself, he was troubled by an observation he had made that morning. He had been riding on a winding path near a village when he first noticed the lingering bitterness of wood smoke and the blackened remains of bonfires. And there were other signs of recent frolics – of country folk venturing into the groves to foretell their future spouses by way of yellow garlands, charred cartwheels and other midnight charms. Nat could have smacked his fist into a wall for not having grasped his mistake. Away from the straight-laced towns Midsummer's Eve was not celebrated on the newfangled date of the twenty-third of June. This first year since the calendar change there was confusion enough, between some fairs and markets keeping to the old date while others moved eleven days forward to the new style. Country dwellers had long memories and to them Midsummer's Eve would always be eleven days later, on July the fourth. Here, the blooming of Saint John's wort was the sign of Vigil Night, and no one gave a fig for Parliament's decree.

If today was Midsummer's Day – and of course it was in the prophecy's 'Old World' – matters were rather different to how he had conceived them. For one, Gunn's prediction might still be proved true, namely that Tabitha's baby would be born today. He struggled with the urge to turn Jupiter sharply around and gallop straight home. For if his and Tabitha's baby was a Midsummer child, was it not still the likely candidate to be this so-called saviour?

Keep a cool head, man, he told himself sternly. He knew he should give out fresh orders to the men but he had not the airiest notion what to say. Tabitha had made a worthwhile point about his not having been prepared for the role of leader to his household and tenants. Where the devil could Gunn be hiding? He pulled out his map of the forest and its environs. It was a patchwork of the tamed and the wild, from the gamekeepers' precincts around the Chamber of the Forest to tracts of emptiness featuring a string of curious names: The Seven Stones, The Old Fort, and Castle Cob. His eyes took in the mapmaker's marks for the scatterings of wells, giant stones and tumuli.

A niggle of a memory surfaced at the back of his mind. Gunn had made some reference to an underground place. But where and when was it? He took a long swallow of ale and closed his weary eyes. The prophecy. He pulled his copy of the pamphlet from his coat and there it was:

And when the rich thieves upturn the common land
*   in war*
The child shall find sanctuary behind earth's secret
*   door.*

Earth's secret door. He called Joshua over. 'Do you know of any caves or tunnels hereabouts?'

'Aye. A few of the ruined forts have crude pits and cellars. But if you're looking for proper tunnels into the earth that would be Briggestone Barrow.'

'Is there space enough to hide there?'

Aye. It's a massy great hill with a flat top. If Gunn is hiding there we could take the dogs to flush him out.'

Nat worked his way through the resting men and asked each and every one if they had passed near Briggestone in the last few days. At first he was met with only a flurry of shaking heads. Then a pair of youths with the look of itinerant labourers spoke up. The older lad pulled off his hat and bowed his head. 'It may be naught, sir. But when we was coming to Relict's Moss this morning, we seen some strangers up on the Briggestone. Wandering along the top of the hill, they was.'

'How many men?' Joshua demanded.

'Three, maybe four. Looking in the distance. Patrolling, as you might say.'

'Did you see any other strangers on the road?' Nat asked.

The younger lad shook his head. 'No one of note, sir. Only on the Saxon Road there were a woman driving a gig. Looked like she were late for summat. Never even gave us a—'

Nat caught Joshua's eye and asked, 'How far is Briggestone?'

'As the crow flies it's no more than three or four miles but it crosses Langley's land.'

Nat called Cam over. 'If my dogs go over Langley land they could be shot,' the blacksmith grumbled.

Nat didn't want to hear excuses. 'I have a notion of how we can do it. Show me the short way on the map, Constable.'

Joshua traced a route through the green area titled *Langley Park & Hall*. It incorporated Langley's pastures and Relict's Moss before reaching common land at Whetstone Well and Briggestone Barrow.

'As I alone have this ridiculous right to take dogs across a gentleman's estate without being shot at,' Nat said, 'I shall lead the pack.'

Joshua nodded curtly. 'Aye, and as an officer of the law I will ride alongside you.'

Cam pulled out a greasy parcel of kippers obtained from the inn's landlord and tied a number of the stinking fish on the end of two long strings. 'All the young scent hounds are trained to follow red herrings this way,' he assured Nat. 'They'll run together as a pack wherever this stink is dragged. Just keep forward of the rest of us and they'll follow where you lead.'

Joshua and Nat each took a clump of fish and let them trail on the ground as they rode away. Soon they were cantering over neatly tended Langley land at a good pace. The dogs were moving well at their rear but the men had fallen back, for some were on foot or ancient ponies. So far, the air was very still with no sign of habitation. The sun was past its zenith and Nat's pocketwatch already showed it was after one in the afternoon. He consoled himself that with luck Tabitha's danger might be over and he already a father.

After half an hour they entered deep arboreal shade cast by enormous yew trees. The forest was different here; the air was silent and smelled of mildew. The Civil War had seen many of England's oldest trees toppled but here amongst the ancient meres there stood stout-trunked behemoths with limbs as crooked as hoary stags' antlers. Joshua murmured that they had reached Relict's Moss, for here the ground was an ancient bog studded with emerald ponds. Here too were more signs of Midsummer Eve's fires and magic. Circles of ashes were trampled in the ground and a girl's torn petticoat hung like a victory flag from the branch of a tree.

Joshua moved his mount up beside Nat's. 'It could be Gunn slipped up here the night Langley's men barricaded the road. I never liked this place, the Langleys are fools to enclose it. Do you recall how dead men have been found here in the bogs over many a year?'

'I do.' Nat looked about himself, into the jade green pools that wore a dull sheen of lichen. 'I read of a body that turned to leather from long marinating here in the mud. The corpse was dressed in what looked like a fox fur and leather shoes. A surgeon attested the fellow had been murdered – thrice. His skull smashed, his throat cut, and the remains of a garrotte still lay deep in his neck.'

Joshua shook his head. 'To die so brutally means a soul can never rest.'

'Perhaps,' Nat ventured, 'the ancients had their great mysteries; think of their giants' stones, too vast to be moved by men alone.'

'Aye,' Joshua said. 'When I was a foolish boy we village lads went on an adventure to Briggestone Barrow. There was talk of hidden gold, the usual dream of lost treasure. It is a maze of a place; we were lucky to get home in one piece. I've long thought it the likely stronghold of those murderers who killed the folk drowned in the bogs. Gunn no doubt hopes we fear it too much to make a proper search.'

It was then Nat noticed their way ahead was barred. Beaufort Langley and a stranger were staring up at them in astonishment, standing in a clearing beside a portable inkstand bearing scrolls of paper.

FIFTY

'Nat De Vallory. Of all the rogues to come trespassing. What the devil are you doing here?' Beaufort Langley blustered.

'We are here on the sheriff's business. That is all you need to know,' Joshua said curtly.

'Wait,' young Langley cried. 'You owe me ten guineas don't you know, for that mangy wolfhound you stole from our kennels.'

Nat guffawed at the accusation. 'What? You mean my father's own dog that you stole?' Pox the man, he had a deal of audacity.

'Ha, sir,' Langley said, turning to his companion, who appeared to be a surveyor or mapmaker. 'This upstart fellow betrays his low birth. All over ten paltry guineas. He is as tight with his wallet as a gnat's arse.'

Nat stared down from the saddle with chilling *sangfroid*. 'How crude you are. And certainly no gentleman. I do not steal dogs – or land.'

A self-satisfied grin broke out across Beaufort Langley's asinine face. 'Since I last saw you I remembered your visage. I saw you at the Kaleyards tavern, did I not?'

'You may have. I questioned Nancy Blair. I was seeking the whereabouts of Maria St John and the name of any who consorted with her.'

Beaufort looked less comfortable. 'What did that loose-tongued hussy tell you?'

'More to the point, what were you doing there the night before she was murdered?'

'Me?' Langley brayed. 'I do like a little low pleasure. I have no wife to hide my appetites from. Whereas I'll wager that damned lively wife of yours would like to know of your visit.'

Nat laughed coldly. 'You shall not rattle me, sir. My wife is an open-minded lady.'

Beaufort leered up at Nat. 'That's not all she keeps open, according to my knowledge.'

Luckily for Langley, at that moment a distant sound reached
Nat from behind his back. Faint but raucous, it was the pack in
full cry. He glanced at Joshua who silently acknowledged he had
heard it too. 'Well, sirs, the constable and I have business to
attend to,' he said coolly.

Disgruntled, Langley continued to stand foursquare before
them, blocking their way. 'Wait. Where is my ten guineas?'

'Go hang for it, Langley. You know as well as I do that your
keeper stole my father's wolfhound.'

Joshua motioned his horse to take a step forward. 'In the name
of the sheriff of Chester, I demand you let us pass.'

Young Langley's temper was rising. 'How dare you come
here,' he taunted Nat. 'You are a by-blow, a nothing. Sir John
must be crack-headed to let such a viper into his home. All the
gentlemen hereabouts are against you.'

Langley's companion spoke for the first time. 'Is your father
hunting today, sir?'

'No, no.' Then, hearkening, Langley asked, 'What is that
racket?'

While the two men turned to scan the countryside for the
source of the approaching hullabaloo, Nat saw his chance. A
document box stood open on the ground. In the guise of turning
Jupiter around, he dropped his battered string of red herrings
inside it.

'What the devil!' cried young Langley as he spotted the
pursuing dogs pelting towards them up the track.

The surveyor was backing away. 'Mister Langley. The brutes
are heading straight for us. Let's run!'

Uncertainly, Langley staggered backwards. Nat signalled to
Joshua and as one the pair dug their heels into their horses' flanks
and set off at a gallop, soon outstripping the pack. Hearing cries
of bewilderment and then fear from Langley, Nat grinned like a
Cheshire cat. Only when the clamour of dogs reached a wild
crescendo did Nat swing Jupiter around to observe the mayhem.

Looking back, young Langley lay prostrate on the ground,
cursing and yelling at the dogs to back away. The surveyor was
pushed up against a tree, ineptly batting at the dogs with the
aromatic box. The hounds were happily ignoring all commands
in the sheer joy of playing with their amusing prey.

'The surprise on their faces,' yelped Nat, his face pained from a volley of laughter. Even Joshua broke his grave expression to chuckle. 'Covered in slobber, they are.'

Finally, Nat called the dogs with a long low whistle. The leading dog, Nipper, lifted her snout at the sound and fixed her eyes on the pair of them. She gave a summoning bark and at once the pack joined her in full cry and trotted gleefully towards Nat and Joshua. Then they were off again, Nat and Joshua and their horses galloping to keep ahead of the feverish hounds, winding along paths and jumping fallen branches, the two men looking keenly ahead for their rendezvous at Whetstone Well.

At the well they waited for the rest of their companions until all were reunited in a whirlwind of fur and hooves and flicking tails. The spring produced a famous cure-all that had once enticed invalids from miles around. Now the dogs sank dripping jowls in the stone troughs set beside the famous pools. Nat, too, drank long and heartily, for the water was sweet with an aftertaste of liquorice. As he wiped his mouth, Jacob Hollingsworth slunk over and drew him to one side.

'Sir, beyond that stand of trees is Briggestone Barrow. The best way would be to ambush them by stealth. No more than half a dozen silent men to scout ahead. And the best scent hound – Nipper – can search for Miss Saxton without raising the alarm.'

Nat did not disagree. What little he knew of leadership certainly allowed for giving your best men full rein. Jacob was a soldier, Cam was a poacher and Joshua had long experience of catching villains. When they were ready Nat addressed all the men. 'Four of us shall go forward. Cam, Jacob Hollingsworth, Constable Saxton and myself. The rest of you wait here. If you hear a musket shot, advance at once with your weapons at the ready. If you hear no signal, stay alert. And keep mum.'

The mood at once became grave. The chosen men assembled, with Nipper on a tight leash. Through the trees Nat could see the flat-topped mass of the ancient barrow. His spyglass showed no figures upon it and not a blade of grass appeared to stir, nor a bird to circle above it.

FIFTY-ONE

D irty, sore, and hungry, Jennet had never felt so miserable. For what felt like forever she had been kept here, imprisoned in the dark. All her desire to fight back had vanished long ago. Now, her sole aim was to draw no attention to herself. If Repentance noticed her, she was made to work, and she hated groping her way down the slippery tunnel to fetch water from the horrid black hole of the well. One time, when she had been made to tend the fire and stir a thin broth, she had been overcome with hunger and spooned a few scalding lumps out of the cauldron into her mouth. That had earned her a wallop from one of those she privately called the True Believers. Her head had been slammed against the solid wall of rock and she had felt blood, for goodness' sake. To her astonishment, the others hadn't cared a pin about her injury. To think, they carried on about all this caring and loving and yet she could have bled to death. Since then, she had hunched in a shadowy recess, where she cried and slept and silently called Tom Seagoes every wicked name under the sun.

Opening her eyes, she found she had been dreaming again. Rubbing swollen eyelids, she tried to cling to those visions of home that had seemed so real a few moments earlier. She recalled her sunny garden and her happy concerns over the hatching of chicks in the henhouse. Why had she run away from such comforts? Reluctantly, she looked around the chamber and found that it was filling with more people than usual. Someone trod on her toes. Lord, it was Grisell, with her hair a wild grey nest and her Sunday gown ruined. Jennet pressed herself deeper against the wet wall so her former companion would not see her. Grisell was one of the True Believers and one of the last people here she wanted to speak to.

Baptist Gunn came in and a little flurry of anticipation passed around his followers. Even he looked exhausted; shadows hollowed his eye sockets and his hair hung greasy and flat. He began to talk of America, of the promised land. Though some of the bedraggled band still mumbled, 'Praise be,' and Grisell cried, 'We are saved,' it seemed to Jennet that as many stayed silent and watchful. She hopelessly wondered if she would get another chance to jump off the cart when they set off again, or if she might hide before they boarded the ship. That was the sort of thing her father, or Tabitha, would do. They would not have been sitting here half-dead with terror like she was.

A few words distracted her from her private thoughts. 'Together we will launch a ship of history,' Baptist was saying. She watched him and found there was still some flame-like quality that drew her to him. He raised a tankard. 'Like all the poor of the earth we have no food. Yet we have water. Today, I ask that you drink with me. For this is my blood. Let us share a last cup together.'

He took a swallow himself and then the cup was passed amongst them. 'I am ready to face death,' he announced in a stronger voice. 'As I am ready each time I return. As I am ready each time I am betrayed.'

Jennet felt the longing rise again in her soul to believe in Baptist. He stood before them like a persecuted saint, his eyes shining. She knew her scripture. Could Gunn be more than a mortal man? She studied him with fresh, scrutinizing eyes. No, she had been tricked into following him to this slimy pit. He was a fraud, a charlatan, just as Tabitha had always maintained.

There was a scuffle in the tunnel that she guessed led to the outside, for Gunn's trusted men, armed with knives and muskets, kept a close guard upon it – not only on those coming in but stopping anyone leaving as well. A familiar female voice rang out, echoing against the hollow stone. To Jennet's fuddled surprise, Sukey Adams strode in and barged her way through to stand at Baptist's side. A victorious grin shone on her face. 'No need to lament, Baptist. I have him. He is here on earth. Here is our saviour.' She raised a white bundle towards Gunn. Jennet strained to see. In the dim tallow light, she noticed the cloth was moving. It was a baby. Judging from her diminished belly, Sukey had given birth to her child. So, had Sukey been pregnant with the saviour all this time? Jennet's mouth fell open in surprise. It had to be the unlikeliest event she had ever witnessed. Surely Baptist was supposed to be the saviour's father? The Bold Hall nursemaid who disapproved of any misdeed, from a clumsy embroidery stitch to a saucy jest – how could she have lain with Baptist Gunn and begot the saviour? Jennet watched, spellbound, as Baptist stepped away from her and studied Sukey, his eyes narrowed and his brows low. He did not appear to share her triumph. The nursemaid moved amongst the group, leaning down to reveal what lay inside her arms. All the time she was repeating phrases: 'Your saviour' and 'He is the chosen one' and 'It is a miracle.'

Sukey Adams came nearer, so close that Jennet could glimpse the child's linen that she herself had helped to create. There was the gown with an oak tree pricked out in holy point lace. A pointed stump of coral set in silver dangled from a ribbon. It was the coral rattle that bore the De Vallory family crest. These were Tabitha's baby's clothes. Sukey Adams had stolen these vastly expensive goods from her mistress. Jennet felt a jolt of outrage.

She turned back to watch Baptist. He was staring into open space as if trying to conjure some better future from the darkness. It was a rare thing for him not to take command as their leader. She caught the puzzlement of the congregation as they waited for him to take charge.

Sukey reached the place where Jennet sat. The beatific expression faltered as she recognized her former companion and a scowl darkened her face. 'Jennet Saxton,' she muttered. 'You are witness to a miracle.' Swiftly she moved on.

Jennet wished she was not so weak from hunger and confusion. She wordlessly prayed that Sukey Adams would not accompany them to America. Hostile murmuring broke into her thoughts. Repentance's voice rose in an ill-tempered complaint. 'Baptist! This cannot be right.' The shrewish woman had marched to the front and whipped around to face them all. 'We cannot let this sinner back into our fold. Salvation was expelled by Baptist himself.'

Sukey Adams froze and turned to face Repentance with a hard expression. 'Look at her,' Repentance yelled. 'She is addled in the head. If we harbour such an abomination as her, God will never forgive us.'

'You are the abomination,' hissed back Sukey Adams. 'Behold!

He is my child. A miracle from God. Tell her, Baptist. Tell her how God has been good to me. How I worked ceaselessly to fetch you all the money for the voyage and have now fulfilled the prophecy as only I can. You need me!'

Gunn stared from one woman to the other. Jennet had a ridiculous urge to laugh. This was the best entertainment she had seen since joining the camp. And as if it truly were a penny sideshow, the sound of a musket firing suddenly cracked the air making more than a few cry out. Next, a noise like the hounds of hell erupted, echoing down the long tunnel, so that all turned fearfully towards the racket.

One of the guards ran in and grasped Gunn's arm, crying, 'They be waiting outside with dogs.'

The gathering wailed and whimpered. Then at last Gunn sprang up, filled with resolution.

He moved fast, darting over to Sukey Adams and wrenching the sleeping infant from her arms. Then to Jennet's horror, he pushed and leapt over the crowd towards her, yanking her arm and dragging her roughly up on to her feet. Not caring how he hurt her, he pulled her roughly after him towards the tunnel and the raucous noise.

'Baptist. Wait for me.' Sukey Adams was trying to catch at his coat. 'I'll tell them it was me! It was me all along.'

With a jerk, he swivelled backwards to shout at her. 'Forget your crack-brained scheming. It's not your damned saviour. It's De Vallory's child. With luck it can get us out of here.'

'You promised me,' Sukey wailed. 'When I unlocked the strongroom—'

'Hold your tongue, woman!'

He barked at the guards. 'Keep them all here until I return. I am going to parlay with our enemies. We are fallen in the hands of sinners. But I will secure safe passage for you all to our New Jerusalem.'

FIFTY-TWO

J ennet stumbled along, trying not to trip on the rocky tunnel
floor. Gunn was almost pulling her arm out from her shoulder.
Behind them they could hear Sukey wailing, 'He's mine. You
cannot have him!'

Gunn was holding the baby all wrong; it was tucked like a
sack of flour in the crook of his other elbow. They stumbled
along till they came to a dead-end where a great pile of boulders
stood heaped up to the roof. The sound of howling dogs had
grown frighteningly close; she could hear them scrabbling at the
rocks, unseen but barely a few feet away.

'I still have goods to trade,' Baptist was mumbling to himself.
His fingers dug like metal hooks into Jennet's arm but she didn't
cry out. 'The constable's daughter. And De Vallory's child.'

Jennet's head jerked up. So that's why she was of value to
him. The constable's daughter. And there it was again: was the
baby truly Nat's child? Her thoughts were muddled but she had
to try to make sense of what was happening around her. Could
Nat have fathered a child upon Sukey Adams? The idea almost
made Jennet giggle, so that she feared she might never stop
laughing in all her days. Why would Nat take Sukey as a
bedfellow? Set beside Tabitha, Sukey Adams was dull and
ordinary. On the other hand, Tabitha was forever complaining
that the doctor had banished Nat from her bed. Heavens, if
Tabitha discovered Nat and Sukey Adams had lain together, she
would explode like a keg of gunpowder.

Baptist pushed the baby towards her. 'Hold it,' he barked and
she did so. 'Stand back.' She edged away as he began to heave
rocks from the top of the heap. They rolled down to the tunnel
floor and in time a thin natural light shone into the place bringing
sweet scented air. Jennet felt her wits reawaken. Gently, she cradled
the warm bundle in her arms and retreated further back down the
tunnel. Peering into the folds of cloth, she found the infant's tiny
face, its eyes shut and fringed with long dark lashes, its miniature

nose and pretty lips lying set and closed. She lowered her own face towards his and felt the child's skin brush her own cheek like warm fruit. He was breathing steadily. She marvelled that through all this hurly-burly he slept on. He looked a little like Nat, she mused, guessing that his hair must be dark beneath the richly laced cap. Or he could be Gunn's child, she supposed, though if so she pitied him for having such a father. As for the notion that the baby was some sort of saviour, that had to be nonsense. With sudden clarity, she grasped that whoever the baby belonged to, Jennet had been placed here by Providence to protect him. She nuzzled his warm brow and inhaled the yeastiness of his skin. Some primitive instinct blossomed inside her and, in that moment, she became less of a child herself and more the mother she hoped one day to become.

'Call the dogs off!' Baptist yelled through the gap in the stones. 'I have Jennet Saxton here. And the baby.'

Jennet strained to hear the reply but could not make out individual words, only that the dogs were called back. Then Nat's smooth, well-educated voice asked, 'Is Jennet unharmed?'

'She's here. Better cared for than at home.' In the shadows, Jennet shook her head in disbelief.

'I'll deliver her safe to her father. In return I want free passage to Liverpool. There is a wagon in a cave a hundred paces down to the left. Get that hitched up and fetch it here. Then I want two days' start to get on my way.'

'Then we get Jennet?' Nat insisted.

'Only if you hurry along. Don't be all day,' Gunn jeered.

Jennet clutched the sleeping infant against her breast, listening as she watched Gunn labour to clear a larger passage to the outside.

A new and deeper voice rang out. 'Jennet?'

Careful of the child, she stepped forward. 'My father,' she said to Gunn. 'May I speak to him, please?'

'A few words.'

On unsteady legs, she stretched up to the gap in the rocks and called, 'Father!'

'Are you well, love?'

'I want to go home.'

Joshua's voice was husky with strong emotion. 'Don't you

fret, sweetheart. I'll get you home.' Suddenly, Gunn dragged
Jennet back and thrust his own head into the gap. 'Get a move
on. Is the wagon ready?'

It was a long wait; Jennet hugged the baby tight, trying to
gather feeble scraps of courage. Eventually, Joshua yelled an
assurance that all was waiting for them. Gunn heaved the final
few stones away so he could clamber through a low opening in
the barricade of stones. Then he leaned down and tugged the
baby from Jennet's arms and held it against his chest like a soldier
strapping on a shield for battle. With his other hand he hauled
Jennet after him. 'Do as I say or there'll be trouble,' he growled.

Jennet had no memory of her arrival at the barrow, for she
had been half asleep and the darkness had been absolute. Now
she emerged from a hole in the hillside on to a great sward of
long grass upon which a circle of men were gathered amongst
a scattering of giants' stones. She knew some of them as
villagers, their muskets trained upon Gunn and their expressions hard and steady. Jennet stumbled and blinked, fearful of
the guns exploding and hurting the baby. Then seeing Joshua,
she cried out, 'Father!' He smiled through tight lips and
motioned to her to be silent.

'You hiding behind a baby now, Gunn?' Nat jeered.

Jennet couldn't see Gunn's face but his reply was mocking.
'Don't you know him, De Vallory? Don't you recognize my
saviour?'

Jennet looked to Nat and saw only bewilderment.

A moment later, Gunn yanked her along at his rear, forcing her
to stumble awkwardly behind him while he gripped the baby tightly
to his front. Through his arm she could feel a deep, steady tremor
of fear. Even I, a frightened girl of fifteen years old, Jennet told
herself, possess more courage than him. He shuffled between them
to where the wagon and horses stood waiting.

When no one moved after him he turned around and began
shouting at his pursuers. 'Don't think of following me. I'll let
the girl go when I'm able. Fair enough?'

Jennet appealed silently to the ring of faces. Above her, the
massy shape of the ancient barrow seemed as dark and brooding
as a beast waiting to spring.

Nat stepped forward. 'No. Release Jennet now.'

'Try and make me.' Gunn was grinning like a crazed jester. Jennet tried to break away to reach her father, but Gunn wrenched her back into place to guard his rear. Then they shuffled on again, awkwardly approaching the wagon. She felt Gunn hesitate as he puzzled over how to reach the driver's seat without relinquishing the fleshy armour of herself and the baby. Jennet was tall but even she would struggle to step up on to the rim of the cartwheel and then heave herself up into the cart. The driver's perch was even higher, and Gunn was considering how best to proceed. He glanced back at Jennet. Here was her opportunity. When he climbed up first, he would have to let go of her. She could take her chance and run.

'You go first,' he said, pushing her forward.

'No. Please let me stay with Father,' she wailed.

'Get up!' Gunn rammed her hard against the cartwheel. Furious muttering broke out amongst the waiting men. Why didn't they do something? Slowly and sulkily, she set one foot on to the wheel spoke, grasped the footplate, and swung her other foot up on the rim, and then heaved her way up to the seat beside the driver's. Before sitting, she swivelled around for a final sight of Joshua. He was watching her, as grim as a statue. To his right there came a ripple in the circle of men as Tom appeared at Nat's side, speaking insistently. Tom wasn't even looking at her. But Nat's expression changed to determination and fixed on Gunn and the baby. The poor child was grizzling miserably. As if Gunn would even care if the baby was hurt, she thought. She could hear Gunn laughing at Nat as if delivering the punch line to some cruel joke.

A movement caught Jennet's attention. High on the flat top of the barrow a man appeared silhouetted against the sky. With a slight nod, he acknowledged her gaze. It was Anna Hollingsworth's wild son, the ragged soldier who had first been suspected of that poor harlot's murder. He was standing very still, a bow stretched tight in his arms, an arrow ready nocked and aimed towards Gunn. With his body the soldier mimed a crouch, telling her to drop down low. Jennet stiffened; she must not alert Gunn. As the preacher set his foot on to the wheel rim, she reached down to take the wriggling infant out of his arms. Gunn's bold brown eyes, which had bewitched her all summer, interrogated her, not quite trusting her. Feeling like Judas himself, she smiled falsely into the preacher's weary face and briskly lifted the baby from him. She stepped backwards to the footplate and instantly dropped down low, protecting the infant beneath her cradling body. With eyes screwed tight shut, she heard Gunn open his mouth to protest, taking in air. His next words were never uttered.

Gunn's death was almost soundless: the soft thud of an arrow in his back and the clatter and thump as he tumbled backwards to the ground. Jennet could not move; she kept her eyes closed; every fibre of her body guarding the infant beneath her banging heart.

Even when Joshua reached her she struggled to open her eyes. Her body was shaking. She let her father help her down and there it was by her feet, Gunn's body lying in a puddle of wet scarlet. Turning away she clung to her father, then buried her face in his shirt.

Nat watched as Jennet lifted a dirty face streaked with tears.

'Thank you, Jennet.' He smiled broadly. 'May I see my baby?'

'So he is yours,' she said. She offered the infant to his father. Nat grasped him awkwardly. The elaborate baby linen was grubby now and the long skirts torn. None of that mattered.

'Tabitha is safe. I've sent Tom back to say you saved this little fellow.' Then he returned to staring at his child with a wonder that overwhelmed his whole being. It was the marvel of witnessing a new life where before there had been no living soul. Gunn might have planned to parade him as a saviour, but Nat understood that to every parent a newborn child is that rarest of events, a private miracle.

FIFTY-THREE

29 September 1753
Michaelmas, New Calendar

After a sparkling autumnal day, the sun was sinking towards coppery evening as Tabitha and Nat made their way along Chester's Northgate Street. Tabitha paid no attention to the sandstone arch that led to the notorious Kaleyard Gate. She no longer fretted that Nat might prefer the company of street girls. Since baby Jack's birth, their love had burned stronger than ever. 'I thank God we were both born to share this existence,' he had whispered one night as they lay in twisted bedsheets. She felt the same, she told him, glad of the darkness that hid a sudden rise of tears. Tonight her only jitters were on Nat's behalf, for the appointed date had arrived to present his paper to the Cestrian Society. That evening, by giving a public account of the events in the forest, he would finally set a seal upon the summer's tragedies. It was a seal she hoped would never be broken.

Upstairs in the Exchange building's imposing meeting chamber, Tabitha fidgeted at the rear of the room as her husband arranged his notes on the oval table. The society's president introduced Nat and he bowed to his audience, an attentive ring of grey-haired and soberly dressed gentlemen. Tabitha was reminded of Nat's return to Bold Hall with Jack in his arms on that dreadful day when Sukey Adams had stolen him. It had been the first time she had seen the foreshadowing of an older, more purposeful man in his youthful features. Now, as he introduced his findings on the history of prophecy, she checked that baby Jack still slept peacefully beside her. Since that harrowing day she could not bear to let her little one out of her sight. He lay motionless in Jennet's arms, save for the occasional sucking of his lips as he dreamed of her, his mother. Jennet nodded in serene acknowledgement; since her ordeal she too had grown in good sense and proved the best of helpers.

'So far, so uncontroversial, sirs,' Nat announced cordially. 'After examining the evidence from the classical age, when sacrifice and oracles were a habit of daily life, I set out to select a living subject for my experiment. My choice was an itinerant preacher, Baptist Gunn. Why so? Firstly, Gunn claimed to practice *oneiromancy* – a term you will no doubt recognize from the Greek term for dreams, *oneiros*. He persuaded his followers that in his dreams he experienced visitations from God and had the power to interpret their meaning. You may scoff, sirs, but this practice has an honourable history. Great heroes recounted in Greek, Babylonian, and Old Testament writings, often received messages in dreams. To recall an example, in the Old Testament, Numbers 12:5–6: God said, "I the Lord will make myself known unto him in a vision, I will speak within a dream." Gunn claimed that these visions arrived fully formed in his mind, either when sleeping or in a state of trance when preaching before his followers.

'My second reason for choosing Gunn was his eagerness to take part in this experiment. That he asked a fee of fifty pounds I mention only in passing. Perhaps to a prophet such as him, my urgent desire to finish this paper made my mind especially easy to read – and my pocket rather easy to pick.'

The club members guffawed politely. Nat raised his arm to display the chapbook titled *The New Prophet of the Forest*, bearing an illustration of a man speaking beside a large tree. 'Some of you will be familiar with Gunn's prognostications from this publication. Those of you who are not will find a copy of this pamphlet set before you on the table.'

After the gentlemen had perused the printed sheets, Nat said, 'As you can see, gentlemen, the prophecies cluster around one fundamental question: who is the saviour whose birth Gunn predicts? To make an answer I will give an account of the dramatic events that unfolded this summer concerning Gunn and his followers. To begin, back in May-time, shortly after Gunn's appearance on my father's land in Mondrem Forest, it was my misfortune to discover the corpse of a young woman known as Maria St John. It was a double tragedy, for upon medical examination it was found that this victim, a prostitute, carried an unborn child who was destroyed along with its mother. While Gunn himself was suspected of involvement, it was in fact his wife, known variously as Salvation Gunn or Sukey Adams, who confessed to this barbarous murder. The cause was her husband's fascination with Maria Saint John and the uncontrollable jealousy this engendered. Mrs Gunn was arrested in July of this year and is being held at Chester Castle. At the recent assizes she was tried and condemned to death by hanging. Then last week, at the request of the prisoner, my wife and I made a visit to Mrs Gunn in her prison cell.

'Imagine our surprise when the gaoler announced that Mrs Gunn has taken the opportunity to "plead her belly" as it is commonly known. In other words, she has been examined by a jury of matrons and is certifiably with child. Now the curious fact is that Baptist Gunn had, according to his followers, cast off his wife because she was barren. Indeed, while living with Gunn, she took the entire blame for the couple's inability to procreate upon herself. It appears, however, that the fault lay with the gentleman. This had long been undetected, for the community was, shall we say, of a promiscuous, free-loving nature. We can therefore also infer that Gunn was not the father of Maria St John's unborn child.'

Tabitha watched the members of the club ingest this information. None of them inquired who then must have fathered Maria's child. Whether conceived from a random lover or even from Beaufort Langley, Tabitha thought no one would now ever know. Poor Maria, who she had tried to redeem after death, not knowing she had hated her so bitterly. The truth was she now felt an even deeper sympathy for Lady Maud's daughter. At every throw in the game her luck had forsaken her until she had lost her life beneath the Mondrem Oak.

'Let us leave Maria's tangled history and return to the malodorous confines of Chester gaol,' Nat continued. 'Mrs Gunn's case was concluded yesterday. By the grace of His merciful Majesty the King, her punishment has been commuted to transportation. Indeed, she will set sail for our American colony on the convict transport named the *Heart of Oak,* three days hence.'

Tabitha was pleased to see expressions of astonishment amongst Nat's audience.

'So, shall we revisit those verses to judge their prophetic

accuracy, sirs? Firstly, that extraordinary events would take place at Midsummer in 1753 where stands the "king of the forest", the Mondrem Oak. Despite a reputation as barren Mrs Gunn insists that she conceived her baby while sheltering in the hollow chamber of the oak at the season of Midsummer. She was found guilty of murder and is therefore the greatest of sinners. Her dalliance with a man not her husband may in many eyes mark her as a harlot. She is certainly a most contradictory personage, being both immoderately modest and yet obscenely violent.

'While I am not at liberty to give out his name, the man with whom she conceived the child was indeed lowborn, belonging to a profession that many despise. Yet, in that profession he has known great honours from a person of the topmost rank.

'The location of "earth's secret door" became apparent only when the forces of the law apprehended Mister and Mrs Gunn at Briggestone Barrow, an ancient druid's hill, where they were hiding inside an artificial cave.

'As for the child's future glory, we know only that he will be born in the New World to a mother of fanatical beliefs. Sirs, are you yet convinced that Baptist Gunn could foretell the future? The man himself is unable to offer any further evidence, having left the world to face his Maker while resisting lawful capture at Briggestone. What I would say is that Gunn was a most exceptional man. As a boy he received an injury to his head which he claimed gave him unearthly powers. In this he supposed himself a visionary of the like of Hildegard of Bingen, who received God's messages while subject to fits or brain fevers. Certainly, he had exceptional powers as a leader and a charmer of the dispossessed. While he lived his followers were drawn to him as irresistibly as iron to an oracular magnet; though upon his death his followers scattered to who knows where.'

Tabitha recalled how rapidly Gunn's followers had dispersed. Her own servant, Grisell, was last seen heading for Liverpool, though whether she ever earned her passage to America, none could say. She was but one of many who had been touched by Gunn's dark flame, by the dazzling fire of his promises, all snuffed out in death and disappointment. Now Tabitha leaned back in her chair, relieved that Nat had eliminated those parts of the tale she had insisted must not be made public. She had no wish for their neighbours to hear of the spirit raised in the chapel, or Mrs Gunn's employment as nursemaid and Jack's abduction.

'So, gentlemen, was our prophet able to predict future events? Within the rules of my experiment I must conclude that Gunn passed the test. It would appear his prophecies have come to pass. Aha, I see expressions of perplexity around the table. So let me reassure you that I too am not persuaded he was a genuine prophet.'

Tabitha nodded. She and Nat had talked long about Gunn's powers. The preacher had cast a messianic spell over his followers but neither believed he had true divinatory powers. Tabitha had recalled each occasion when she had watched him preach. 'It is almost as if he repeated some other person's visions,' she had protested. Now she listened intently to Nat's argument.

'His falling into sleeping trances at public meetings, for example, appeared to me too neat and timely. In observing Gunn, I saw much in common with both the *haruspices* who inspected entrails for Caesar and the mountebanks who tell fortunes at Chester fair. They all peddle what their followers most wish to hear. In Gunn's case, his captivating message was that the old world of Britain was oppressive and unfair, and that he alone gave hope of a new life of liberty across the Atlantic. His prophecy of a holy birth carried all the weight of the Bible's supreme language. And in a community where many young women were happily going forth to multiply, he could expect a suitable newborn candidate to appear at any moment to take the saviour's crown.

'Let me leave you with a few thoughts on why, in this rational, modern age, we continue to be gulled by such sleight-of-hand men and prognosticators. As every meeting of this society reveals, we now live in a place and time of technical marvels. Here in this room we have observed demonstrations of the powers of electricity, of magnets, and in Monsieur Diderot's *Encyclopaedia,* seen machines that appear to think and labour for us, their human masters. So why, amongst these practical inventions, should our newspapers and almanacks be crammed with tales of ghosts and oracles and fortune-telling? Why, when mankind creates the world anew do the old spirits of superstition fight back, unwilling to be forgotten? I can only speak as one who has lived by the pen and comprehends that the multitude has always been bewitched by bloody murder, tragedies, devils, lost children, dreams and prophets. Even in the distant future I hope that the capacity to marvel at what is beyond our sight will continue. Yet that is not to say that these visions are real, only that I love to feel my spine shiver at a good ghost story as well as any other.

'I will leave my last words to the great lexicographer, Doctor Johnson. On the subject of the supernatural, he wisely maintained that, "It is undecided whether or not there has ever been an instance of the spirit of any person appearing after death. All argument is against it, but all belief is for it."

'Gentlemen, as a member of this esteemed society I would refashion the good doctor's paradox: could a man such as Baptist Gunn foretell the future? In his case, rational argument appears for it, but all credible belief remains against it.

'Gentlemen. I am obliged for your kind attention.'

FIFTY-FOUR

Until at last there rises a new constellation
And the child leads the man, for his name shall be a nation.

The New Prophet of the Forest

31 October 1753
All Hallows' Eve

The green days of summer surrendered to the dominion of grey-cloaked winter. Inside Bold Hall, they fought the damp and cold with vast, log-piled fires and merry company. Nat invited Mister and Mrs Rix for an evening's entertainment at Bold Hall's chapel to celebrate All Hallows' Eve, when the Unseen press their closest to humankind. As the company assembled, Tabitha maintained a cheery aspect in spite of her reluctance to return to the dilapidated chapel. It felt an age since her collapse by the chantry window. According to Doctor Caldwell, her blood was now sufficiently strengthened by steel powders and rich beef. But she was convinced that happiness fortified her better than any medicines.

Beyond the ancient windows, the night was as black as soot. Once again, candles guttered in the sconces casting an ever-shifting gloom. Nat had set four chairs in a row exactly where they had both sat on the night of Gunn's visit. She was glad Nat had insisted that Jack be put to his cradle early with Jennet watching over him. Thankfully, this time she had remembered her warmest fur mantle and Nat drew it tight around her shoulders.

'I want you to enjoy my entertainment, sweetheart,' he murmured, setting a kiss on her brow. 'You might call it a catharsis. It was a shocking trick that imposter Gunn played upon us. In the spirit of Hallows' Eve we shall purge ourselves of his mischief.'

Nat made his way to the very spot where Gunn had given an apparent sleeping prophecy that distant summer's night. She assured herself that there was nothing to fear; their fortunes had recovered more thoroughly than they could ever have expected. Lady Maud had exerted pressure upon her father and the Langleys had ceased all claims to Sir John's land in Mondrem Forest. True, not all the contents of Bold Hall's strongbox had been recovered from Gunn's wagon at Briggestone Barrow, but they had sufficient coin to keep the estate intact. And Nat's confidence was up; now he beamed with pleasure as he stood before them in his new French coat stitched with spangles that glittered in the candlelight. Tabitha could not help but smile with pride.

'I welcome you to this gathering, friends. Tonight, we celebrate the occasion that has since days immemorial been celebrated as the Feast of Samhain, or Summer's End. It is a night of mischief, when ghosts and strange spirits appear to the unwary. Tonight, to glimpse this other world will be simple. I only ask that you join me at this dimly lit window.'

They all stood and moved towards the empty frame of the chantry window. Through its unglazed frame came a soft illumination such as had glowed on the night when Tabitha had feared her own dead mother walked again. A sudden qualm made her lean on Sophie's arm. Then, recovering herself, she attempted laughter. 'Goodness knows what phantom Nat will have conjured for us.'

'Heavens above,' declared Mister Rix, who had reached the window first of all. 'What the devil? Oh, De Vallory, that is remarkable.'

Nat was grinning like a schoolboy. 'Very well,' said Tabitha, bracing herself. 'Do your best to terrify me, you rogue.'

Reaching the window, she pressed her face to the metal frame and gave a little cry. Before her lay a baby. Their own baby, Jack. He lay asleep upon a carved table. Yet, simultaneously, she could see directly through his bundled body. The outlines of the table's carved surface could be seen through his bonneted head.

Beside her, Sophie said, 'Oh my heart. Is it a ghost of little Jack?'

'Not at all,' Nat exclaimed. 'Though he does have an oddly transparent appearance, does he not?'

'I believe I have guessed your secret,' Mister Rix announced.

'Well, I have not,' protested Sophie. 'Do you know how it is done, Tabitha?'

Tabitha scrutinized every inch of the apparition of her child, utterly perplexed as to how Nat could have conjured their child in this semi-transparent form. 'Is he still asleep upstairs?' she asked in wonderment.

Nat chuckled. 'I am not so ingenious. I must give credit to Signor Giambattista Della Porta and his inventive mind. Step inside and I'll show you the science of this apparition.'

Nat put his arm around her waist and led her into the narrow chapel. 'You remember how the door was locked that night? It was an essential part of the trick.'

Gazing about, Tabitha was at first horribly perplexed. The table on which she had just seen baby Jack stood fearfully empty. Next, she noticed that every wall was draped with black fabric, completely covering the altar and memorial statue. Nat turned her gently by the shoulders to face the hidden corner of the room behind the door. There stood a great pane of glass such as the gardeners used for a glasshouse window, propped against the wall. Behind it stood the exact same tableau as that glimpsed through the window – an identical table upon which lay the entirely substantial body of baby Jack. Jennet sprang forward too, from where she had waited in the shadows.

'Heavens. Are you part of the trick, too?' Tabitha did not know whether to scold the girl or congratulate her. 'I still don't see how it was done.'

Jennet reached to adjust an oil lamp, which cast a powerful beam upon the infant sleeping on the table. Suddenly, Jack's sleeping form sprang into place upon the carved table by the window. The image was a perfect replica and yet its form was insubstantial and half-transparent.

'Absolutely extraordinary,' Mister Rix declared. 'I never saw such a thing in my life.'

'It is you I should thank for the loan of Della Porta's *Magia Naturalis*. In there I found a chapter titled "How we may See in a Chamber Things that are Not". That ingenious Neapolitan had a great interest in a type of camera obscura not unlike our modern magic lanterns. It was Della Porta's name I saw on Gunn's bookshelf and thus discovered the origin of his theatrical illusion.'

'Who do you believe played the part of the spirit?' Mister Rix asked.

'I believe it was Gunn's assistant.'

Tabitha looked intently into Nat's face. 'No, no. It could not be. I never took my eyes from him.'

Nat nodded. 'I know. Then I recalled that the servants had said there had been no callers or visitors save for Gunn and his assistant all that day. Expecting trickery, I left orders that their cart must be left in the stables and that the main house be forbidden to them. Higgott observed how the youth passed back and forth around the house to the stable and we all thought nothing of it.'

'And? Gunn's assistant could not be in two places at once,' Tabitha insisted.

'The solution, like most fairground illusions, is rather mundane, my love. It is a classic case of *occultis aperta* – the solution is concealed in open view. Do you recall a pair of twins at the camp?'

Tabitha groaned. 'I do. Not by sight, but I heard of them. There was a woman named Abundance who claimed not to know which of the two was her child's father.'

'I believe Gunn generally kept the twins apart so he could use them for such switches. I only saw them as a pair at the Briggestone, and even then I thought nothing of it. Only when I recreated this illusion did it occur to me that amidst all the to-ing and fro-ing from here to the stables an extra person must have slipped inside. He needed only to hide and wait for his cue to appear. And later, in all the confusion, Sukey Adams no doubt led them to the strongroom.'

Tabitha marvelled at such cleverness wasted on mere deception, seeing again in her mind the shrouded figure moving painfully towards the chantry window. 'So why, when I asked who my enemy was, did he name "Salvation"?'

It was Jennet who gave the answer. 'Spite. I saw what they thought of Sukey in Briggestone Barrow. Gunn's followers knew

she was a murderess. They were not all bad folk, Tabitha. They
hated her and feared her, too.'

Later, Tabitha carried the baby up the carved oak staircase,
pausing at the portrait of Sir John as an infant, studying the
artist's mirror-like rendition of the De Vallory rattle hanging from
the child's apron. She relived Sir John's first sight of his grandson,
when he had stretched his sinewy hand to tap the silver bells on
the De Vallory rattle with a grunt of pleasure. The new generation is the dying generation's solace, she reflected. As it did very
often these days, her mind drifted to Sukey's baby, which would
be born in the spring. It was certainly uncanny that this unborn
saviour had already performed his first miracle, namely saving
his mother's neck from the hangman's noose. Moving on to her
chamber, Tabitha wondered what name Sukey would give him?
What was the prophecy? 'His name will be a nation.'

She reached her chamber and set Jack down with extreme
tenderness, so he would not wake. As she rose from bending,
she remembered how last summer they had talked of names.
Sukey had always shown tight-lipped disapproval of a name as
unexalted as John, even though it represented the De Vallory
family line. Then bitter Grisell had piped up with that newborn
religious enthusiasm of hers.

'There will be a great number of children named Philadelphia
when Mister Gunn reaches the New World. He says the city was
named after the church spoke of in the Apocalypse.'

'What a tongue twister. I am not calling my child Philadelphia,'
Tabitha had said. 'Would you do so, Sukey?'

The nursemaid had looked modestly down into her lap. A slow,
secret smile spread across her lips, as if she saw something quite
different from the intricate Tree of Life lace she was working
on. 'No,' she said, stroking the fabric. 'Philadelphia is but one
city. I think the new realm itself would be better.' Tabitha had
imagined that the nursemaid had been thinking of Jerusalem or
Eden or Heaven itself. Now it was perfectly clear what she had
meant. The child would be named America.

At peace beside the De Vallorys' elaborate oak cradle, Tabitha
turned over what she had learned of Sukey's fate. By now she
must be chained in the dark bowels of a wet and heaving convict

transport. She was certain Sukey would survive the voyage, for she had the iron will of an evangelist. Once on land she would be made to disembark in shackles and be consigned to a master as an indentured servant. Doubtless there would be churches aplenty in the new city and she would find a malleable preacher with an eye for a wholesome, fertile woman. In her reverie, Tabitha could see the tale unfold: the baptismal ceremony at which the parson congratulated her on the patriotism of her child's choice of name. He might well think her a bright and comely personage sent by God to be a fitting housekeeper, or even a wife.

It was time to make a clean breast of her secret. Unpacking her mother's box, she sorted through the written prophecies found in Grisell's chamber, numbered on little slips of paper in a precise hand. Most were familiar but a few were novel and strange. When Jennet knocked at the door and joined her to watch over Jack, Tabitha bundled them into a flowered reticule and returned downstairs to join the others for supper.

In the dining room the table stood resplendent in the light of scores of flame-tipped candles that sent golden beams glancing over the great silver punchbowl, the crystal glasses, and the glistening pies and tarts. Nat's eyes sparkled too as he rose and welcomed her. They celebrated the best of All Hallows' nights, with liberal toasts, and spiced soul cakes, and a wild performance of the *Souling Play* by a bunch of rowdy village boys. And when the four of them were once again alone, Tabitha emptied her reticule and spread the handwritten prophecies across the polished table.

'Is this another parlour game?' asked Sophie, who had perhaps drunk too much of her husband's excellent arrack punch.

'Of a sort,' said Tabitha. 'For I have one final revelation in this story of Gunn and his wife. Here is the letter she sent to us requesting we visit her in gaol.' Tabitha placed the grubby paper beside the handwritten prophecies. 'Look. The writing is the same. I believe that Sukey – or Salvation Gunn, if you will – supplied her husband with the products of her own troubled dreams. Recall that it was she who was named a "sybil" in the handbill from Lancashire. And Jennet told me that when Gunn deserted his wife at the Briggestone, she cried out after him, "I will tell them it was me. It was me all along." Being the superior showman, he performed the prophecies to his followers. Yet I believe it was Sukey who had the extraordinary powers. Perhaps she gave these to Grisell for safekeeping. Grisell could not have written these. She could neither read nor write.'

Nat stared at her, impressed. 'So you believe it was Sukey Adams who had the prophetic power? It was she who foresaw the saviour's coming? Death and fire, she must have been hoping to get with child ever since Gunn cast her off.'

Tabitha nodded. 'I am sure she would rather have presented her own child to Baptist. It was our misfortune it took her so long to conceive.'

Their guests riffled through the little papers while Nat stared thoughtfully at the candle flame.

'Listen to this one,' Sophie Rix exclaimed. '*Tall towers of glass shall come to pass. A flag of stars, a sign of George's sorry loss.* Your prophet – or should I call her prophetess – had some odd fancies.'

Nat said nothing, reading a series of slips with close attention. Mister Rix peered at another through his lorgnette. 'Tell me, what happened to that soldier fellow who fathered Mrs Gunn's child?'

Nat looked up. 'His regiment was recalled to Ireland. I don't suppose he'll ever discover that the child exists.'

'And is it true that this fellow held great honours?' Rix continued, pouring himself another bumper from the decanter.

Nat held his own glass out to be refilled and recalled the story. 'The fellow fought at the Battle of Dettingen by all accounts. The king, God bless him, was troubled by a bolting horse. It seems Jacob Hollingsworth was one of those who protected His Majesty while sheltering beneath an oak tree.'

'Goodness me,' Mister Rix exclaimed. 'Not another oak tree.'

Nat moved around the table to sit beside his wife. 'How do you interpret these rhymes, Tabitha?'

She circled the rim of her wine glass with her forefinger. 'I am puzzled by this talk of a flag of stars. The American colonies fly the red flag of America bearing our own Union Jack, do they not? The first prophecies also tell of a new constellation. The lines Sophie just recited seem to suggest we might lose our American colony.'

'Salvation Gunn will be pleased at that,' Sophie chimed in.

'Her child may yet meet his father if there is war and the Cheshires are sent over there,' Nat said dreamily.

Mister Rix chuckled. 'Goodness me. The king may be ageing but even he would not be so foolish as to lose our American colony.'

It was very late when Nat and Tabitha walked along the oak-panelled passage up to their bed, past the watchful eyes of long-dead De Vallorys. Jennet was relieved of her vigil and disappeared to sleep in a guest chamber. Before retiring Tabitha sat by the window nursing the babe at her breast, blessing her great good fortune. The Hallows' Eve gale rattled the casements and Nat crossed the room in his nightshirt to fix the latch.

'Look at the moon,' he said. Through the glass they watched the frost-white globe shining over the silver-bright flower beds of Bold Hall's garden.

Tabitha surrendered to its fascination; so distant yet dream-like in its strangeness. 'Only think, it is the same moon that must be shining somewhere far away, above the *Heart of Oak* as Sukey Adams crosses the Atlantic.' She looked down on the sweet, bonneted head of their child as he suckled sleepily. 'Sometimes I fancy there is a curious connection between little Jack and Sukey's unborn infant.'

Nat came and stood behind her, resting his hands gently on her shoulders and dropping a kiss on the top of her own – and then their son's – head. She didn't tell him the odd thoughts she often had; that a mere twist of fate had prevented Jack taking the place of that other child on the fateful voyage. To her it was like a tale of a mortal child miraculously saved from being switched with a fairy changeling. All she said was, 'I am glad that thousands of miles of ocean keep them from us.'

Then she settled Jack in his cradle and they went to bed, where they made gentle love that was all the better for being quiet and sweetly slow. Afterwards, Nat's strong arms clasped her tight as she pressed into the warm crook of his body. This was contentment; a bright star of a moment to treasure.

'I wonder what Sukey Adams dreams of tonight?' Nat murmured sleepily.

'Whether crosses or crowns,' Tabitha said softly, 'only pray let her dreams not be of us. Or Jack.'

As she tumbled into sleep, for a moment she glimpsed the ceaseless tumult of those wild revelations, bottomless and teeming. And, for herself, she was thankful to be beached here on the brink of now, not knowing, merely hoping, surrendering to tomorrow.

ACKNOWLEDGEMENTS

When I first set out to write a sequel to *The Almanack*, my idea was to place a utopian sect on the Bold Hall estate and thereby unsettle Tabitha and Nat, the hall's new residents. At first, I was afraid this might be perceived as too unlikely in the middle of the calm and uneventful Enlightenment. However, when I began my research it proved that history is indeed stranger than most fiction.

The customary image of the eighteenth-century clergyman is of a conservative, well-connected gentleman, inhabiting a handsome rectory in return for delivering a dull weekly sermon. This was certainly the case, but at the same time a quest was evolving amongst the less privileged for a more exciting spiritual awakening. Large crowds gathered at open-air sites to hear preachers such as the Methodist leader John Wesley, alongside many other mystical leaders whose names are now lost. Wesley himself was a keen believer in the prophetic power of 'remarkable dreams' and collected countless examples of them on his evangelistic journeys.

Particularly fascinating are the Sleeping Prophets, who appeared to become possessed and utter prophecies to crowds while seeming to be asleep. In the early eighteenth century a number of groups had emerged in south-eastern France who manifested spirit possession, prophecy, and visions. These in time influenced English ecstatics, some of whom became known as Shakers in their native Manchester, and eventually took their beliefs to America in 1774.

Though not based upon any single individual, hedge-preachers such as Baptist Gunn certainly existed and drew crowds of followers. I enjoyed putting a pinch of Samuel Taylor Coleridge into Gunn's character, for the youthful poet wrote at length of his project to set up a utopian group in America called Pantisocracy, though the scheme was later abandoned. After considering such cult leaders down the ages, I also placed the monstrous instigator of mass suicide, Jim Jones, in the mix, for any review of religious charismatics does sadly unearth a less admirable parade of false prophets, madmen, confidence tricksters and psychopaths.

A second surprise came when I uncovered the serious conflict in England's woods and forests between Whig grandees enclosing common land and the poachers who defied them. In 1723 the Black Act had been passed after a series of raids by poachers known as Blacks, named from the precautionary measure of painting their faces to go hunting at night in large gangs.

The Act introduced the death penalty for over fifty criminal offences, including being found in a forest while disguised, and was infamous for punishing men and dogs by death in countless cases. Yet still poaching continued; buoyed up by the words found in Genesis, country people insisted that animals were made for the sport of all of men, not only red-coated squires.

A more widely known conflict is the one this period witnessed between the emerging and largely male medical profession and the more ancient traditions of female midwifery. Newly elevated into society, Tabitha would have faced a choice as to which source of advice to turn to. Certainly some physicians of the day continued to insist on the mother avoiding 'maternal impressions' from distressing events and situations in case they injured her unborn baby.

Regarding location, my forest is not so very different from modern Delamere Forest, Cheshire, which is the remnant of the ancient medieval forests of Mara and Mondrem. Though partly imaginary, it shares with Delamere a good number of barrows, hillforts and sacred wells. The forest was also the home of Anna Hollingsworth, the so-called 'Wise Woman of Delamere', a refugee from Germany whose quaint home and good character I hope prove of interest.

A great many books, articles, people and experiences helped me in writing this book but the following deserve a special mention:

David Cressy, *Birth, Marriage, and Death: Ritual, Religion, and the Life-Cycle in Tudor and Stuart England* (Oxford University Press, 1997)

Clarke Garrett, *Spirit Possession and Popular Religion: Origins Of The Shakers: From The Old World To The New World,* (The Johns Hopkins University Press, 1998)

E P Thompson, *Whigs And Hunters: The Origin of the Black Act* (Penguin, 1990)

Thompson; Hay; Linebaugh; Rule; Winslow, *Albion's Fatal Tree: Crime and Society in Eighteenth-Century England* (Pantheon, 1976)

Clifford A Pickover, *Dreaming of the Future* (Prometheus, 2001)

Steve Roud, *Monday's Child Is Fair of Face . . . And Other Traditional Beliefs About Babies and Motherhood* (Random House, 2008)

R M Bevan, *Tales of Old Delamere Forest* (CC Publishing, 2008)

Keith Thomas, *Religion and the Decline of Magic* (Weidenfeld and Nicolson, 1997)

P Broster, *The Chester Guide: Or, an Account of the Antient and Present State of that City* (1781)

Anthony Storr, *Feet of Clay: A Study of Gurus* (Harper Collins, 1997)

Jennifer Mori, *Magic and Fate in Eighteenth-Century London: Prosecutions for Fortune-Telling, c. 1678–1830* (Folklore, 129:3, 2018)

I would like to thank the following people for their help and inspiration.

My faithful writer friends, Alison Layland and Elaine Walker, who gave me invaluable feedback, guidance, and some terrific ideas to improve my story.

Also, to my friends in The Prime Writers, a group of writers who have all had their fiction debuts commercially published at the age of forty or more. Thank you, especially to those who so kindly found time to read early drafts.

An intense period of writing on retreat at Ty Newydd Creative Writing Centre in Wales was made possible by the generosity of a grant from the Francis W Reckitt Art Trust.

For crucial encouragement and belief in the novel, many thanks to my agent, Charlotte Seymour, and all the team at Andrew Nurnberg Associates.

Thank you to all at Severn House, especially Kate Lyall Grant and Sara Porter, for having faith in a sequel and for their hard work and support.

And finally, I'm grateful as ever to my son Chris for his

positive encouragement, and to my sisters Marijke and Lorraine for playing their part in encouraging new readers. Finally, thanks to my husband Martin, for happily accompanying me to iron age forts, ancient houses and churches, and then reading and critiquing my early drafts.